HELSINKI HOMICIDE:

BEHIND CLOSED DOORS

JARKKO SIPILA

Translated by

Katriina Kitchens

Originally published in Finnish as *Suljetuin Ovin* by Crime Time, Helsinki, Finland, 2012.

Translated by Katriina Kitchens

Published by
Ice Cold Crime LLC
5780 Providence Curve
Independence, MN 55359

Printed in the United States of America

Cover by Ella Tontti

ISBN-13: 978-1-937241-10-0

Also by Jarkko Sipila

In English:
Helsinki Homicide: Against the Wall (Ice Cold Crime, 2009)
Helsinki Homicide: Vengeance (Ice Cold Crime, 2010)
Helsinki Homicide: Nothing but the Truth (Ice Cold Crime, 2011)
Helsinki Homicide: Cold Trail (Ice Cold Crime, 2013)
Helsinki Homicide: Darling (Ice Cold Crime, 2014)

In Finnish:
Koukku (Book Studio, 1996)
Kulmapubin koktaili (Book Studio, 1998)
Kosketuslaukaus (Book Studio, 2001)
Tappokäsky (Book Studio, 2002)
Karu keikka (Book Studio, 2003)
Todennäköisin syin (Gummerus, 2004)
Likainen kaupunki (Gummerus, 2005)
Mitään salaamatta (Gummerus, 2006)
Kylmä jälki (Gummerus, 2007)
Seinää vasten (Gummerus, 2008)
Prikaatin kosto (Gummerus, 2009)
Katumurha (Gummerus, 2010)
Paha paha tyttö, with Harri Nykänen (Crime Time, 2010)
Muru (Crime Time, 2011)
Suljetuin Ovin (Crime Time, 2012)
Valepoliisi (Crime Time, 2013)
Luupuisto (Crime Time, 2014)
Mies Kuumasta (Crime Time, 2015)

In German:
Die weiße Nacht des Todes (Rohowolt Verlag, 2007)
Im Dämmer des Zweifels (Rohowolt Verlag, 2007)

In Italian:
Morte a Helsinki (Aliberti Editore, 2011)

HELSINKI HOMICIDE:

BEHIND CLOSED DOORS

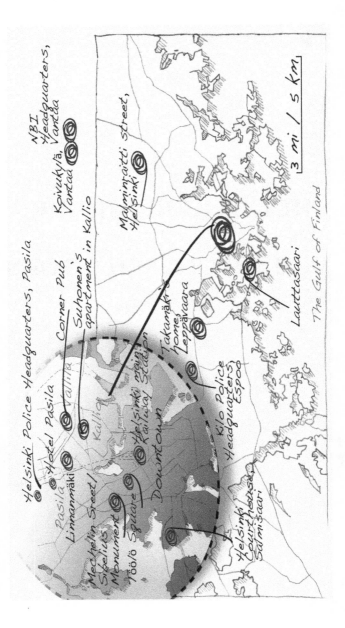

Helsinki Police Headquarters, Pasila

NBI Headquarters, Vantaa

Koivukylä, Vantaa

Corner Pub

Suhonen's apartment in Kallio

Malminraitti Street, Helsinki

Pasila

Hotel Pasila

Valma

Liimanmäki

Kallio

Helsinki Railway Station

Takamäki's home, Leppävaara

Mechelin Street / Sibelius Monument

Töölö Square

Downtown

Kilo Police Headquarters, Espoo

Lauttasaari

Helsinki Courthouse, Salmisaari

The Gulf of Finland

3 mi / 5 km

CAST OF CHARACTERS

Kari Takamäki.....................Detective Lieutenant,
Helsinki PD Violent Crimes Unit

Suhonen....................Undercover Detective, VCU

Anna Joutsamo...................VCU Sergeant

Mikko Kulta....................VCU Detective

Kirsi Kohonen....................VCU Detective

Karhu.....................HPD Head of Narcotics

Jaakko Nykänen ....NBI Head of Intelligence

Eero Salmela.............Suhonen's old friend and ex-con

Raisa Mäenpää...................Rape victim

Veikko Sandström...................Rapist

Nea Lind...................Defense attorney

Sanna Römpötti...................TV crime reporter

Juha Saarnikangas..................Ex-con, former junkie

Härkälä...................Special Prosecutor

Strömberg...................NBI investigator

Rahkonen...................NBI investigator

Jari Tanner..................Released convict

Kimmo Aarnio...................Prisoner

PROLOGUE
END OF SEPTEMBER
BANGKOK, THAILAND

The man felt a shove in his back and stumbled into the room. The black bag covering his head came off, revealing a flushed, gaunt face and scalp matted with sweat. He inhaled sharply to catch his breath. In the stifling heat of the car trunk, he had somehow managed to fight off the growing nausea.

The dimly-lit room had no air conditioning. Sunlight filtered in through the slats in the blinds, striping the floor with shadows. Above them, cigarette smoke snaked around the room under the fan's heavy blades.

A broad-faced Thai was sitting behind a desk. The man couldn't pinpoint the Thai's age—nonetheless, he was not young. The man knew the Thai behind the desk was called Suradech, but he wasn't sure if that was his first or last name. *Mr. Suradech.* He had learned that the Thai man was particular about the "mister."

Twenty minutes earlier the man had been relaxing poolside, with a cold Singha beer in hand. After raining cats and dogs that morning, the clouds had parted, and he took a dip in the hotel pool. That was one of the perks of owning a hotel in Thailand.

Suradech's goons had surprised him as he was climbing out of the pool. He knew resisting would only have made things worse.

"*Perkele,*" Suradech cursed in Finnish. With a Thai accent, however, the attempt sounded more like a pig's squeal. The man understood it though; and to be fair, he hadn't exactly mastered the English language, either.

"Where's the money?"

"I'll pay up," the man said calmly. "I swear."

"You swear?" Mr. Suradech echoed with a cold chuckle. "I've heard that many times."

"But you always get your money. I've had temporary setbacks," the man said.

One of the thugs whacked him behind his knee with an iron pipe.

The blow knocked the Finn to the vinyl floor.

"I don't think you understand."

"What the hell was that?" the Finn managed to get out between groans.

Barely noticeably, Suradech shook his head. The Finn hoped this meant the beating was over, yet he knew a blow to the head could come at any moment.

"Don't you get that I have to pay my debts, too? I give you food, drink, and workers for your hotel. They cost money. Understand?"

Wish you'd send some customers while you're at it, the man thought, but didn't say it. The deal had seemed good until Suradech implemented a unilateral raise in his rates.

"Sure. But the Finnish girl's food poisoning last month was bad for business."

His lip twitching, Mr. Suradech said, "No excuse for not paying me."

"As long as the food you deliver is good."

"She could've gotten it anywhere."

"Bullshit," the man said from the floor. "That chicken salad sat out in the heat for four hours."

Suradech got back to the point.

"You still owe me."

"I'll pay you tomorrow. I'm sure it'll work out."

"That's what you told me last week," Suradech said in an icy tone.

"There's been a slight setback," the man tried to explain. "Business is slow, on account of your salad. That kind of shit spreads like wildfire on the internet. We need to renegotiate our deal."

Mr. Suradech lit another cigarette, though smoke was still coiling up from the one in the ashtray.

The Finn had bought the hotel from Mr. Suradech's acquaintance, an old building that had seen its heyday in the 1970s. The thirty-room hotel wasn't large, but it had a nice pool, and the outdoor restaurant's food met even the high Finnish standards, at least most of the time.

The menu was a big improvement from the prison grub the man remembered only too well. Owning a hotel was his dream come true, and returning to Finland's slushy, snowy winter wasn't an enticing option.

Thoughts buzzed in his mind. Had he been taken? Was Suradech aiming to get the money from him and then get rid of him if things didn't go according to plan? He wondered who had owned the hotel before him.

A quick look at the expressionless man from Thailand convinced the Finn that Mr. Suradech would conduct business with a snap of his fingers. He glanced sideways and recognized the other thug. The same guy directed traffic around the hotel, dressed in a uniform. Gimme a break, the Finn thought.

He simply didn't have enough customers. His agreement with a Finnish travel agency had gone sour—probably because the police had tipped off the agency about his past. Of course! That had to be it. Damn cops.

"Fuck," he cursed from the floor. His knee stung, but what bothered him even more was the entire predicament. In Helsinki, he would've had the power to fight back, but here he was on foreign ground. He could easily bring some guys from back home to deal with Mr. Suradech, but then he'd be in trouble with the Thai police. His only option was to play by Suradech's rules.

Coming up with the money was problematic. He couldn't even think of dealing drugs; it would land him in a rat hole for decades. He was starting to get tired of Thailand, but didn't have anything better at hand. Now that he thought of it, Thailand was the best thing he'd had going for him in years.

Paying Suradech was easy enough. He still had thirty thousand dollars in the safe of his rental condo on the coast. The problem was he'd had a lot more last January. Paying Suradech the ten grand would leave him with twenty. That would give him two months, and then he'd be broke for real.

It looked like he had better get back to Finland. All of his contacts were there, and it would be easier to make money there.

He had a couple of months. Eventually the hotel would prove profitable—he just needed more time. If travel agencies didn't want to work with him, he'd have to get customers by word of mouth. A couple of tattooed goons patrolling the pool could keep Suradech in check.

And this was exactly what he wanted to do: live in a warm country and run a legal business. Granted, the opportunity had presented itself out of the blue, but he wanted to hang on to it. He had already invested more than a hundred thousand dollars, and had even fixed the roof himself. Renovation of the rooms was underway. He couldn't walk away from it now.

Looking Suradech boldly in the eye, he said, "Send the boys to collect the money tomorrow."

"Promise?" the Thai man behind the desk retorted with a chuckle.

"You can always count on the word of a Finn."

"Is that so?"

The Finn got up despite the pain in his knee. He mustered an expression that was as cold as a February night in Helsinki.

"If I gave you my word that I was going to kill you, you wouldn't see the sunrise on the day after tomorrow," the Finn said.

"You don't say," the Thai man replied, paling slightly.

"You can take a Finn at his word."

"Understood," Suradech said.

"Killing you is not my priority right now. I'll get you the money tomorrow, and then I'm heading back to Finland to negotiate a few things. It may take a while. You keep things going here. Or else…"

"Or else…what?" Mr. Suradech asked, perplexed.

The Finn was surprised at the Thai man's hesitancy. Maybe he should've abandoned politeness for assertiveness all along.

"Or I'll have to rethink my priorities. Business at my hotel…*my* hotel…runs smoothly or you'll never see another dollar from me."

Mr. Suradech nodded at the thugs behind the Finn. One of them picked up the black bag and started pulling it over the man's head.

"Go fuck yourself," he said in Finnish, shoving the bag away. Mr. Suradech shook his head at his goon.

THURSDAY,

OCTOBER 18

CHAPTER 1
THURSDAY, 9:30 A.M.
HELSINKI COURTHOUSE

The two men were as opposite in appearance as possible. The well-groomed attorney Risto Niemi sat square-shouldered behind the courtroom table. His distinguished, gray hair was combed, his suit was recently pressed, and his shoes looked spit-shined. Next to him sat Veikko Sandström in a pair of dirty jeans, with greasy, messy dark hair and a rip in the sleeve of his black T-shirt.

But Nea Lind knew that either one of them could have been a rapist. You couldn't judge that book by its cover.

Today they had been arguing the case for twenty minutes or so. It was following the usual formula: at first, as the court did every time it reconvened, the prosecutor had read the charges, the defendant had then pled not guilty, and some other procedural items were discussed. Soon the prosecutor would finally have a chance to explain the details of the case.

The attorney glanced at her client. Lind was glad that Raisa Mäenpää kept her gaze forward and never looked at the suspect.

Lind took in Sandström's acne-covered face once again. It was difficult to determine his age, but Lind had noted from the documents that he was thirty-six.

Niemi, sitting upright, was a bit older. Lind and Niemi knew each other from various cases. The two would greet each other in the courthouse cafeteria, but never share a table. The district court was filled with dozens of attorneys like Niemi. If Risto Niemi were ever to get slapped with a DUI, no crime reporter would identify him as a prominent lawyer, and the incident would hardly make the news.

Lind was startled when Sandström's gaze met hers. The man's sharp eyes didn't match his otherwise haggard appearance. She averted his glance.

"Well," the judge began, in a tired tone. The blonde woman was in her fifties, but her face revealed deep wrinkles. Being a judge apparently took its toll.

"We will hear the defendant next," she said.

The red light outside courtroom 408 indicated that the case was being handled behind closed doors. The only people in the beige-colored room were the judge, the prosecutor, the victim, the suspect, and the two attorneys. The case had begun three months ago. No outsiders, including the press, were allowed in—though it was unlikely anyone would have been interested.

"May I cross-examine my client?" Lind asked.

Raisa Mäenpää sat on Lind's left. The difference in their appearance was as vast as that of the two men sitting fifteen feet away. Lind was wearing a gray suit with a navy blue silk scarf. She was nearing forty and had dark, straight, shoulder-length hair. She wasn't the beauty queen type, but she was pretty. Her long hours meant that she now carried a few extra pounds.

Mäenpää, however, was about thirty pounds overweight. She was wearing a dark cardigan and her dirty-blonde hair was pulled into a sloppy ponytail. She had a few blemishes on her cheek.

It wasn't obvious by the women's appearance which one was the rape victim. As a matter of fact, they both had been raped.

Mäenpää was twenty-five years old. Lind had asked her the first time they met why she had left the bar with the perpetrator. Mäenpää had looked at her and asked, "Why not? For once, someone was interested in me."

Lind was proud of Raisa for reporting the incident to the police. Too often these crimes were not reported, allowing rapists to escape punishment. Lind's job was to get the man behind bars, but she wasn't at all convinced the prosecutor shared her goal. He seemed to have adopted a rather relaxed approach.

"Yes," the judge said. "But let's follow procedure here so we can make progress. The prosecutor will question her first, after which you, as her attorney, can supplement as needed."

Lind nodded. She had no choice. While she would've preferred to open the questioning, it was up to the judge. Lind knew from experience how important it was to manage a cross-examination delicately. She had even arranged for Raisa to enter the courthouse through a side door to avoid seeing Sandström in the lobby. Some attorneys demanded a room divider between the victim and suspect, but Lind disagreed. The case was about a heinous crime, and the victim shouldn't appear compromised. A divider would only serve to bolster the sense of power the rapist had sought in the first place.

The judge turned to Raisa and sternly reminded her that she was to state the whole truth and nothing but the truth.

"Please tell us what happened," the prosecutor said kindly, but in a rather stilted tone that seemed more practiced than genuine. He was the youngest of all the attorneys in the room. His suit may have been the same shade of gray as Niemi's, but Lind knew that he had no experience with rape cases.

"Why don't you start with the events in the bar," Lind interjected.

"Counselor Lind," the judge reprimanded. "You'll have an opportunity to pose your questions later."

Raisa Mäenpää cast a confused look from Lind to the prosecutor.

Prosecutor Rantala attempted to look friendly. The charges he had read earlier were plain and to the point.

According to the charge, Veikko Sandström had invited Raisa Mäenpää to his apartment in the Kallio neighborhood of Helsinki on July 12, threatened her with violence, and raped her. Sandström's defense attorney had denied the charge, claiming that the sex was consensual. It was useless to try to deny the fact that sex was involved; the medical exam had detected loose pubic hairs matching Sandström's DNA.

Nea Lind knew it was his word against hers, and Raisa Mäenpää's story against Veikko Sandström's. Was the sex consensual or not?

The prosecutor removed his glasses and turned to Raisa.

"Let's start with the bar, the Corner Pub. What happened there?"

"I was…" Raisa began weakly.

"Speak up," the prosecutor interrupted. "This is being recorded."

Lind moved the long-necked microphone on the table closer to Raisa's mouth.

"Proceed," the prosecutor said.

"Well, um, I was at the bar, and at some point this guy Veikko came over to chat."

"You mean the accused?" the prosecutor specified, glancing at Sandström.

"Well, who else?" Raisa asked, without looking at the suspect.

"Don't get cute," the judge remarked. "Just answer the questions."

The prosecutor looked pleased.

"What happened next?"

"We talked some more," Raisa said, disconcerted.

"What did you talk about?"

"This and that. I can't remember exactly."

"Okay. Then what happened?"

"After last call we decided to go to Veikko's apartment."

"We?" the prosecutor interrupted. "So, both of you?"

"It was Veikko's idea, and I agreed."

The prosecutor put his glasses back on and glanced at his papers.

"The police report here states that you're the one who suggested it."

"No, it was Veikko."

"What was his wording exactly?"

"I can't remember."

"Try. Think back through the evening," the prosecutor probed.

Lind felt like rolling her eyes, but kept her cool when she noticed the judge looking at her. Raisa needed to recount what happened that evening, but she shouldn't be made to relive it.

"Well, maybe it was something like, 'Let's go to my place.'"

The prosecutor looked at his papers again and was quiet for a moment. Then he asked, "Why did you agree to go to his apartment?"

"It was after last call, and he said he had a bottle of wine at his place."

The prosecutor paused again, annoyingly, and asked, "To have some wine?"

"Yeah."

"Sandström's apartment is located right off the Beltway, about a five-minute walk. What did you talk about on the way?"

"I really can't recall."

Raisa shivered at the thought of that horrible evening's events. She'd had the same feeling at the police station when the lady cop had interrogated her.

"How come you don't remember?"

"We'd been drinking over the course of the evening."

"How much?"

"Well, several beers and ciders."

"How many?"

"I don't usually keep count."

"Alright," the prosecutor said.

Raisa glanced at Lind, who said, "Relax, you're doing fine."

"What happened at the apartment?" the prosecutor asked.

Raisa tried to catch her breath. She felt as if she was being raped all over again. It kept happening in her nightmares, and the medication the doctor had prescribed wasn't helping.

"I'd rather not…" she began, but stopped.

"You'd rather not what?" the prosecutor jumped in.

"Well, actually, I'd rather not think about anything that happened in the apartment."

"Unfortunately, we have to," the prosecutor said, grabbing his glasses again.

"But I already told the police."

The judge looked over and said sternly, "Counselor Lind, haven't you advised your client as to the proceedings?"

"Yes, I have," Lind replied.

Her eyes on Raisa, the judge continued, "You must recount the events exactly as they happened in the apartment. You are required to tell the truth. In case you didn't understand the instructions, I can repeat them. The court convened here to learn the truth, and in this case it comes down to the credibility of you and the accused. Speak now and tell the truth."

Lind saw the crooked smile on the defense attorney's face. He whispered something to Sandström.

"Prosecutor, go ahead," the judge snapped.

"How did things proceed in the apartment?"

Raisa swallowed.

"We, um, we went in. I took off my shoes. I didn't have a coat—it was a warm summer night."

"And?"

Raisa had trouble speaking and her sentences were choppy. She was looking at the ceiling.

"I sat down on the couch... Then he brought two glasses of wine.... And he tried to kiss me. I told him no and tried to push him away. He wouldn't budge. And then he said that...we had come here for sex, and he was gonna beat me up if it didn't happen. And then he did it."

Raisa felt nauseous.

"You didn't resist more than that?" the prosecutor asked.

Nea Lind noticed Raisa's moist eyes.

"I didn't dare. I've been beat up before, and I didn't wanna go through that again... He was a lot stronger than me. I just laid there still; I didn't dare do or say anything."

Raisa remembered the sickening stench of the man on top of her.

"What happened after the rape?"

"I...I said I had to go to the bathroom, and then I ran out of the apartment."

"Where did you go?"

"I...sat crying on the Kallio church steps for probably an hour. I... I..."

"You went to the police that same night, correct?"

"Yeah."

"Did you call anyone?"

"Who would I have called? And bragged about getting raped? No, I didn't call anyone."

"Not even..." the prosecutor searched for the words, "your best friend?"

Tears streamed down Raisa's cheeks as she shook her head and said, "I don't have one."

The prosecutor nodded. "No further questions."

The judge offered the floor to Lind, but she said she had no questions. She didn't want to prolong the situation and hoped Niemi would also see that it wasn't necessary to beat up on the victim any further.

"Niemi, do you have questions?"

"A few," the counselor said, turning to Mäenpää. "How often do you go to the Corner Pub?"

"Well, now and then."

"Several times a week?"

"I guess so."

"How much alcohol do you consume on average?"

"Um, about the same as everyone else."

"Most people don't go to the Corner Pub several nights a week," Niemi said with a smirk. "Do they?"

"Your honor, this is irrelevant to the case," Lind protested.

"Make your point, Counselor," the judge said.

"Yes, Miss Mäenpää, what were you wearing that evening?"

"What was I wearing? I had on a longish, black skirt and a black T-shirt. What's that got to do with it?"

The prosecutor's expression was icy.

"Your job is to answer the questions. How much alcohol did you consume that night?"

"I already told you, several."

"Ten?"

"I couldn't say for sure."

"So you were definitely intoxicated?"

"I guess. Define intoxicated."

"Were you able to walk straight?"

"I guess. I dunno."

"Who paid for the drinks at the pub?"

"Well, I paid for some of them, and then later the man sitting next to you did."

"Did you know each other before?"

"We didn't exactly know each other. But we'd met before."

"At the Corner Pub?"

"Mainly."

"Mainly?"

"It's possible we met at some other bar."

Sandström stared straight ahead with a cold expression.

"A few question about what happened in the apartment. My client claims you wanted to have sex. How come you don't remember that?"

"Objection, irrelevant," Lind inserted.

"You don't have to answer that," the judge said.

Nea Lind couldn't believe that Niemi would stoop this low.

After a short pause, Niemi continued, "Please explain why the medical exam found no signs of struggle on your body— not even a bruise. And your skirt was completely intact."

"I… I…" Raisa began. She struggled to talk through her tears. "I told him to stop."

"Why didn't you sustain any injuries?" Niemi went on.

"My client already answered the question," Lind interrupted.

Raisa Mäenpää buried her face in her hands and sobbed.

"Does your client need a moment?" the judge asked.

"No," Raisa said through her hands. "Let's get this over with."

Lind handed Raisa a tissue, and she wiped her eyes and blew her nose.

"When I was seventeen, a guy beat the crap out of me. I didn't want that again. I just didn't."

"What did my client say to threaten you?"

"Well, he said he'd hit me if I didn't give it to him…"

"Are you sure about the wording? At the police interrogation, you used the word beat."

"It's the same thing."

"But I asked you what wording he used to threaten you."

"I…"

Lind looked sternly at the judge, who was allowing this to happen.

Niemi continued, "You don't remember? Is it possible that you're imagining the threats?"

"No, no, no! He threatened to beat me," Mäenpää said.

"Hit you or beat you?" Niemi insisted.

Unable to keep quiet, Lind said, "Completely irrelevant."

Niemi put on an innocent face. "I'm only trying to establish the victim's credibility."

"Proceed," the judge said.

Picking up his papers, Niemi asked, "Did you undress yourself?"

"I... Yeah, he said he'd beat me if I didn't take off my skirt."

Lind knew that in Raisa Mäenpää's mind she was being raped in the courthouse for the second time within a short period. First with the prosecutor's questions and now with Niemi's.

"You also took off your underwear yourself?"

"Yeah," Raisa Mäenpää said.

"Last question. Did the man use a condom?" the attorney asked.

"Uh, well, yeah, I already told the police that."

"Was it his or did you give it to him?"

"I don't understand. I didn't give it to him."

"Do you carry condoms?"

"I don't..."

"Answer the question."

"I usually do..."

"You're talking to a man in the pub," Niemi went on, looking at Raisa Mäenpää. "The evening is going along nicely. You leave with him to go to his apartment for some wine. You carry condoms in your purse. You undress yourself and your skirt is intact. You have no injuries. You can't remember what words the man used to threaten you. Do you still claim you were raped?"

"I didn't want to… I just didn't want to."

"No further questions," Niemi said.

ONE MONTH LATER

MONDAY,

NOVEMBER 26

CHAPTER 2
MONDAY, 11:10 P.M.
HOTEL PASILA, HELSINKI

Suhonen knew he was drunk, but he wasn't as plastered as his homicide-unit colleague Anna Joutsamo. She had trouble walking straight, and Suhonen was escorting her by the arm to the taxi station.

Their plan had been just a couple of beers to take the edge off after a tough shift. Detective Lieutenant Kari Takamäki and VCU Detective Mikko Kulta had joined them at the bar in Hotel Pasila, and the evening had stretched on. It was only eleven, but since they'd started drinking around three in the afternoon, the pints had added up. Kulta had even bought them a round of shots. An hour earlier, Joutsamo had suggested they find a karaoke joint. She wanted to sing Elvis's "Suspicious Minds" as a duet with Suhonen. That's when Suhonen realized how bombed she was.

Suhonen had his arm around the brunette sergeant to hold her up, and she leaned firmly into his side.

A tram clanked by on Pasilanraitio Street twenty yards away. Joutsamo could ride it home, but Suhonen knew tonight it was time for a taxi. The taxi station was near the hotel and, luckily, Joutsamo didn't live far away. She wouldn't have time to fall asleep in the cab.

"Listen," Joutsamo began.

"I'm putting you in a taxi."

Joutsamo whirled around to face Suhonen, grabbed his head and kissed him. It caught Suhonen totally by surprise, and he didn't know what to do. The kiss lingered for a few seconds, and he tasted alcohol in the woman's mouth.

"Let's go to my place," Joutsamo mumbled into Suhonen's ear.

Suhonen wondered if the woman could really be this wasted. He found her perfectly attractive, and neither of them was currently in a relationship, but a workplace romance that started in a drunken slosh just seemed like a really bad idea.

"Get in the cab," Joutsamo said, pulling Suhonen by the hand. She swayed, but Suhonen's grip kept her upright. There was only one taxi waiting at the stop and Suhonen hoped it wouldn't leave without them. Suhonen decided he needed to see Joutsamo home and they made it into the Mercedes without falling over.

"To Töölö, Tykistö Street," Suhonen said. "By Mamma Rosa." Suhonen knew his colleague's address because he'd picked her up for work a few times.

The cab took off. Joutsamo laid her head on Suhonen's shoulder and wrapped her arm around his waist. She purred something, but Suhonen couldn't make out what it was. She smelled good. He hesitated for a moment and then stroked his colleague's coarse, dark hair.

* * *

Takamäki chuckled to himself on the backseat of his taxi and debated if he should send Suhonen an Elvis-themed text, but decided against it. Takamäki was familiar with the song. Kulta had looked it up on his iPhone and seen that Elvis recorded "Suspicious Minds" in 1969, when it rose to the top of the charts. *Rolling Stone* magazine ranked it 91st on the all-time Top 500. The song stuck in Takamäki's mind after Kulta played it over and over in the bar.

On Beltway I, the taxi took the exit ramp before the tunnel and continued onto the old Turku highway. The light was green. The railroad, Leppävaara station, and Sello mall all passed by on the left as the taxi looped under the beltway bridge.

The much-needed evening out with the team had been fun. Early fall had been busy at the Pasila Police Station. The Helsinki PD was focused on saving money—not its personnel. Takamäki couldn't ask his investigators to put in extra hours anymore if they weren't getting paid for the overtime.

An earlier reorganization at the Helsinki PD had messed up their workloads, as it usually happens. Workloads didn't get distributed evenly; some units got too much, while others did just fine. No one had too little on their plate—Takamäki could've used a couple more detectives.

This latest reorganization had split the VCU into two groups: one for long-term cases and a separate one for routine investigations. Back when the VCU had been assigned follow-up of petty thefts on the street, including grocery store holdups, it had received six additional detectives. Now that these same crimes were transferred to a routine investigations team, twenty-two investigators went with it.

Takamäki's team stayed in the long-term investigations group, but sometimes had to lend a hand on routine cases due to that group's overload.

That morning they had wrapped up the investigation on a homicide case that had drawn a lot of publicity. The motive, jealousy, wasn't unusual, but since the crime took place in the upper-class neighborhood of Kulosaari, it became a media sensation. Mrs. Von Alftan, sixty-seven, had killed her husband, about the same age, when he had threatened to leave her for a younger woman. She had shot her sleeping husband in cold blood.

They had been a wealthy couple. The woman had taken 250,000 euros in cash and the jewelry from the house safe and headed for the airport. She might have made her escape if it wasn't for some bad luck. She had forgotten to cancel the cleaning lady, who showed up an hour before her flight was scheduled to depart for London.

Thanks to Joutsamo, Mrs. Von Alftan was picked up after she'd boarded the plane. The ever-suspecting Joutsamo had checked the passenger lists of ships and flights after she couldn't reach Mrs. Von Alftan on her cell phone. The London flight proved to be the winner.

At first, Mrs. Von Alftan wouldn't confess, but finally broke down after a few days of interrogation. Takamäki's team had handled the case as a murder one investigation; it had been clear-cut—and even though they had just delivered the case files to the prosecutor around noon today, Takamäki knew that the verdict would be life in prison.

After putting in the hours on such a high pressure case, a spontaneous celebration was called for. When they planned evenings out ahead of time, everyone usually had a beer or two and then went home.

Tonight they'd been drinking beers for a cause.

Takamäki yawned.

"Long night?" the cab driver asked in the rearview mirror.

"And wet," Takamäki replied. "Luckily, tomorrow is my day off."

"Not for me," the driver said.

"Well, even though your night may be long, I hope it's not wet."

The taxi passed several apartment complexes and turned onto a narrow street lined by townhomes. Takamäki sensed something was wrong. Blue flashing lights slashed the smoky air. He realized it was fire trucks.

"I think I'll leave you here," the driver said, stepping on the brake a hundred fifty feet from the nearest fire engine.

"Yeah, okay."

Takamäki paid cash for the ride and got out, concerned. From this distance it was hard to say which unit was burning, but he knew it was his building.

Another fire truck drove up and Takamäki stepped out of the way onto the sidewalk. Some residents had come outside to watch.

Takamäki thought through the morning's events. He hadn't used the sauna. He had made coffee, but turned off the coffeemaker. The television was off, too. None of the electric appliances seemed a likely cause, but of course many of them stayed plugged in all the time.

He counted five fire trucks. His beer buzz disappeared as he walked up closer. The worry became a grimace as Takamäki realized the firefighters were focusing on his unit.

The flames rose high in the dark sky.

* * *

The taxi stopped in front of a light gray apartment building on Töölö Square. Suhonen pulled a wallet out of his breast pocket and handed the driver a twenty.

"Keep the change."

The driver thanked him.

Suhonen had planned on leaving Joutsamo at her place and continuing in the taxi to his home in Kallio, but he changed his mind. Joutsamo's arm was limp and a soft snore confirmed that she was asleep. He'd have to help her into the apartment.

"The lady decided to take a nap, so I'll lift her out on the other side," Suhonen said to the driver.

The cabbie turned around and said in a worried tone, "All the same to me, as long as she doesn't puke in the car. That'll cost you five hundred."

Suhonen got out from behind the driver and rounded the taxi to the other side.

Trying to pull Joutsamo out by the hand was useless. Shit, he thought. He knew the only way to get her inside was to wake her.

"Hey, Anna," Suhonen said, reaching into the car. He wrapped his arm around the woman and pulled her out of the cab.

The street was lined with parked cars, but the sidewalk was deserted. Suhonen was glad no one was around to watch. He managed to get Joutsamo on her feet as she was waking up.

The light-gray, 1930s-era apartment building stood behind them.

Joutsamo perked up from moving around in the crisp weather.

"Darling, you're such a sweetheart," she cooed, smiling. "Where are we?"

"In front of your place. Do you have your keys?"

Joutsamo stuck her hand in her pocket as the taxi drove off. She pulled out a set of keys.

Suhonen had an idea and grabbed his cell phone.

"What do you say we preserve this moment in a picture?"

"Of course," Joutsamo said with a smile.

Suhonen stretched out his hand and Joutsamo moved close to him. As the cellphone camera flashed, shedding light on the photo op, Joutsamo decided to plant a kiss on Suhonen's cheek.

"Is it a good one?" Joutsamo asked.

Suhonen looked at the screen and said, "Helluva good shot. The urban photo of the year. Eight million stories in the city, and this is one of the best. The most interesting of the evening, at least."

"Let me see," Joutsamo chirped and Suhonen turned the phone.

"It's great, right?"

"Damn, my eyes are so screwed up I can't really see."

"I don't think I can hit the lock," Joutsamo said and handed Suhonen the keys.

Suhonen kept his arm around the woman's waist as they walked to the door. He had never asked her how she could afford living in Töölö. Her last apartment had been closer to downtown, but even in this part of Töölö the rent for a one-bedroom was over a thousand euros. On the other hand, a VCU sergeant made almost four thousand a month, so that was probably enough. Of course, Suhonen had never asked if she owned the apartment or just rented.

The front door required a code, which Joutsamo managed to punch in correctly on the second try. They stepped into the warm hallway.

As they entered the elevator, Joutsamo kissed Suhonen again.

"Fourth floor," she said in the middle of the kiss.

Suhonen pressed the button and the elevator took off with a jerk. He felt her chest pressed against his.

* * *

Takamäki noticed a police car and an officer with a crew cut dressed in blue coveralls standing next to it. As Takamäki got a few feet away from the car, the officer turned to him.

"Who are you?" the boulder-of-an-officer asked.

"I live in that burning house," Takamäki said solemnly.

"Do you know if anyone's inside?"

"Nobody's inside," Takamäki said, shaking his head.

His wife had passed away a few years ago in a car accident. His older son was studying in Vaasa, north on Finland's west coast, and the younger son had gone into the army the previous summer. Back in Takamäki's day, the army kept the boys three out of four weekends and sent them on leave once a month, but now it seemed the opposite; apparently the military wanted to save on the cost of the meals. But Joonas was on the Santahamina military base on duty this weekend. Takamäki had called him earlier.

"What's your name?" the officer asked.

"Kari Takamäki."

The officer sniffed the air. The smell of alcohol was evident even in the midst of smoke.

"And where have you been? Securing an alibi at a local pub?"

In principle, Takamäki liked the officer's attitude. Everyone was a suspect. But in the glare of the fire he wasn't impressed.

"My alibi is foolproof," he said a little too sharply. "I have three police witnesses. No need to question it."

"Is that so?" the officer retorted in a challenging tone. "If that's your attitude, we best continue this at the Kilo police station after you've sobered up."

Takamäki reached slowly into his breast pocket, telling the officer that he was only going for his wallet. He showed his Helsinki PD ID card to the young officer, who took a close look at it.

"Okay, you're a cop yourself. I didn't recognize you."

"Now, could you tell me what's going on here? That's my place."

"It's burning."

A fireman was spraying water from a truck. The smoke had turned into a light-colored vapor.

"Why?"

"No idea. You should know the investigators can't go on the site until the fire is out."

"Where are the crime unit guys?"

"At home, I guess," the officer said with a chuckle. "They probably won't be here until morning, if then. Of course, if we happened to find a dead body inside, they'd be called. But you said there's nobody in there."

Takamäki looked at his home. The high flames had subsided, but he could see a glow of fire inside.

The situation looked grim. The place wouldn't be livable for weeks, or even months. At least the firefighters were able to confine the fire to his unit.

"Shit," Takamäki burst out.

"I know," the officer said. "It's a hell of a thing...Do you have somewhere to stay?"

Suhonen was lounging on the living room couch in the one-bedroom apartment. A glass of cider sat on the low, gray Ikea sofa table. Joutsamo had brought him the drink and then said she needed to use the bathroom. Judging by the continuous sounds of vomiting, the toilet bowl encounter would take a while.

Suhonen took a sip of the cold drink. It tasted good—nice and dry, and not as sweet as some of the American ciders he had tried on his trip to the States a few years back. The television sports channel showed highlights of last night's NHL games. The announcers raved about the Detroit Red Wings player Valtteri Filppula in his red jersey making a classic pass to the back post, which the right winger slammed into the empty net. Suhonen played hockey, too, and had trained with the police hockey team in the fall.

Joutsamo was home safe and sound; Suhonen could have left by now. But on the other hand, she had brought him the drink and he didn't want to leave a full glass on the coffee table. And this way he could keep tabs on Joutsamo. Alcohol poisoning could be hard on those who weren't heavy drinkers.

Suhonen was glad that Joutsamo had kissed him; it didn't lead to anything sexual but felt nice. With her inhibitions lowered by the alcohol, he had seen tonight what has been lurking in her thoughts.

Joutsamo's hangover, however, would be gruesome. That's why he had taken a picture of her. He wasn't sure if it would make the situation better or worse, but it was some kind of proof anyway.

He heard a phone ring and recognized it as his. The phone was in the pocket of his leather jacket, hanging on a hook in the entryway. The call was from Takamäki; Suhonen noted the time as 11:48 P.M. This wasn't unusual for Takamäki, since his late night calls were always about work, and crime took place at all hours.

However, a couple of years ago in May, Takamäki's late night call was personal, and he had asked Suhonen to come over right away. Suhonen wondered, but went as asked. Kari then told him that his wife had died in an automobile accident that afternoon, and they had talked well into the night.

"Suhonen," he answered, then added, "What's wrong? Lost your keys?"

"Got the keys, lost the house," Takamäki said.

"Huh?" Suhonen returned to the couch. Joutsamo was still throwing up in the bathroom.

"My place is on fire. It's quite the show. About ten fire trucks are trying to make sure the fire doesn't spread into the other units."

"Wait..." Suhonen replied. "Come again?"

Takamäki's voice was surprisingly calm, and he sounded as somber as a radio newscaster.

"My house is on fire. No idea of the cause. It's pretty grim."

"Do you want me to come over?" Suhonen asked.

"No need. The Espoo detectives will look through the place tomorrow."

"Arson?" Suhonen asked.

"No idea. But I know the sauna wasn't on, and I didn't make oatmeal this morning."

"You been getting any threats lately?"

"Nothing acute like this."

"So expect the detectives from Espoo bright and early?" Suhonen asked. He tried to remember if he'd heard any recent threats against Takamäki, but couldn't think of anything.

"I don't think there's anything else to be done."

"The house of a Helsinki homicide detective is burning due to an unknown cause. Sounds like a case for the National Bureau of Investigation."

"Well, let's wait to see what they find about the cause," Takamäki said. "Who knows, the television might've set itself on fire."

"What a shame," Suhonen said. "Did you lose everything?"

"Yeah, it's a total loss. I don't think there's anything left. Luckily, my most important photos are on a flash drive at work. The flames looked pretty menacing when I got here."

"Where are you going to sleep?"

"The Kilo Hotel, I…" Takamäki didn't finish the sentence.

"Well, I'm at Joutsamo's place at the moment. Maybe you should come here."

After a pause, Takamäki asked, "Joutsamo's place?"

Suhonen laughed. "Miss Suspicious Minds is puking in the bathroom. She's pretty messed up. I thought I'd stay here long enough to get her head out of the toilet and onto a pillow. It'll take at least an hour or two. Hop in a cab and come over. We can fit two on this sofa bed."

* * *

Suhonen startled awake and cautiously opened his eyes. Takamäki's face, still asleep, was a foot away from his. He'd had more attractive things to wake up to, but nothing that got him up this quickly.

Suhonen glanced at his watch: 8:23. He looked up and saw Joutsamo in the bedroom doorway, in a white T-shirt and panties. Her face pale, she headed for the bathroom.

Suhonen stood up and felt a bit dizzy, but his hangover wasn't too horrible. He put on his jeans and went into the kitchen. He looked for a coffeemaker, but found only an electric water kettle. Of course, no coffeemaker—Joutsamo never drank coffee at the station either. Suhonen poured water into the kettle, and started it.

He opened the refrigerator and poured himself a glass of apple juice. He pulled a thin slice of Parma ham out of the package and stuffed it in his mouth. Then he took the package of ham, some cheese, and a tub of margarine to the small table in the corner of the living room. A basket of bread was already there.

The apartment was a typical five-hundred-forty-square-foot, one-bedroom in Töölö. The kitchen was between the bedroom and the living room, and the bathroom was by the entryway. The décor was modern, but not particularly feminine.

Joutsamo came out of the bathroom and jumped when she saw Suhonen in the kitchen.

"What are you…?"

Her voice was hoarse from too much alcohol the night before, and having just awakened. Her dark hair was a mess.

Suhonen gave her a grin and said, "You invited me in."

"Shit," Joutsamo grunted. She disappeared into the bedroom and quickly returned wearing a pair of loose, gray sweatpants.

As Suhonen was setting the breakfast table for three, Takamäki opened his eyes slightly and grunted a "good morning."

"So all three of us came up here, huh?" Joutsamo said, sitting down at the table. She chugged her glass of juice, then refilled it.

"Actually, no," Suhonen replied. He was glad Takamäki had ended up joining them. He'd have less to explain if he wasn't here alone.

"Fill me in. I seem to be having trouble piecing my memory back together. The last thing I remember is you wanting to go to some karaoke bar to sing Elvis songs."

"You were the one who wanted to go," Suhonen corrected her.

"I can vouch for that," Takamäki inserted. He had put on his jeans and was headed for the bathroom. It dawned on him that the only clothes he owned now were the ones he was wearing—aside from the suit coat, white shirt, and blue tie he kept at work. He'd have to buy some underwear.

"I see," Joutsamo said. "I hope we didn't go."

"We didn't," Suhonen told her.

Takamäki was at the bathroom door.

"The Ibuprofen is in the medicine cabinet," Joutsamo said.

When Takamäki disappeared into the bathroom, Suhonen pulled out his cell phone.

"I'll show you a picture…"

"A picture? Dammit."

"Yeah, maybe it'll shed some light. After Takamäki and Kulta left the Pasila bar, you were adamant that we come here to continue the party."

"I was?"

"Yep," Suhonen said. "Well, you were so totally wasted that I thought it best to see you home." He spoke fast, hoping to finish before Takamäki came back from the bathroom.

"Okay," Joutsamo said.

Suhonen showed her the picture where she was kissing him on the cheek.

"We got a cab, and I brought you here."

"We didn't…," Joutsamo began, looking up at Suhonen. "Did we?"

"No," Suhonen said, shaking his head. "You went into the bathroom right away and got friendly with the toilet. I decided to stay for a while and make sure you were okay."

"Thanks, that was sweet of you," Joutsamo said sincerely.

"Anytime," Suhonen replied with a smile. "I don't guess you want to save it?"

Shaking her head, Joutsamo handed Suhonen the phone, and he deleted the picture.

"And how did the boss end up here?"

"That's a more dramatic story. Fire trucks were at his place when he got there. His house was in flames."

"No!"

"Yup. Apparently it was really bad. Nobody hurt, though. The boys were out."

"But why?"

Takamäki came back from the bathroom, and Suhonen asked him, "So, still no information on the cause of the fire?"

"No. The firefighters said it was aggressive and spread fast."

"And this morning, I kept wondering where that slight smell of smoke was coming from," Joutsamo said.

"My clothes. I don't have anything else to wear."

"You think someone started the fire on purpose?"

"It's possible."

Takamäki brought the tea kettle and a box of tea bags to the table.

"Anybody threaten you lately?" Joutsamo asked.

"Nothing serious. But we've always said that the loudmouths who make threats aren't nearly as dangerous as the sinister ones plotting in secret."

"So now what?" Joutsamo asked.

"Guess I need to go over there to see the damage. And then I'll have to go buy socks, underwear, shirts, and a toothbrush."

"You remember what we agreed last night?" Suhonen asked in a serious tone.

"Yeah, but that was a bunch of drunken bull," Takamäki said with a nod.

"No, we'll stick to it. We already had the conversation."

Takamäki chuckled and made himself a sandwich.

"What did you agree on?" Joutsamo asked.

"Kari will stay at my place until he can find his own apartment to rent."

Joutsamo drank her strawberry tea, shaking her head.

"All in all, it was quite a night," she said.

CHAPTER 4
TUESDAY, 11:00 A.M.
LEPPÄVAARA, ESPOO

The sun shone low in the sky, with a north wind blowing, on the crisp, clear fall day. Standing in front of his townhouse, Takamäki smelled the smoke that had infused his clothes. The Espoo Police Forensics' white van plus two vans from a private damage restoration company were parked on the street. Since nobody was outside, they must be inside.

Smoke had blackened the townhome's cream-colored wall, especially above the broken windows. The tin roof was torn open. Charred truss pieces and burnt furniture had been thrown into the front yard. The lawn was a pool of mud from all the water and firemen's boot stomps.

Takamäki had homeowner's insurance, and the association which actually owned the townhouse structure also had insurance, so the losses would be covered.

He hesitated for a moment, then decided to walk closer. Instinctively, he looked for clues. The front door was busted—probably by the firemen. The smell was even stronger there. Takamäki opened the door to the heartrending sight. The whole main level was completely black, with a few pieces of mangled furniture left on the wet floor. Even the kitchen table was burnt to a crisp.

He had come through the door a thousand times into this home that no longer existed.

"Who are you?" asked a man in white coveralls from the far end of the living room. He was holding a camera.

"Detective Lieutenant Takamäki from Helsinki Homicide," Takamäki replied. Being clear about his rank might spare him from having to explain.

"Is this fire related to one of your cases?" the man asked.

"No. I live here."

"In that case, I'm sorry," said the round-bellied officer in his fifties, who introduced himself as Markus Kuusela from the Espoo PD.

Takamäki looked around his home. At Helsinki PD, fire investigations were handled by the arson division, but Takamäki had seen plenty of ruined houses that criminals had torched in order to destroy evidence.

"It looks like a hefty fire," Takamäki remarked.

"Yep. That's what made me wonder at first. Usually a place will end up looking like this only in the far corners of Espoo where it takes fire trucks a while to reach the scene. But here, the Leppävaara fire station is only a few minutes away."

Takamäki didn't say anything. Memories flooded his mind. His family had lived here for over a decade. His kids had grown up here. They had played floor hockey and Legos on the living room parquet floor that was now charred. His eyes teared up.

"We'll get the dog in here soon to help us sniff out and locate any chemicals, but you can smell it now, can't you?" Kuusela said.

Now that Kuusela mentioned it, Takamäki detected a sharp smell amidst the smoke.

"Tests will confirm it, but I think it's pretty obvious. The smell, the extent of the destruction, and the quick pace—I'm sure it was gasoline. I can't tell if they used commercial gasoline or some sort of homemade napalm."

"Arson," Takamäki pondered.

"It's obvious that someone came in and poured the gas up and down, then set it on fire and fled the scene. Luckily, it's a newer building, and the roof was built in sections. Otherwise, the rest of the townhomes would've burned, too."

"Then that's the only good thing," Takamäki said gravely.

"Wonder if it's related to your job," Kuusela said. "That's not part of my job description though. The detectives will contact you shortly," he added.

"Who's in charge of the investigation?"

"I don't know, actually," Kuusela said with a shake of his head. "Someone from the Espoo VCU."

Takamäki glanced at the blackened staircase and asked, "How's the upstairs?"

"It looks exactly the same as down here. That's why I think the gasoline was spread into every room. You'd better hit the mall today and get yourself some underwear. Everything here is junk. A fireproof cabinet might have made it, if you have one."

"I don't," Takamäki said. He realized that the fire had destroyed all the family's documents, including passports, insurance papers, and bank statements. Luckily, he had the passwords for his internet banking in his wallet, so the arsonist couldn't have stolen them, and he wouldn't have to close his bank account.

Takamäki said goodbye to Kuusela and turned to face his home. It was totally gone. He decided never to return.

* * *

Attorney Nea Lind took another look at the verdict. It made her furious. Some hefty curse words were on the tip of her tongue, but they wouldn't do in the office of the Helsinki District Court.

That morning, Lind had defended a man accused of theft and driving under the influence. Afterward, she had come to read the verdict in Raisa Mäenpää's rape case.

Lind knew she needed to calm down before heading to the courthouse cafeteria. With its glass walls facing the main lobby, the cafeteria, which was often packed at noon with attorneys, suspects, and prosecutors, was a great place for curious onlookers to observe judicial behavior. Once in the cafeteria, she set her leather purse on a chair at the only available table, and joined the line. A moment later, she sat down with her coffee and a sweet roll. Lind read the district court's decision again, huffing at some of the judge's arguments.

"Okay if I sit here?" a woman asked.

Lind looked up. Crime reporter Sanna Römpötti was dressed all in black. The forty-year-old reporter's tight hair bun pulled her cheeks taut.

A bad luck bird, Lind thought.

"Of course," she said.

Römpötti sat down. She had bought a cappuccino and a savory Karelian pastry warmed up and loaded with egg butter.

"Something eating you?" Römpötti asked.

"Is it that obvious?"

Römpötti took a bite of her pastry, and crumbles of egg butter fell onto the plate.

"Look at this," Lind said. The decision had been stamped "Confidential," but in her rage she didn't care.

Römpötti leafed through the ten pages.

"You were Mäenpää's attorney?"

"Yeah. It was a pretty miserable case."

Römpötti sipped her hot cappuccino as she read the verdict.

"Wow," the crime reporter said as she got to the last page.

"Right?"

"I'm glad he was convicted, but a suspended sentence of a year and three months for a rape isn't very much."

"Yeah. It was basically the least possible punishment."

In Finnish law, the minimum conviction for rape was a year in prison.

"And the damages for pain and suffering was fifteen hundred," Römpötti added, still looking at the document.

"Do you know what a garden dormouse is?" Lind asked.

"No," Römpötti said, wondering.

"It's an endangered animal. If you were to kill one of those, the fine would be the same as the one in this rape case."

"Was it a straightforward case?" the reporter asked.

"It was largely based on the victim's statements."

"Then I understand... Well, I don't understand it, but I get the district court's logic. The crime aspect is a bit unclear to the judge, which makes it easy to only give probation. Just in case the perpetrator happened to be innocent, at least he stays out of prison."

"But if he's guilty, he goes without punishment."

Römpötti could relate to the attorney's frustration. Lind had been a victim of rape herself only the year before. In her case, the punishment was far from lenient. The rapist had gotten life in prison, because he was also convicted of two murders.

Lind had been on sick leave for practically the entire winter and returned to the courthouse just last spring.

"How did Mäenpää handle reliving the rape in court?"

"The proceedings were full of shit. The judge let the defense harass the victim in the courtroom. She left with tears running down her face."

"Who represented Sandström?"

"Risto Niemi," Lind replied. "He's a pig."

Römpötti kept sipping her cappuccino. She had finished the pastry.

"He is pretty aggressive. I've been in the courtroom with him a few times. Listen, if I were to do a story on rape convictions, would you comment on air?"

"This case was heard behind closed doors, so I wouldn't be able to comment in detail. But in general, absolutely."

Römpötti pondered the angle for the story. It wasn't all that uncommon to get probation for rape; the reporter knew that it was given in four out of ten rape cases. A rape was about violence, whereby the perpetrator wanted to oppress the victim. It wasn't about sex; rather it was using someone of perceived lesser value to inflate the rapist's self-image.

"Do you think Raisa would be willing to talk to the camera, maybe with her back to it?" Römpötti asked.

"I don't know, but I can ask her."

Römpötti had asked the same question of many victims. Only a few were willing. The reporter wondered why there was always so much shame attached to rape cases, as if the victims were to blame.

Lind had spoken on television talk shows about her rape. Something she had said had stayed with Römpötti: "The rapist doesn't deserve to have me wallowing in my trauma. Am I supposed to refuse to live happily, and vow to hate men? The answer is simply no."

Lind was known as the rape specialist. But she only represented victims and refused to take on suspects' cases. This fact, along with the publicity Lind had accumulated on the subject, likely irritated some district judges.

* * *

Joutsamo had been relaxing on her couch, watching television, when the prosecutor had called to tell her that Veikko Sandström only got probation. Takamäki's team had ended up with the case because the sex crime investigators were tied up with a serial rapist case from the summer. Joutsamo had been in charge of the Raisa Mäenpää case. The investigation had been simple for the most part, but to determine exactly what happened in the apartment was complicated.

Joutsamo decided to use her hangover day to think about the verdict. Of course, it wasn't exactly her business—it was up to the police to investigate, the prosecutor to prosecute, and the court to judge.

But probation for rape? The problem, in Joutsamo's opinion, was that the punishment usually wasn't harsh enough.

Philosophers and law students throughout the ages had wondered why criminals were sent to prison in the first place. One theory claimed it was about revenge. If society as a whole didn't react to crime, then individuals would—the victims' families would pursue an eye for an eye. A well-functioning society's role was to dish out punishment for crime. But if the punishment wasn't severe enough, the victims' hunger for revenge wouldn't be satisfied. The scales of Lady Justice, the Roman goddess, would be off balance.

The scales were never even when it came to suspended sentences because it presented no concrete consequences for the crime. In Finland, the only crime that came with a sizeable punishment was murder, with a prison sentence of about fourteen years.

In Joutsamo's experience, fear of punishment was no deterrent. Rather, the lack of serious consequences served as an incentive for criminals. Prison math and the economy had completely changed the picture. If the punishment for manslaughter was ten years, first-time offenders would get off with half of that and repeat offenders with two thirds. Those under twenty-one would only have to serve a third of the ten years.

Cost cuts had been levied to offset the expense of prisoner care. Parole shaved another six months off the sentence. Short sentences were changed to community service with electronic ankle bracelets. Even hardened criminals now ended up in low-security prisons.

Police work was frustrating since it was the same criminals who kept causing people harm. It seemed of little use to find the perpetrator, knowing that the same individual would be back on the streets in short time or, in the case of a serious crime, in just a few years.

Veikko Sandström had raped a woman and got off with punishment noted only on paper. For a guy like him, probation meant nothing.

Joutsamo's headache had returned, and she decided to concentrate on the sit-com.

CHAPTER 5
TUESDAY, 1:55 P.M.
KALLIO, HELSINKI

Raisa Mäenpää walked into the Corner Pub on Helsinki Street in the Kallio neighborhood. The bar was half full, which was pretty typical for a Tuesday afternoon. Happy Hour was to start at three o'clock. It was warm in the bar, and Raisa took off her down coat. Outside, a cold wind blew through the apartment-building canyon of Helsinki Street.

Raisa had worked her nine-to-one shift at the grocery store. The store called her at eight in the morning on the days they needed her to come in. Her wages and her various welfare payments were enough to pay for a few beers in the pub.

Raisa looked around for her friend Salla, who hadn't gotten there yet.

Lind had called and told Raisa about Sandström getting probation. Raisa thought the man should've gone to prison, but she wasn't overly concerned. She and Veikko had avoided each other in the pub, and hadn't talked about what happened. The others didn't even know about it because the case was handled behind closed doors. That suited Raisa fine.

She was pleased with the fifteen-hundred-euro compensation. According to her attorney, though, it would take a while to get the money.

The bar counter was near the front door, and the room narrowed toward the back. The sound system was playing Eppu Normaali's melancholy tunes from the early '90s. The old television sets had been replaced by flat screens a few years ago, but the brown wooden tables were still from the same era as the music. The black cigarette burn marks on the tables told of the time when smoking was still allowed in the bar.

Raisa liked the place. It felt comfortable and she was one of the crowd—a regular, who belonged there. She said hello to the familiar, mustached bartender and asked for a cider.

"How's it going?" the bartender asked.

Rane wasn't tall, but he had broad shoulders. Raisa knew he'd been known in the Tampere powerlifting circles a decade ago.

"I'm doing alright," Raisa replied, wondering why he'd ask. "I worked this morning."

Rane wasn't usually interested in the customers' lives. Time and again, Raisa had watched him ignore the drunkards bearing their souls, and say that he was there to pour booze, not to listen to people's problems.

"Why do you ask?" Raisa continued.

"Here's your drink," Rane said, handing her the glass.

Raisa knew the price and paid with a five-euro bill. The bartender slipped it in the cash register and handed her a euro coin and the receipt. Raisa stuffed them into her jeans pocket. No tip was expected for anything under five euros.

The dry, cold cider had a nice edge. She was glad the court case was over. Her attorney had suggested she appeal, but she didn't want to.

She grabbed an evening paper from the counter and flipped through it. The front page article about a singer and a member of Parliament asked if it was appropriate for a twenty-year-old pop star to be seeing a man in his fifties. Raisa didn't feel strongly about it—she felt it was their business.

A small article in the newspaper said the police were looking for a rapist in Tampere. Seeing the article brought her own rape back to her mind. She had repeatedly chided herself for going with Sandström. She'd been so helpless, paralyzed. She should've fought him. She felt dirty somehow and had started showering twice a day. Many nights, she could only sleep with the help of alcohol.

Somehow, the events of that night seemed distant now. But she still kept a careful eye out while on the streets, especially at night. She checked behind her each time she opened her front door. She couldn't even dream of dating a man, and didn't want to talk about it with Salla. There was no need to burden her friend, and she couldn't bear the thought of her friend growing tired of the story. It was better to stick to, say, the affairs between politicians and singers. Today Raisa would probably say she thought the man was using the young woman, unless Salla had a different view.

Raisa took a long sip of her cider. Fuck, she was such a pitiful creature. But it felt good to be at the Corner Pub. She couldn't face being alone today.

Rane returned from the back of the bar, carrying empty glasses. He loaded the dishwasher behind the counter, filled a beer mug, and took the money for it.

The bartender stopped next to Raisa and said, "Listen, Raisa, I wonder if it's smart for you to be here."

"What do you mean?" Raisa asked.

"Well, Sandström is over there in the back."

"Oh?"

Rane nodded.

"What's that got to do with me?" she continued.

The man thought for a moment, then said, "Well, based on his stories, I just thought I'd warn you."

"What stories?"

After a moment's hesitation, the man said, "He's talking about the district court decision he got today."

"He's talking about it?" Raisa asked, stunned.

"Yeah."

"What's he saying?"

"You don't wanna know," Rane said and immediately seemed to regret opening his mouth. The bartender wouldn't lie, out of principle, so it was usually best to keep quiet, especially if he wasn't sure how the truth would be taken. He also hated the arguments he had to listen to on the job, especially those of married couples. There were plenty at the Corner Pub.

"I do wanna know."

"No, you don't."

"Tell me word for word what he's saying about it," Raisa demanded. She glanced around and wondered how many in the bar already knew she had been raped.

"He's bragging about it."

"How's he bragging about it? He was convicted."

A raucous laughter erupted in the back of the pub.

"He's saying mean things."

"Tell me what he said!"

"Remember I warned you," the bartender inserted.

"Spill it."

"Well, he says that according to the court you're so ugly that it's legal to rape you without punishment. That kind of thing, and a little worse."

Raisa Mäenpää stared at the bartender in silence.

"Yeah," the bartender said. "I don't think we need a scene between you two. So maybe you could finish your drink and leave. And keep your distance for a while."

Raisa Mäenpää didn't stay to finish her drink. Tears were streaming down her cheeks before she reached the front door.

CHAPTER 6
TUESDAY, 8:30 P.M.
KALLIO, HELSINKI

Takamäki was out of breath and his legs were aching, but the top of the long hill was already in sight. With only about a hundred yards to go, he didn't want to give up. Helsinki Street rose up into the Kallio neighborhood past the Töölö Bay and botanical gardens. The half-mile long and quarter-mile wide bay stretched north from the six-to-eight-story Helsinki skyline. During summers, a tall fountain graced the center of the bay, but it had been turned off months ago.

He ran under a train bridge.

The cool weather didn't bother him, but the strong headwind made the hill more challenging. Takamäki had been running in his brand new sweat suit for almost an hour, covering the grounds around the park of the Olympic Stadium. Built for the 1940 Summer Olympics, which were cancelled as World War II broke out, the stadium finally welcomed international athletes in 1952 when Helsinki hosted the summer games.

Takamäki preferred the asphalt to the old, mushy sawdust track in the park, but now he was almost done with his run. He hadn't planned on a last moose-like spurt up the hill, but now adrenaline was taking over and he felt he had to.

The physical strain of running usually cleared his mind, but not this time. The taxi ride, the burning house, and the sight of the destruction whirred in his head. He wondered how he'd been able to react so calmly. Maybe it was a state of shock that triggered his police instincts. But investigating an arson and being the victim of one were two completely different things.

The red bricks of the Aurora, a building for Lutheran social and health care services, flashed by as Takamäki drudged up the hill. A passing taxi driver gawked at the crazy runner. The intersection at the top of the hill was his finish line. Takamäki forced himself to think about maximizing his last bit of strength and lengthening his stride. The last yellow-green house. His sight blurred; all he could see was the traffic light. It was red. The last ten yards. His legs and lungs burned.

Takamäki touched the gray light post at the Third Avenue intersection. He stood leaning his hands on his knees and breathed fast for thirty seconds. Can't stay here, he thought, and felt his legs stiffen. He straightened his back and started down Helsinki Street in a light jog.

The image of the burned house and the face of his dead wife, Kaarina, filled his mind.

WEDNESDAY,

NOVEMBER 28

CHAPTER 7
WEDNESDAY, 8:55 A.M.
WEST UUSIMAA POLICE HEADQUARTERS

Takamäki parked his Toyota station wagon in the lot next to the West Uusimaa Police Headquarters in Espoo's Kilo neighborhood. He could hear the traffic hum from the Turku expressway a quarter mile away. Low-hanging clouds turned the sky even grayer than a typical November morning, and Takamäki was sure it would rain today. The shape of the police headquarters built in the early 1990s suggested that the architect might have drawn his inspiration from cereal boxes on his kitchen table: one in the middle with an additional box sideways on each end. However, the wing on the right, which housed various government agencies was four or five times the width of the six-story police station. At the other end of the long structure were the Espoo district court, prosecutor's office, and the debt collection agency.

Takamäki locked his car with his key fob. The car was almost the only thing he owned now. At the time of the fire it had been parked in the Pasila police station's garage, where he kept it now as parking spots were tight near Suhonen's apartment in the heart of Kallio.

The detective had stopped by Pasila on his way to Espoo. An assault case from the night before had been turned over to his team. The attacker had been caught in the act. Takamäki assigned the case to Kulta.

Takamäki had begun to suspect that the quick and easy cases were being thrown his way to boost the unit's "cases solved" numbers.

He headed for the main entrance. The metro area police units worked together closely, and he knew the place well. But since the Espoo Police had become West Uusimaa Police, teamwork had become much more complicated. Their district reached all the way to Hanko, Finland's southernmost city about seventy miles southwest of Espoo, and then some twenty miles northwest to Vihti. The East Uusimaa Police Department extended beyond Loviisa, about sixty miles east of Espoo. Rather than having the suburban departments reach all the way outside of the city, Takamäki would have preferred having the metro area police departments within Beltway III—Helsinki, Espoo, and Vantaa PDs—merged into one unit. That would have made more sense than including Hanko, seventy miles away, in the same district with Espoo, only a few miles from downtown Helsinki.

The thought process wasn't always logical; and the likely reason behind the new districts was to insure that the metro area chief of police couldn't appear too powerful next to the national police commissioner.

But Takamäki wasn't interested in the game of politics; he wanted to solve crimes.

He was asked to wait in the lobby. About thirty people were in line for passports, firearm permits, or other documents. All of it could have been taken care of online, but the police organization was light years away from perfecting customer service. After all, the target customers for the police were those who broke the law.

Criminals had to be put away for what they had done, but the police had no control over the prosecutor's office, the courts, or the Prison Department. In Takamäki's opinion, every phase of the system had too many large, unnecessary holes. Prosecutors might decide not to prosecute, even when the perpetrator was obviously guilty. Naturally, the courts would throw out the cases that were inadequately investigated; and, punishments were always doled out from the minimum end of the scale. On occasion people were sent to prison, but the Prison Department would seek to release them as soon as possible.

Takamäki wanted criminals off the streets, but since all efforts were made to cut costs, the detective's efforts were thwarted. The whole criminal justice system was compromised by budget cuts, and naturally the police department wasn't immune.

It had crossed his mind that the job didn't make much sense anymore, and at times he wasn't sure why he or any other police officer should even try.

Every damn night people were beaten, their skulls hitting a cement floor, the pavement, or the sidewalk. In the worst cases, lives ended. People got stabbed in the stomach, spleen, or ribs. Men and women were raped, children were sexually abused, and babies shaken to the point of brain injury. People were shot, poisoned, or hung themselves; and many died alone on their couches of alcohol or drug overdoses, unattended illnesses, or plain loneliness.

These cases came to the homicide unit, to Takamäki. Sometimes it was just all too much.

Takamäki was escorted from the police station lobby to the Violent Crimes Unit office. The sign on the door read "Long-Term Investigation." He was handed a paper cup of police-grade coffee and led into an interrogation room with the same gray walls as at the Helsinki police headquarters.

Detective Sergeant Mari Ranta was in her fifties, stern-faced, with dark hair. Takamäki thought she resembled what Joutsamo would look like in another twenty years.

The woman sat at a brown desk, her eyes fixed on the computer screen. Takamäki knew the routine. It would take a few minutes to record his personal information, as well as his statement and indication of whether he wanted to press charges.

"According to the report I got from the location of the fire, you arrived at the scene in a taxi about fifteen minutes after the fire started. When did you leave your home?"

"I left for Pasila, where I work, at quarter to eight in the morning."

"And everything was normal at that time, correct?"

"Yes."

"Did you drink coffee? Take a sauna? Did you cook something on the stove or bake bread in the oven?"

Takamäki looked impatient. He understood why Mari Ranta had to ask the questions, but it seemed pointless somehow after what the crime scene investigator had told him.

"I drank coffee, but I turned off the coffeemaker. I always do a routine check to make sure all electric appliances are off."

Mari Ranta typed, "The victim says he checked to make sure no electric devices were left on."

For Pete's sake, Takamäki thought. This would take all day.

Ranta asked him about the television, computer, and candles. Based on Takamäki's answers, none of them could be the culprit.

Takamäki finished his coffee.

"So," Mari Ranta began. "I'm sure you know we have to go through this. We need to look into everything."

"Have you talked to the fire investigators?"

"That's none of your concern," she quipped, looking up.

Takamäki stared at the woman. On second thought, she didn't resemble Joutsamo in any way. Anna would've gone straight to the point instead of wasting time on useless questions.

"When was the last time your freezer was vacuumed?" Mari Ranta asked.

"What?"

"When was the…"

"I heard the question, but I don't get why you ask."

Ranta squinted and said, "Electrical problems cause the most fires, a couple of thousand annually, but appliances don't self-ignite. Their incorrect use or placement, or neglected care, can be the culprit. So, when was the last time your freezer was vacuumed?"

"I have no idea."

"What about the refrigerator?"

"No idea."

Ranta looked pleased as she typed the answers.

"And I couldn't tell you when the television, computer, or candles were last vacuumed either," he added.

Takamäki studied the gray walls and waited for the next question.

"How is your financial situation?" Ranta asked, looking Takamäki in the eye.

"And what does that have to do with…?"

"Are you a cop or not?" Ranta asked, but didn't wait for the answer. "If yes, then let me ask the questions and you answer them."

"My finances are fine," Takamäki said. The question was obviously about insurance fraud.

"In that case, you'll agree to give me permission to request a bank statement."

The police had easy access to suspects' bank account information, but they couldn't get into a victim's account without signed consent.

"My house was burned down and you suspect me of insurance fraud?" Takamäki asked, sounding upset.

"I didn't say that," Ranta replied. "But do I have reason to?"

Takamäki cursed under his breath and said, "You certainly don't."

"I see," Ranta said, hinting at multiple meaning in her words. She paused and then continued, "Will you give your consent to a bank account inquiry?"

Takamäki's bank account activity was simple. The detective's pay was a little under five thousand euros, and a third of that went into taxes. He ended up with about three thousand per month. He made his mortgage payment, bought food and other necessities, and transferred small amounts to his boys' accounts. He figured the current balance was about eight thousand euros.

"No, I won't," Takamäki answered.

"Do you have a reason?"

"I don't deem it necessary."

"I see," Ranta said and typed the refusal into the computer.

The door opened behind Ranta, and Jaakko Nykänen, the handlebar-mustached head of intelligence from the National Bureau of Investigation, walked in.

"Hello," the man in the gray sweater said. Nykänen knew Takamäki well. He had been a detective on Takamäki's team about ten years back until he was promoted to detective lieutenant at the Espoo narcotics unit, and then ended up as one of the bosses of the NBI's organized crime unit.

"Excuse me," Ranta said, turning around. "We're in the middle of an interrogation."

"No need to continue," Nykänen replied, his eyes fixed on Takamäki.

"I'll decide…"

"You'll decide nothing," Nykänen interrupted in a sharp tone. "The NBI has taken over the case."

Nykänen shook Takamäki's hand and said, "Unfortunate as hell. Let's go get some coffee."

Mari Ranta remained in the room as the two walked out. A bunch of good old boys working the system, she thought to herself.

* * *

Nea Lind stepped into her two-room office on Dagmar Street and switched on the light. The décor was conservative, with oversized furniture, because she wanted to portray an aura of dignity to her clients. Lind would have been happy with simpler furnishings, but the style lent a sense of trust to the elderly, wealthy ladies from Töölö, who came to write their wills. After all, trustworthiness was at the heart of an attorney's success.

Lind had considered hiring an assistant, but hadn't found the right one yet. From time to time, she had hired law students for short internships, but lately she hadn't had any need for that. Her long sick leave the previous winter had cut the number of her cases, and business hadn't picked up until fall.

Nea Lind was tired. She had spent a long, restless night thinking about the court decision on Raisa Mäenpää's case. She knew she shouldn't take the court proceedings personally, but she couldn't help it. She wondered if she should have acted differently in the courtroom. Was she overly hard in her interrogation, causing her client to collapse in tears? Should she have delivered her final statement with more emotion, emphasizing her client's suffering? Should she have thrown calmness and coolness out the window? Those things might have affected the judge, but it would have been much more traumatic for Raisa.

The office, formerly an apartment, had a small kitchen alcove in what was now a meeting room. Lind switched on the fancy coffeemaker. She kept clean cups in the cupboard and milk in the refrigerator. She also kept a couple of bottles of champagne handy, just in case.

Lind warmed some milk in the microwave and made a cup of double espresso. The result was a cup of good office coffee.

She carried her steaming cup of coffee into the other room and pressed the power button on her laptop. Instead of a landline in the office, she used her cell phone. After careful consideration, she had decided to leave her cell phone at the office unless she had good reason to bring it home. She did the same with her laptop. Otherwise, she'd spend all her evenings working. She had another phone and computer at home, but she had to draw the line somewhere.

Lind checked her cell phone in its stand by the pen holder on the desk and saw a message.

She tapped the PIN into the phone. The screen displayed no name, but she recognized the number.

The message had been left at 2:14 A.M. and it had a typo, but its content was clear: "Good bye."

Lind let out a cry, and, with shaking hands, dialed Kari Takamäki's number.

CHAPTER 8
WEDNESDAY, 9:25 A.M.
KALLIO, HELSINKI

Mikko Kulta stood behind the custodian and urged him to hurry and unlock the door.

He had called the man from the police station right after Takamäki called him. Kulta and Kirsi Kohonen had double-parked an unmarked car outside, and the custodian had been waiting in the stairwell when they barged in.

They might have rushed for nothing, but you never knew. An ambulance was on its way, just in case.

The long-haired custodian in blue coveralls finally managed to unlock the door, and Kulta walked in. He smelled vomit, which was a bad sign. A winter coat and shoes lay scattered on the entryway floor. The apartment was a one-bedroom of about three hundred square feet, with the bathroom by the front door. On the left was a wardrobe, and beyond it the living room. The kitchen table stood in front of the window and a couch sat on the left wall.

Kulta noticed the cans of beer and cider on the sofa table. Behind the entryway wardrobe was a bed, in an alcove-like space.

A heavy-set young woman lay on her back on the bed. Her eyes were closed. She was wearing a T-shirt and panties. There was vomit on her shirt and on the bed by her head, with some stuck in her hair.

Kulta put on his rubber gloves and felt the woman's neck. No pulse.

"On her side," Kulta said, and Kohonen grabbed the hips. The woman had urinated on the bed.

Kulta bent down and scooped vomit out of the woman's mouth with his hand.

"I think we're too late," Kohonen said. She lifted the woman's shirt, and they saw red and purple streaks on her ribs. Both of them had also felt her stiffened limbs—*rigor mortis*.

Kulta removed his finger from the woman's mouth and cursed.

He saw various medicine bottles and an empty bottle of white wine on the nightstand. He looked at the labels without touching them. Sleeping pills and antidepressants.

The paramedics came charging in, and the detectives stepped aside. Kulta took off his rubber gloves.

The detectives took a closer look at the apartment. A poster on the wall depicted a Mediterranean seashore. Kulta recalled seeing one somewhere before. Clothes were strewn on chairs and on the floor. On the couch were magazines and a small, brown, smiley stuffed dog with floppy ears. Candy wrappers and a page torn out of a notebook lay on the table.

Kulta read aloud the words penned in girly handwriting: "I can't go on."

The red-haired Kohonen walked over to Kulta. Her head came up to the amateur basketball player's bicep.

"You can't go on?"

Kulta showed her the suicide note and added, "Well, I can't go on much longer, either."

A paramedic in a white coat walked over to the detectives.

"If I had to take a guess," he offered, shaking his head, "I'd say it wasn't the pills, but choking on her vomit, that killed her."

Kulta had seen it before. Normally, coughing would've kept the vomit from getting into the windpipe, but the alcohol and pills must have knocked her out. The lack of oxygen caused by the blocked trachea had caused her death.

Kulta thought about the phone call from Takamäki. The detective had said that Raisa Mäenpää had sent a text message to her attorney just after two in the morning. It confirmed Kulta's suspicion that this was more a call for help than a serious suicide attempt. People trying to overdose on medication often ended up with only foiled attempts.

This time it was different.

Even though the case seemed like an obvious suicide, it was best to be thorough and investigate the apartment. Any fingerprints found on various surfaces, such as on glasses, might help them identify someone else who could shed light on the situation, or even turn the case from a suicide to a murder investigation.

* * *

Kulta stepped into the Corner Pub with Kohonen on his heels. They had come up with a plan, just as they used to do while partners in Patrol: Kulta was in charge, and Kohonen watched his back. On the way, the pair had thought back to their Police Academy training, remembering always to focus on communication and to maintain a safe distance from those being interviewed.

Rain had dampened their coats during the short walk from the car to the front door of the pub. Several customers sat at the wooden tables, even though it wasn't quite ten in the morning. Some cradled their morning beers in both hands.

Rane, the mustached bartender, finished wiping the counter with a damp cloth before walking over to Kulta and Kohonen. Kulta unzipped his down jacket and pulled his police ID out of his breast pocket. He showed Rane the blue-and-white card.

"Looks authentic," the bartender said coldly.

"It is."

"Can't always be so sure. We see some winners here, especially at closing time. Sometimes I feel like half the cops in the city and the county alcohol inspectors try to get in here when they're drunk."

"We're sober," Kohonen said with a smile.

"Coffee?" asked the bartender. "It's on the house."

"Why not. A large vanilla latte," Kulta smirked.

"We only have black," the bartender grinned back. "But it's definitely good brew. Not as good this early in the day as in the afternoon, though. Few order coffee in this joint."

"Black's fine."

Rane set two cups on the counter and filled them with thick, black coffee. Neither detective wanted milk.

"Can I help you with something?"

"You had a female customer here yesterday…"

"I had several."

"This one was Raisa Mäenpää."

"Yeah, Raisa. A chubby young woman."

Kulta pulled a photograph out of his pocket and said, "Her."

"Yep, that's Raisa."

Kulta had brought the picture with him from the apartment. In it, Raisa Mäenpää sat in a lounge chair, sipping a colorful drink through a straw. The photo was obviously taken on a beach trip.

"Did she stop by here yesterday?"

The receipt they'd found in Raisa's pants pocket showed that she had ordered a four-euro drink at the Corner Pub the day before. Kulta had been involved in the investigation for Raisa's rape case last summer and remembered that Raisa frequented the Corner Pub. It made sense to start there and ask about her comings and goings.

"Did something happen to her?"

"I'll tell you after you answer my questions," Kulta said, sipping the coffee that tasted even worse than it looked. "So, was she here?"

"Yeah, she was here yesterday."

"And she had a cider?"

"Yeah, how did you...?"

"I'll ask the questions," Kulta interrupted. "What kind of mood was she in?"

The bartender looked thoughtful and shifted his weight from one foot to the other.

"Well, how should I put it... She wasn't at her happiest."

"What do you mean?"

Rane told them about Raisa's time at the Corner Pub, and how he had warned her about the conversation at the back table.

"Then she took off and left her drink sitting here."

"Who was talking at the back table?" Kohonen inserted aggressively.

The bartender threw her an agitated glance. Kulta thought fast and asked Kohonen to wait outside.

Rane waited for the disgruntled woman to leave before continuing, "Well, it was the rapist. He was bragging about only getting probation."

"The guy who raped Raisa? Veikko Sandström?"

Rane glanced around as if afraid to be considered a snitch for the cops. No one seemed to be listening.

"Yep, he's known around here as Veke the Zipper."

"I'm not familiar with that nickname. What does it mean?"

The bartender chuckled and explained. "He got his balls stuck in a zipper once when he was drunk and ran in here with his bloody crotch, screaming and hollering for an ambulance."

"Did Raisa and Veikko see each other here yesterday?"

Shaking his head, Rane said, "Raisa left as soon as I warned her. I don't know if I should've said anything."

Kulta didn't comment, but asked, "How long was Veikko here?"

"He sat here until midnight. We could check the surveillance video. Did somebody kill Raisa?"

"She's dead, but…"

"Suicide," the bartender uttered, barely above a whisper.

"It's possible. And you think she was depressed when she left?"

"Yeah. Real down."

Kulta nodded and pulled a two-euro coin from his pocket.

"I told you it's on the house."

"Your coffee was so bad that I don't have the heart to take it free," Kulta said, with a small chuckle.

Kohonen waited outside under a nearby store canopy. The cold November rain came down sideways.

"That was a mean move," Kohonen protested as the pair marched toward the car parked at the corner of Brahe Field.

"Was it? I thought you pulled the 'aggressive bitch' attitude on purpose, so he'd talk to me."

"Am I an aggressive bitch?"

"Should we go back and ask the bartender?"

"Nope. He can leave a comment on the police website if he wants to. What did he tell you?"

Kulta pulled the car keys from his pocket and pressed the remote button. The car lights flashed as the doors unlocked.

"In short, Sandström bragged about practically getting off scot-free after the rape. Then Mäenpää left, really down."

"That supports the suicide theory."

Kulta opened the door and quickly sat down in the driver's seat.

"I think the bar visit plays a central role in Raisa's decision to overdose on the pills."

CHAPTER 9
WEDNESDAY, 11:10 A.M.
HELSINKI POLICE HEADQUARTERS

Takamäki, Joutsamo, and Nea Lind, Raisa's attorney, sat in the homicide unit conference room. Takamäki had postponed his conversation with NBI's Nykänen about the fire after Lind's phone call, and beelined his way to Pasila.

Windows on one side of the room looked into the courtyard; opposite them was a glass wall that had been covered with tape six feet high for privacy. Fluorescent light shone over the boringly beige furnishings. The room's crisp, clean ambience resembled a hospital examination room.

Kulta had just finished going over his findings from the apartment and the Corner Pub, and had passed around photographs of Raisa Mäenpää's body. He and Kohonen then left for lunch.

Joutsamo glanced over her laptop at Takamäki and Lind at the table.

"I just want to double check something," she said. "We're conducting a cause-of-death investigation, which is deemed confidential. I mean, should the attorney be present?"

"I think Nea can help us with this," Takamäki said. "Let's consider this an unofficial background discussion. It's not a confidential meeting nor an interrogation. Let's just see if we can make some progress."

Joutsamo nodded, and Lind stayed quiet.

"Nea, did Kulta's report sound logical to you? Did it fit the picture you have of Raisa Mäenpää?"

"I'm not a psychologist, and I don't actually know that much about the young woman's background. We talked during the rape investigation, and I tried to put a picture together as best I could. But this sort of thing is tough on a woman, and getting over it requires strong self-esteem. At least it did for me."

Takamäki and Joutsamo agreed. They both knew Nea Lind had been a victim of a heinous rape the year before.

"I'm thinking mainly about our criminal justice system," Takamäki said. "Can we find an angle we could use to put Veikko Sandström behind bars?"

The detective had looked up Sandström's information on the computer. Over the years, the man had accumulated a long rap sheet, which seemed to cover at least half of the crimes listed in the books: theft, grand larceny, DUIs; a couple of crimes involving a firearm; a drug-related crime; resisting arrest; domestic assault; several counts of unlawfully operating a motor vehicle; terroristic threats; a few counts of endangering traffic safety; credit card fraud; several counts of unlawful use and theft of a motor vehicle; three assaults; one assault and battery; frauds; possession of a dangerous item; a couple of counts of vandalism.

The guy appeared to be a professional criminal, but not a good one. Sandström had managed to get off most of the charges with just probation or fines. He had been to prison twice. Takamäki wondered what else Sandström might have done without getting caught.

Lind pondered Takamäki's question, shuddering at the memory of the greasy-haired, repulsive Sandström in the courtroom.

"Do you mean something like aiding in a suicide?" Lind asked.

"Yeah," Takamäki replied. "It's obvious, from what we've seen, that Mäenpää took the alcohol and pills on her own,

70

around the time she sent you the text message. Nothing points to anyone else in the apartment."

Lind stared at the table, without a reply.

"I didn't mean to stress you out about the text message," Takamäki said, apologetically.

"I know," Lind said, slowly lifting her head. "I'm just kicking myself for not bringing the phone home. Raisa would be alive, if I... But you can't always be on duty. You just can't."

"That's pointless speculation," Joutsamo joined in. "You can't put that on yourself. But the idea of possible aiding or abetting with a suicide is interesting. I browsed through the laws, but couldn't find any mention of it."

"If it's not in the statutes, it's not punishable," Lind said. "Of course, in Finland this has been more of a euthanasia issue. Killing someone even at the person's sincere request is illegal, at least for now. But suicide is not a crime. The general criminal laws state clearly that it's illegal to aid or abet only when the act itself is punishable."

"So if I rig up a noose and someone hangs himself on it, I can't be punished?" Joutsamo wondered.

"Well, the question is..." Takamäki inserted. "Did they do it voluntarily?"

"That's different," Lind interrupted. "Let's get back to the matter of suicide. The law discusses a possibility that the person aiding or provoking it could be considered responsible, if the person committing suicide is not of sound mind."

"Could this be applied to Veikko Sandström?"

"I don't think you can find a prosecutor willing to stretch the definition of manslaughter that far," Lind said, shaking her head.

"Well, the prosecutors have never been a problem for us," Takamäki said with a light chuckle. "But convincing the judges is a different ballgame."

"So, bullying someone to death is not a punishable act?" Joutsamo reiterated.

"Not if the person decides on her own to do it," Lind said. "Think about a teenager who commits suicide. How could you interrogate the parents as suspects, instead of investigating the cause of death? How could we estimate the amount of provocation in Raisa Mäenpää's case? She took the pills herself and flushed them down with alcohol. She might have survived, had she not fallen asleep on her back and suffocated from the vomit... Sandström is clearly a piece of shit, but it would be impossible to get legally binding evidence when the only person that could give it to us is dead."

"What if we had a letter, a video, or some other message with the deceased talking about the bullying?" Joutsamo continued. She was immensely bothered by the case.

"I don't think that would be enough. Maybe if it was about defamation of character or spreading an offensive rumor about her private life, but those things don't qualify as homicide. If he's been bragging about the details of the court proceedings in the bar, we could get him for disclosing confidential information."

Joutsamo typed in a web address on her computer and found a section on criminal law on Finlex's website.

"Um, the section on provocation states that whosoever commands, hires, bullies, or in any way purposefully persuades or seduces another to commit a crime... It does mention bullying."

"Yes, to commit a crime. Suicide is not a crime."

"Yeah. And that goes for aiding, as well."

"I think the only time the aiding and provoking would be interpreted as a valid concern is in the case of a paraplegic who was unable to carry out the suicide. Someone could set it up so a nod of the head would release the toxic injection."

"I see that more as a moral issue than a criminal one," Takamäki inserted. "I wouldn't consider it a crime under those circumstances. In fact, euthanasia happens in nursing homes on a regular basis. Coverage for the care of a poor elderly person is discontinued, and she's pumped full of pain meds."

"What about neglect?" Lind suggested. "If someone watches another person die, isn't it about neglecting to rescue?"

"Normally, yes. But I feel like criminal law isn't meant to be applied in all situations," Lind said with sadness.

"In other words, Veikko Sandström is walking again," Joutsamo added.

"Unfortunately," Lind said, shrugging.

Suhonen entered the room and two men in dark overcoats stepped in behind him.

"Am I interrupting?" Suhonen asked.

Takamäki glanced at Joutsamo and Lind who both shook their heads.

"No, we're wrapping up—though we never really got started."

Suhonen missed the implication, but didn't care. He introduced the two men behind him.

"Meet Ikonen and Marttila from the NBI. They don't waste smiles," Suhonen said.

The men didn't as much as smirk at Takamäki.

Joutsamo and Lind got up and the two men took their seats. Suhonen stayed by the door.

Ikonen waited for the women to leave, then glanced at Suhonen and said, "We won't need you, either."

"Suhonen stays," Takamäki said.

"Is that so?" Ikonen asked.

"Yes."

"You know why we're here," Marttila said matter-of-factly.

Of the two tough-looking detectives, Marttila looked to be in his late thirties and Ikonen just over forty. Both had dark hair, trimmed above the ears. All the NBI guys at the Jokiniemi fortress-like headquarters seemed to have the same haircut.

"You're the guardian angels from Nykänen's unit," Takamäki said. Nykänen, the head of intelligence, had told Takamäki in Espoo that he was sending two men from protective services to meet with him.

"That's an old joke," Ikonen said.

"And neither of us goes to church on Sundays," Marttila added.

Takamäki thought he detected a faint smile on Marttila's face, but he could've been wrong.

Ikonen leaned forward and asked, "Have they found anything new about your situation?"

"I was hoping you guys would have something to tell me."

"Another unit is in charge of the investigation. Our job is to keep you safe, Detective Lieutenant Takamäki."

"How about we go by first names," Takamäki suggested.

"That's fine," Marttila said with a nod. "But sometimes we find that a police officer who has become a victim of crime tends to downplay the severity of the situation."

"It's like they try to save face," Ikonen joined in, "to show they've got it under control. How is your family? Wife? Kids?"

Takamäki was surprised to see Suhonen hadn't briefed the detectives for their assignment.

"My wife was killed in a car accident two years ago. One of my sons is going to school in Vaasa and the other is in the army."

"So no acute threat to them," Marttila said with a nod.

"Well, no," Takamäki said. He was starting to think the detectives were trying to over-control the threat aspect. "The problem is we have no idea who set the fire. We don't know if the arsonist knew I was away, or if the intent was to kill."

"We should start with the latter," Ikonen said.

"No," Takamäki grunted, and followed with his favorite catchphrase, "Never assume!"

"This isn't a crime investigation," Ikonen said, shaking his head. "It's about protecting you. We always start with the worst case scenario and plan accordingly."

"And the worst case scenario is…?" Takamäki asked.

"You're a public figure, and the news of your murder would end up on the front page in afternoon tabloids," Ikonen said, keeping his expression blank. "When perpetrators realize they've failed, they'll keep trying until they succeed."

"That right?" Takamäki said and glanced at Suhonen in the doorway.

"You wanted to know the worst case scenario. Our job is to make sure that sort of thing doesn't happen," Marttila added. "Let's look at the facts. Where are you staying now?"

"In Suhonen's apartment."

The NBI men kept their eyes on Takamäki.

"And the address?"

"Can't tell you," Suhonen barked from the door. "That's classified information, due to my undercover work."

"Is that so?" Marttila said.

Suhonen could have given the NBI his address, but his principle was simple: the fewer people that knew it, the smaller the possibility of a leak.

"The Helsinki Police emergency dispatch has the same classification on my address as they do on the Presidential Palace. In case of an emergency call, we get the same number of patrol cars."

Takamäki glanced at Suhonen again. He knew Suhonen wasn't far off. The emergency dispatch did have various classifications for addresses, depending on who lived there, but he wasn't sure if Suhonen was quite at the same level as the president. Then again, maybe he was.

Takamäki didn't want to complicate things.

"It's a two-bedroom apartment in Kallio. Given Suhonen's undercover work, security is tight," Takamäki explained.

Marttila turned to Suhonen next and asked, "Alarm system?"

Suhonen nodded and added, "And a Rottweiler named Ronja. Hundred and ten pounds of pure muscle."

Takamäki knew that was a lie.

"Good," Marttila said and pulled a stack of folded documents from his breast pocket. "These are instructions for what to do in various scenarios. They may be obvious to you, but I encourage you to read them anyway. Best not to divulge the address, so don't type it anywhere online or give it to the video store. You need to vary your routes and keep an eye out for anyone who might be following you. It's possible that there are lookouts around the police station."

Takamäki knew that was a possibility. The Skulls, the motorcycle gang that Helsinki Homicide had tangled with at various times, had done that in the past.

"I'll read it," he said with a nod.

"What about your car?"

"What about it?"

"Will the information lead to the apartment?"

"Not to Suhonen's apartment. And not to the smoking ruins, either. I also have a confidential address."

"Doesn't look like it worked very well for you," Marttila said.

Ikonen and Marttila asked for Takamäki's phone number, and each sent a text message to his phone. They watched to make sure Takamäki saved both numbers and added them to his speed dial.

Ikonen looked Takamäki straight in the eye and asked, "Is this situation causing you anxiety?"

"Yes," Takamäki said, honestly.

"I understand. We also have therapists available, if you need that."

"I think peer support is all I need, for now. Suhonen, that is."

"That's what I figured. Any questions?"

Takamäki shook his head.

"Good. We'll go see Mari Ranta, the Espoo investigator, and naturally we'll be in touch with our own unit. But if anything comes up, you need to contact us immediately. If need be, we'll get you 24/7 protection, but you don't seem to need that at the moment. What do you think? We're not doing this to toot our own horns—we're doing it for you."

"No need for protective measures," Takamäki said.

His opinion of the two had changed in the course of the discussion: They were professionals.

Takamäki would have liked to be a fly on the wall when Mari Ranta told these two that she suspected insurance fraud.

The two men's handshakes were firm, as expected. They didn't shake Suhonen's hand, because he'd gotten a phone call a moment earlier.

* * *

Mikko Kulta was returning from the cafeteria as Takamäki was seeing the NBI detectives out. Before the recent remodel, the walls in the police headquarters had been dingy yellow from decades of cigarette smoke. Now the hall was terracotta, and the rooms had glass walls, but were covered six-feet high for privacy.

Kulta walked to the team's shared office and sat down at his computer. Joutsamo's desk was a few feet away behind a set of white shelves.

"Who were those guys?" Kulta asked as he signed in on his computer.

"Who?" Joutsamo asked absent-mindedly, looking up from her work.

"The two guys Takamäki was escorting out."

Joutsamo squinted at Kulta and said, "If I told you, I'd have to kill you."

"Hah. No, but really. Security Intelligence Service guys?"

Joutsamo replied in a low voice, "You have to whisper that name here in the new building. It might activate the bugs."

"Seriously?" Kulta said, annoyed.

Joutsamo stopped goofing around.

"They weren't secret agents from Rata Street, but were NBI boys from Jokiniemi. Chatting about security precautions due to the arson."

"They find out anything new?"

"Not that I've heard," Joutsamo said, shaking her head.

The tall detective was quiet for a moment, but then decided to ask.

"Listen, Anna," he began.

Joutsamo perked up her ears. Kulta rarely called her by her first name, so this had to be important.

"It's not really any of our business, but…"

"But what?"

"Well, that attorney at the meeting today. That's pretty unusual, right?"

Joutsamo agreed, and waited for her colleague to go on.

Kulta had hoped for a comment from Joutsamo, but when she didn't say anything, he continued.

"It's pretty rare for attorneys to attend our meetings. But I guess Nea Lind did know the victim. And, it wasn't an acute crime investigation."

"Yes," Joutsamo said, her tone encouraging him to go on.

"Well," Kulta grunted, "what's the point of beating around the bush? Are Takamäki and Lind in a relationship or something?"

"Did someone say they were?"

Kulta didn't like spreading rumors, but if anyone knew about the two, it would be Joutsamo.

"There's been a rumor. Don't tell me you haven't heard."

Joutsamo chuckled and said, "I've heard at least a hundred times that I'm seeing Takamäki, or Suhonen, or you."

"Well, that's no news. But what about Takamäki and Lind?"

"I've heard something like that around the cafeteria," Joutsamo said tilting her head. "Ask him."

"I'm calling him right now... So is it serious, then?"

"I don't know," Joutsamo said sincerely.

"So you don't deny it?"

"Ask Takamäki."

* * *

Nea Lind took a tram from the police station to her Töölö office—both stops were conveniently located so she didn't have to walk far. A taxi would have been faster, but the tram was cheaper, and she was in no particular hurry.

Takamäki had asked Lind to come and discuss the death of Raisa Mäenpää. She was bothered by the young woman's fate, but knew she couldn't control the past: not her divorce, nor getting fired; not getting raped; and not her client's death. She learned from past experiences, but she couldn't change any parts of what had happened. Life didn't have a delete button; if it did, it worked only as the final step.

She had to either get over or around it; she needed to keep looking forward.

Lind glanced at the National Museum from the tram window. Its granite façade and soapstone decoration reflecting Finland's medieval churches and castles make it was one of the country's most important examples of national romanticism.

She moved closer to the tram door. Some drunkard in a sloshy stupor had just tried to tell her something, but she had quickly barked, "Don't talk to me, loser."

It worked. Almost all shady characters had at least one relationship that had left an unfortunate memory in their brains, which were mostly destroyed by alcohol and drugs. The memory of an angry woman usually stuck with them and kept them quiet, at least in public places. Dark paths in the woods were a different story.

The tram came to a stop and Lind stepped out. She opened her umbrella and walked from the stop in the middle of Mannerheim Street toward the city center. She waited about twenty seconds for the green light, while raindrops pelted her umbrella. While she waited, she made a decision.

She pulled her cell phone out of her pocket and dialed a number. In ten seconds she heard the reply.

"Römpötti," said the hard female voice.

Lind knew the reporter well, and the official tone surprised her.

"It's Nea."

"Oh, hi. Sorry, I don't have my glasses on and couldn't read the caller ID."

"Did I catch you at a bad time?"

"Define bad time," Römpötti said with a chuckle. "Guess it wouldn't be a bad time if I was in a hotel bed in Nice with somebody else's hubby, as long as I wasn't on the rebound."

"Or as long as the caller wasn't his wife."

"Yeah. Well, unfortunately, I'm not in Nice. And there's not one guy here in the office that could take me to France. Even if they met all other requirements, they never seem to have enough money," Römpötti said.

"In other words, it is a pretty bad time," Lind poked. She was now in front of the Botta nightclub near the Parliament House. She turned toward Museo Street and tried to evade the puddles in the uneven pavement. The Töölö area was built between 1920-1930 when the rapidly-growing city needed more housing. Its typical Nordic classicism architecture was restricted to a height of seven stories by the maximum length of the Helsinki Fire Department's ladders. It has now become one of the most desirable and expensive housing areas in the city.

"So, what's up?" Römpötti asked, now serious.

"Do you have time to stop by my office on Dagmar Street?" Lind asked.

Römpötti hesitated.

"I've got an interview this afternoon. I'm supposed to do a story about whether prosecutors should head crime investigations instead of the police."

"Sounds boring."

"Do you have something better?"

"Maybe," Lind said and turned the corner by the Restaurant Manala onto Dagmar Street. This street began by the restaurant, was cut by Arbis Park, and continued at a higher level on the other side of the park. Near a grove of trees was a ramp down to a parking garage that doubled as a bomb shelter. It was a small park—just a few trees, some playground equipment, and a dog park.

This park also housed Lind's favorite statue: Gunnar Finne's sculpture of Saint George standing in the middle of the fountain, slashing a dragon's neck with a sword.

"What is it?"

"Come to the office. We don't know who might be listening to your calls."

"If anyone was listening, they'd already know you called. Tell me what it's about. I've got to do the story by tonight, or the editor-in-chief will be very unhappy with a news program that's too short."

"Raisa Mäenpää killed herself after Sandström bullied her."

Römpötti was quiet for a moment and then asked, "Will you speak on camera?"

"I might."

"A dramatic turn of events. I'll be there in an hour."

"Okay," Lind said.

She had walked to the statue and stopped. Saint George was the hero of all the knight stories. In the classic final scene, he slayed the dragon with his sword. She mused about her conversation with Römpötti. While the sword of the police hadn't worked in Raisa Mäenpää's case, perhaps the pen of the press could prove more powerful.

CHAPTER 10
WEDNESDAY, 1:15 P.M.
STURE STREET, HELSINKI

"What's this about?" Suhonen asked from the front passenger seat. The car was an old '90s red Nissan Primera with a back spoiler. Over the years, the sun had bleached the black plastic on the dashboard. Paper cups and other pieces of trash sat around Suhonen's feet. The windshield wipers weren't keeping up, more due to their condition than the density of the rain.

"We'll take care of it quickly," Eero Salmela said. He was driving east on Sture Street. The men noticed the pleasant aroma from the nearby coffee factory.

Salmela, in his fifties, was wearing an old sheepskin coat. His long, gray hair was messy and his five-o'clock-shadow too long.

Suhonen had been at the station when Salmela had called and asked him to come along for a ride. He said he had some interesting information. But before he'd share the news, Suhonen would have to help him with something.

He drove the Nissan past the old, white Functionalist-style house at the corner of Sture Street and Teollisuus Street built back in 1942 that now housed a Volvo dealership. In 2000, the dilapidated building was condemned, but the National Board of Antiquities had wanted it preserved. To the Board, the cost of preservation was irrelevant, since the money wasn't coming from their budget; it was the owner who was responsible for all preservation costs.

Salmela drove on. He had told Suhonen they were going to an address on Viola Street in the Hermanni neighborhood. All Suhonen needed to do was to be there. Salmela would take care of business and then give Suhonen an important piece of info.

The two men had a long history. They were friends as teenagers in Lahti. By chance, they ended up on opposite sides of the law. Both had belonged to a gang that did small burglaries, but the day the group got caught, Suhonen was at home with a fever. Salmela got a mark on his record, while Suhonen stayed clean and was later able to attend the Police Academy.

Over the years, they stayed friends, despite the fact that one of them was a cop and the other a career criminal. Suhonen had given a pass on some of Salmela's crimes, in exchange for leads on the criminal underworld.

The car turned onto a small street lined by apartment buildings. Suhonen was familiar with the area, because he'd done drug busts in several of the apartments in the past two years.

Salmela parked the car in front of a dirty, brown, four-story building. Suhonen remembered it well. A man was stabbed to death there four years ago. The couple had met at a bar in Malmi and gone to his apartment for more booze. The woman claimed he had tried to rape her, and she stabbed him with a kitchen knife. Suhonen didn't recall the verdict—there were so many cases just like it. But he never forgot a location.

"This is the place," Salmela said, but didn't get up. He sounded nervous.

"What place?" Suhonen asked. "What's this about?" Salmela had lost a lot of weight lately. He'd had a severe heart attack a year ago, but had recovered. His health problems and rough lifestyle showed on his face. He used to operate in Helsinki's stolen goods market, but all he had to show for it now were lines on his criminal record. Salmela was as pitiful as the drug addicts he had ripped off.

"Just come with me, I'm picking something up."

"Picking something up?"

"Yeah."

"Like what?"

Salmela dodged the question. "You don't have to do a thing, and there's no danger. You just watch my back."

He got out of the car, and Suhonen followed him briskly to the front door.

"Why do I have to watch your back, if there's no danger?" Suhonen asked.

Salmela walked in the door without a reply. Despite the usual buzzer panel on the wall, the front door was unlocked.

On the second floor Suhonen caught up with Salmela and grabbed him by the collar. "Stop. What the fuck is going on?" he said. "I'm not going anywhere with you until you fill me in."

"Hey, take it easy. It's nothing. I just don't know these guys that well."

"What are you picking up?" Suhonen asked, with a poignant look.

Salmela attempted a smile, but realized it was useless.

"A couple of grams of hash."

"Don't…" Suhonen grunted.

"That's what this is about. Since the heart attack, I've had all sorts of pain. Hash is the best thing for it. All the shit the docs have doped me up with makes me fuckin' lethargic. Using hash keeps me somewhat together."

The stairwell was empty.

"Why, Eero?"

"Um, my daughter lives in Berlin," Salmela began, looking at the concrete floor. "My ex-wife and I went to see her. We were supposed to go on the honeymoon, but my heart attack screwed that up. Anyway, we took the train to

Amsterdam, and I got a few hits there. I can't believe how much it helped me… Made me feel so much better. Is that a good enough reason?"

"And you decided to bring me along on this shit gig?"

Salmela forced a smile and said, "I've got a real good lead for you."

"Fuck! I can't be involved in a hash purchase."

"Think of it as undercover work. It's important."

"Okay, who are you buying the stuff from?" Suhonen asked with a smirk. "Why did I have to come with you? A couple of grams is such a small thing, nobody's getting robbed."

"Well, it's more like twenty."

Suhonen looked incredulous.

"Okay, we agreed on fifty grams," Salmela said. "But it's all for me. For pain. I'm not selling it."

"You didn't answer my question. Who's selling it?"

"Some skinheads," Salmela began. "They quoted a good price in the bar, but you never know."

Suhonen felt his Glock in the holster under his arm.

"You never know."

Salmela grinned, but his voice was a whisper.

"And after I finalize the deal, you can give the tip to Narcotics. They can bust these guys, and make the news. The skinheads deal in kilos. The press will be interested for sure."

Suhonen felt sorry for his friend. After a long spiral downwards, his life had gotten back on track about a year ago. He'd been living clean for a while, but now he had obviously drifted back into the world of crime. Clearly he was desperate, since he had brought Suhonen with him to protect him in a drug deal. Salmela must not have had anyone else he could trust.

"Let's go," Suhonen said.

A smile spread on Salmela's face.

"This'll get you some good shit."

Suhonen pushed Salmela's fragile body against the wall and said, "I'm not interested in the shit, Eero. I'm doing this for you. And only this once. I'll make sure nobody steals your money and that you make it out in one piece."

"Thanks, that's all I need," Salmela said. "I need you...but...I'm sorry about all this. Remember that."

"I will. And you remember that, too."

"You got it."

The men walked up to the top floor. The name Heiskanen was on the mail slot. Suhonen knew that didn't mean anything, because the name could be someone else's from long ago.

Salmela knocked on the door three times. It might have been the code, or then again maybe not. Suhonen wasn't interested, so he didn't ask.

A short, bald man with a bloated face opened the door. He was about five foot six and looked like he weighed well over two hundred twenty pounds, maybe closer to two sixty.

The guy didn't say anything, but motioned for them to come in. Salmela walked in first and Suhonen followed.

Suhonen had seen hundreds of apartments like this in his career. No one lived there, or if they did, they didn't care about a thing. In some of the worst drug holes the garbage didn't even get picked up. Here it seemed like the trash had been taken out, but no one cleaned or vacuumed. Suhonen wouldn't have wanted to walk around barefoot in here. Food leftovers, junk, and dust balls covered the floor. The CD player blasted Metallica. Someone turned the music down, which told Suhonen at least one other person was in the apartment.

It was a one-bedroom apartment, with the bedroom on the left of the small entryway. The living room was on the right. Salmela walked in first.

In addition to the fat guy, two men in their thirties were in the living room. They both sat on the couch in front of the television. An XBox war game was playing on the large TV, now paused due to the surprise guests.

The fat guy grinned at the other two and said, "It's fine, we're good."

The men looked at Suhonen. He noticed the red, empty beer cans on the floor and quickly estimated there were a dozen. He didn't see any syringes or needles. The two men were clearly more interested in Suhonen than Salmela.

The fat guy disappeared into the kitchen and came back with a small package wrapped in plastic. Salmela took it in his hand, unwrapped it, and inhaled deeply.

"Smells good, seems okay."

"It's Moroccan," the fat bald man said. "This is the only good thing that comes from there."

Salmela handed him a wad of rolled-up bills. The bald guy counted the money, lifted his head, and smiled. "All here."

"Good," Salmela said and turned around.

Suhonen took another look at the two men in front of the television. He'd recognize them again, if need be. He turned around, as did Salmela.

Suhonen walked into the stairwell and Salmela followed with the package in his pocket. The door closed behind them.

"That went well," Salmela said with a smile, and they walked down the stairs. Neither said anything else.

Once outside, Salmela unlocked the old Nissan Primera's doors and Suhonen sat down in the passenger seat.

"That was easy," Salmela said and started the engine.

Suhonen was quiet.

Salmela drove slowly on the narrow Viola Street toward Häme Street. Cars were parked in the oncoming lane, practically making the street a single lane.

"Where'd you get the money?" Suhonen asked.

"Should I drop you off somewhere by the police station?" was Salmela's reply. The drive was only a few miles. Viola Street didn't have access to Sture Street, so they had to turn onto Häme Street and head north. Salmela got in the left lane. In a few hundred yards, after the tram stop, he could make a U-turn.

Suhonen didn't answer. He was peeved at his old buddy for pulling the stunt. This wasn't how it was supposed to work. They exchanged information, and he was willing to help Salmela when needed. But why did he have to go on a two-bit drug deal like that? The whole thing was peaceful with no apparent risk.

Was Salmela trying to gear up for future deals? Did he want to send the message that he had help if he needed it? Suhonen couldn't think of any other reason.

Salmela made a U-turn and drove down Häme Street to the Sture Street intersection. The right lane would lead toward Töölö on the broad street lined by apartment buildings. The windshield wipers kept trying, but the result was weak. The windshield was foggy, and Salmela changed the fan setting.

"Oh, the lead," Salmela said.

Suhonen didn't reply.

"I heard some attorney's place is gonna be burned down soon."

That got Suhonen's attention.

"Burned? Where?"

"In Leppävaara. I'm sure you guys can figure out who the intended victim is. I doubt many lawyers live around there."

Suhonen was wired.

"When is this supposed to happen?"

"Any day now. Good thing you came with me, huh? That's valuable info."

"Who and why?" Suhonen asked.

"I don't know for sure. Something about a disagreement, I hear."

They turned from Sture Street onto Teollisuus Street, still headed for Pasila.

"Where'd you hear this?" Suhonen insisted.

Salmela focused on driving, but Suhonen noticed a slight tremor in his hands, despite the tight grip on the steering wheel.

"Why do you need to know that? It's hard to say with some of this shit—you should know that by now."

"Just tell me," Suhonen said, his tone calmer. He knew it wouldn't do any good to press Salmela, at least not from the get-go.

Salmela attempted a grin and said, "Some guy at Hakaniemi Square. Or maybe I overheard someone talking on their cell phone in the metro."

"Don't give me that shit."

Salmela was quiet for a minute, then said, "Didn't I just help you? You'll figure out who the target might be and go over there in an electric company van to do a stakeout. Then you catch the guy with the canister. Sounds like a pretty good plan to me."

Suhonen wasn't about to tell Salmela about Takamäki's house, but he wanted to get a name for the investigation.

"If memory serves, Leppävaara has about sixty thousand people," Suhonen began. "That's the same number as in Vaasa or Seinäjoki. I'll bet dozens, if not hundreds, of lawyers live there. It's impossible to set up a stakeout for that many targets. We need something more specific."

Suhonen knew that the Leppävaara lead would help him find defense attorneys who worked with organized crime, but he needed a name. Salmela's hint might well have to do with Takamäki. It was easier to hire an arsonist to burn down an attorney's house than a cop's.

Salmela kept following a slow-moving bus. Suhonen would've passed it by now.

* * *

Kulta walked into the Corner Pub first, with Kohonen right behind him, Rane looked surprised to see the detectives again.

"More coffee?"

Kulta shook his head and scanned the back of the bar, but couldn't see his target.

"Is Sandström here?"

The bartender hesitated for a moment, but then nodded.

"He's sitting over there, way in the back."

Kulta headed that way, undoing the buttons on his winter coat. Kohonen did the same. They both were carrying their weapons, as a precaution. In Finland, only the beat cops routinely carried guns; detectives did only if they expected to run into a problem.

The hallway to the back was only a few feet wide with the bar counter continuing on the left. A sign pointed to the restrooms. In the narrow passage, the detectives stepped out of the way of an overweight, fifty-year-old woman wearing too much makeup.

The back room of the pub had four or five tables. The detectives immediately recognized Veikko Sandström out of a group of four men. The greasy-haired scumbag still looked the same as he did in the police photo taken that summer. Kulta had escorted the man to the police station's holding cell for the rape investigation.

The original light-lacquered wood on the round tables was barely visible through the dark spots caused by countless cigarette burns.

Kulta made a mental note that the hunchback sitting on the wooden chair on the right was the biggest threat. He was about thirty years old and had probably been in very good shape a few years ago, judging from his large, muscular body. Since then, too many beers had added some padding on those muscles. The hunchback resembled Rane, the bartender, but was twice his size.

Sandström took a quick sip from his half-full beer mug.

"Sandström," Kulta said without a hint of hesitation. "Let's head out to Pasila."

The man looked genuinely surprised.

"Why? What have I done now?"

"We'll talk about it in Pasila."

Kulta saw anger creeping into the man's face. From the look of his eyes, he'd had a few beers.

"I haven't done shit. I don't have to go anywhere!"

The others were looking at the detectives. One of the men pushed his chair back, scraping the floor. He didn't get up.

"Okay, let's take it easy."

"Fuck you, pig," the hunchback snorted, empowered by his intoxication.

Kulta stared at the man coldly and said, "We should probably check out your rap sheets, too."

The man was quiet for a moment.

"How do we even know you're real cops?"

This wasn't the first time Kulta had heard that. He pulled out his blue-and-white police ID and stretched out his hand toward Sandström to show him the laminated card.

"I can't see a thing," Sandström said and tried to grab the card. He couldn't reach it.

Kulta slipped the ID back into his pocket. The rule was to keep it out of strangers' hands. It would certainly have been flung across the room in this case.

"If you refuse to go with us now, that's disorderly conduct, which will get you a fine to three months in prison," Kohonen spouted from memory. "If any of you refuse to cooperate, we're talking resisting an officer. That's four months to four years in prison."

"Hah," the hunchback snickered, looking at Sandström. "That'd be parole, anyway."

"Okay, let's quit playing around and go to Pasila."

"Fuck you," Sandström said.

Kulta was beginning to think this might end up in a wrestling match. He didn't want to pull the gun unless it was absolutely necessary. The guys at Pasila would just laugh at him for not being able to handle a couple of losers at the Corner Pub without weapons. He could take Sandström and two others, but the hunchback would be a tough one. Kulta remembered an incident from his time in Patrol, when he had told a defiant drunk that they could talk about it first, but that he could then beat up the guy if he didn't do as he was told.

It was completely the wrong approach, but that's what he'd done.

The chair crashed on the floor as the hunchback got up. He looked like an even tougher case than Kulta had estimated. Kulta was six foot four, but this guy was another two inches taller and probably weighed more than three hundred thirty pounds. He had accumulated fat around his waist, but looked like he had pumped a lot of iron in his day. He would probably be slow, but Kulta didn't have room for any ninja moves in the back room's confined space.

"Pile, show him!"

Kohonen threw a panicked glance at Kulta. She thought of her pistol. Kohonen was five foot two and slender—completely useless in this situation without a weapon.

"Pile," Kulta hollered. "Sit down!"

"Screw it. You're a clown."

The hunchback moved between the tables and chairs to the narrow hallway. Kulta raised his hand. There was no room to step aside. He hoped Kohonen would step back, and keep out of the way. He needed to get the hunchback down, and it would be easier in the bar lobby with more room. He had to avoid a wrestling match in close quarters. He thought of his gun again. It was starting to be a viable option.

"Fuckin' cop," the hunchback challenged and took a step forward. His large hands reminded Kulta of the Russian champion wrestler Karelin.

This was it. Kulta realized he wouldn't have time to reach for his pistol.

"Sandström," a male voice boomed from behind the detectives. "Let's not make a scene."

The hunchback stopped and the drunk men at the table turned to look at Rane. The chair crashing had alerted him.

Sandström looked past Kulta at the mustached man and uttered, "No scene?"

"No," the bartender said, shaking his head. The hunchback they called Pile stepped back quietly, picked up his chair, and sat down.

"Okay," Sandström said and finished his beer with one gulp.

He made his way to the hallway.

Kulta glanced at Rane, who shook his head.

"The décor sure does need to be updated, but I don't think the National Board of Antiquities would like that, as there aren't too many of these original pubs from the early '90s left. We'd probably get fined for failure to protect a historically significant bar. Besides, if twenty cops came busting in here, they'd shut the place down. I wouldn't get paid all my tips."

Kulta looked at Rane as Kohonen put handcuffs on Sandström.

CHAPTER 11
WEDNESDAY, 7:20 P.M.
MALMINRAITTI STREET, HELSINKI

Suhonen had found the address for Jari Tanner in the police tip database. Detective Lieutenant Kaunisto from NBI's Turku Unit had entered it. The detective had found a lead while investigating another case. According to the file, Tanner was not currently under investigation.

His apartment was on Malminraitti Street in the heart of the Malmi neighborhood. Suhonen's unmarked Skoda Octavia was parked by the red brick, three-story building. Downstairs was Malmi's Dog Pub, the local equivalent to the Corner Pub in Kallio.

In front of police headquarters, Salmela had finally given Suhonen Tanner's name. Suhonen had had an ace up his sleeve: threaten to arrest Salmela for the hash—but he didn't need to use it. Maybe Salmela had sensed that Suhonen really wanted a name. It was difficult to come by as Salmela seemed very scared of Tanner.

Salmela said Tanner wasn't the one who had told him about the arson gig, but he was the one to contact if anyone was interested.

Suhonen didn't recognize Jari Tanner's name, but had looked up his information: Tanner, 43, had mainly operated around Turku, a hundred miles away on the West Coast, which explained why Suhonen didn't know him. He had the usual list of drug busts, assaults, and robberies on his record. He'd been released from Saramäki prison just two months prior after his latest stint.

Suhonen figured he was a mid-level operator at most.

The man lived in Malmi now, which surprised Suhonen. Criminals didn't tend to move around much, but stayed close to their buddies. All of Tanner's previous addresses were in Varissuo, a neighborhood in Turku. Maybe he had to run off because of something he'd done.

The tip file didn't mention Tanner associating with a motorcycle gang or any other organized crime groups.

The phone book listed several people by the name of Jari Tanner, but no one was a match. No doubt the man had bad credit, and wouldn't have been able to get a regular cellphone plan. The prepaid phones didn't show up in the phone book. The man didn't have a Facebook page or other social media connections. None of the ones with the same name matched the photo in the police file. Facebook links had been a big help in the past in searching for wanted criminals. If the detectives couldn't find the suspects at home, they could go ring the doorbells of Facebook friends.

Suhonen wondered if he should check the pub, but in the interest of time decided to try Tanner's apartment first. It would be useless to wait at the bar, if the guy was at home watching TV.

Suhonen parked his Skoda in the car dealership's parking lot across the street.

He didn't have a clear plan. Posing as an arsonist might have worked, except the deed was probably already done.

Suhonen planned to ring the doorbell and then ask a few questions. His choices were to pose as a cop or as a criminal. Pretending to be a TV license inspector would raise questions rather than present opportunities, since the Finnish Broadcasting Company's budget had been approved, and collecting license fees had been suspended for a while.

He walked to the front door of stairwell B, evading the puddles in the gravel yard. The rain had stopped.

The door was locked. Suhonen tried pulling it, but it was shut tight, with no gap to pry it open with a wire. A buzzer panel was on the wall by the door.

Suhonen didn't see Tanner's name on the list, but the NBI guy from Turku had recorded the apartment number in the file. The report was from two weeks ago, so it was likely the man still lived there. The letters SaBG were next to number eight.

SaBG? Suhonen wondered.

A light came on in the stairwell. Someone was coming out and Suhonen would have a chance to get in without ringing the buzzer.

Suhonen waited. It would be a good time for a cigarette, but smoking was no longer an option for any of his aliases.

He stood slightly to the side, where he could see inside the building. A young woman in a red down coat and beige knit hat came down the spiral staircase. She pulled a blue baby carriage from behind the corner. It took her a minute to get the baby settled. Then she walked to the door, pulling the baby carriage behind her.

Suhonen pretended to happen to the door just as the woman opened it, and he pulled on the door politely. Dark red hair spiraled down from under the knit hat, reaching the woman's shoulders in tumbled disarray.

She looked at Suhonen, who was still holding the door open, and stepped outside with the baby carriage.

"Who are you?" she asked.

Suhonen knew he couldn't say he'd forgotten his keys.

"I'm here to see a friend..."

"Why don't you use the buzzer?" the woman asked. Her eyes were stern and her face was tense. Suhonen guessed she was twenty-two years old. She was nice-looking, but Suhonen sensed something was wrong.

"Nah," he said, sidestepping the question.

"Shit," the woman snapped and laid her palm on the buzzer panel, pressing all the buttons at once. "That's how everyone does it."

"Okay," Suhonen said.

"Shit. Teresa woke up when some idiot pressed the buzzer, and she's been crying ever since. She'll only calm down in the stroller. I'm just tired of making the same rounds three times a day. The same dog walkers, the same drunks, the same wiener-whacking losers."

The woman's problems didn't particularly interest Suhonen, but here was his chance.

"You have to walk all by yourself?"

The redhead gave a forced laugh and said, "Yeah, you men... fuck, yeah. Why am I even telling you this or anything else?"

"Go ahead and tell me. I'm not in a hurry."

"You're not?" the woman said with a small smirk. "Teresa's father left me two months before she was born. Said he couldn't handle the demanding lifestyle change... Shit, in reality, he ran after a blonde vagina. And I've been alone ever since. Well, it's the two of us now."

"He sounds like an asshole."

The woman let out a small laugh and her expression softened a little.

"He doesn't merely sound like one."

Suhonen peeked in the baby carriage and saw the bundled infant's nose and eyes.

"Cute. Teresa, is it?"

"Yeah. She's three months old and her bright future is already behind her."

Suhonen looked into the woman's eyes. The anger had turned to sadness.

"I don't think so. Can't tell with someone so small," he said.

"I'm so fucked up," the woman said, shaking her head. "Sorry to unload on you, but I don't have too many people to talk to these days… The clowns in the park just flash their dicks at me. I don't much feel like talking to those idiots."

"What's your name?"

"What's it to you?" she asked, her cheeks flushing slightly.

"Well, we're having a conversation and my zipper is closed."

The woman laughed and said, "Niina. And you are?"

"Just call me…" Suhonen hesitated for a moment. "Suikkanen."

"Suikkanen? Don't you have a first name? That would be like everybody calling me Alho."

Suhonen's expression hardened.

"I haven't had a first name for forty years. Everyone calls me Suikkanen—even my mother in the institution, or so they say."

Suhonen regretted having reduced to lying on a whim. He had no reason to lie. The woman had nothing to do with police business and yet he had used an alias. Shit. But he couldn't change it now.

Niina and Suhonen looked at each other for a moment. The baby made a sound in the carriage.

"I should go," the woman said, pushing and pulling the baby carriage back and forth. "Teresa's gonna cry if the carriage isn't moving."

Suhonen pulled a piece of paper from his back pocket. He wrote down his prepaid cellphone number he always answered as Suikkanen. He propped the door open with his foot.

"Gimme a call if you ever need someone to talk to."

Niina Alho took the piece of paper and stuffed it into her pocket. Suhonen watched as the mother and baby disappeared around the corner. He turned and looked at the buzzer panel. The name Alho was on the top floor.

Suhonen stepped into the stairwell, and the door closed behind him.

* * *

Anna Joutsamo sat in the gray interrogation room. Despite the air conditioning humming, she smelled the beer on Veikko Sandström's breath. His face was starting to look as gray as the walls.

The man was precisely as unpleasant as he had been during the rape interrogations last summer. Joutsamo thought of the photos taken in Raisa Mäenpää's apartment after she had died from suffocating on her vomit. She had re-read the file on Mäenpää's rape.

The police were certain that Raisa had been raped. She had come directly to the police to report it, which was always important when it came to presenting the evidence in court. The victim telling a friend what happened was also important. Both the police and the judge considered these valuable pieces of evidence. The doctor's exam in the early morning hours also supported the woman's story. When interrogated, one of the regulars from the Corner Pub said he had heard Sandström brag several times in the course of the evening that he intended to screw someone that night.

Joutsamo's view was blunt. A woman or a man had the right to say no at any point, even after they'd already gotten under the covers. If the sex was by force, it constituted a serious crime. A suspended sentence should not have been an option.

The cellphone picture of her and Suhonen, as well as the story he told of Monday night had made Joutsamo think about alcohol's effects. Sober, Joutsamo would never have ended up in bed with Suhonen. But apparently, though she had no recollection of it, she was ready to do it when she was sufficiently intoxicated.

What would her reaction have been the next morning? Would she have felt like she was raped? The new section in the statutes made it illegal to have sex with an unconscious person. But what if she had just been horribly drunk? What if she wanted to have sex with Suhonen at night, but would have changed her mind in the morning? It was complicated; according to the law, the act had to be intentional to qualify as rape. That's why the victim's immediate reaction, such as contacting friends or the police in the middle of the night, was so important.

Suhonen was a gentleman, but Sandström was a piece of shit.

Joutsamo's problem in the interrogation room, however, was that she couldn't accuse Sandström of any actual crime in conjunction with Raisa Mäenpää's death. That's why, instead of a full interrogation, she could only question him as part of the cause-of-death investigation.

Sandström wasn't a suspect, so the phone company wouldn't release information about his cellphone calls. The information could have been useful to determine his whereabouts that night.

Joutsamo had Raisa's phone, but there was nothing in its memory concerning the night of her death. No one had called Raisa, and she called no one. The phone only showed the text message she had sent to Lind in the early morning. Joutsamo had requested information from the phone company, but had not yet received it.

Kulta had checked Sandström's cell phone, but it didn't show any calls to Mäenpää.

Joutsamo had done a routine check, just in case. The police could get information from the phone company on an IMEI code and any SIM cards for the phone without a court order. This was helpful when there was reason to suspect the person was alternating several prepaid SIM cards in one phone. Sandström's phone had only one SIM card.

The phone didn't provide any reason to suspect the asshole sitting opposite Joutsamo of events leading to Raisa Mäenpää's death. However, if Sandström were to say anything in the questioning to make him a suspect, the investigation could quickly change course. Joutsamo didn't have high hopes, but she was going to try.

Joutsamo was supposed to open the discussion by telling Sandström he wasn't accused of any crime. But Kulta had told her about the trouble in the Corner Pub, and Joutsamo decided to take another approach.

She looked the man in the eye.

"Raisa Mäenpää is dead. What do you know about it?"

The man squinted and muttered, "Raisa is dead? Huh?"

"Yes," Joutsamo said, nodding.

"How?"

"The forensic investigation hasn't been completed yet. I don't know the exact cause."

"I didn't have anything to do with it," the man said, wiping his forehead.

"You didn't?"

"No. Did somebody kill her?"

Joutsamo knew to be ready with her reply; a simple "no" wouldn't do.

"Raisa is dead. I'm trying to find out why."

"Shit," Sandström said. "I...I've got nothing to do with it... Oh yeah, you know about the rape case, of course..."

Joutsamo interrupted him. She wanted to make him uncomfortable.

"Of course I know about it. I'm the one who interrogated you last summer."

"Oh. You female cops all look alike," Sandström said with a grin.

Joutsamo didn't smile, and said, "You were convicted of raping her."

"Got probation."

"That doesn't matter. You raped Raisa Mäenpää. The court gave the verdict yesterday and now she's dead. What was your relationship?"

"We didn't..."

"Cut the shit. You're a rapist. Do you know what that means? You're among the most pathetic criminals in the world, not counting those who kill children."

"I didn't rape her," Sandström said, rubbing his head.

"Veikko Sandström, look me in the eye."

The man raised his head obediently.

"You forced her to have sex. You raped her. Do you get it? Hell, you raped the woman. Is that the only way you can get action? Probably."

Sandström lowered his gaze on the table.

"I don't wanna comment on that."

"No need," Joutsamo continued to press. "It's obvious, you rapist. You pathetic rapist."

The conversation wasn't recorded, so Joutsamo didn't have to worry about her tone. She could turn on the recorder with a press of a button, if she wanted to.

"Okay, fine," the man said. "The court found me guilty."

"Say that the court found you guilty of rape."

"Yeah," he said. "I did it."

Joutsamo was happy about winning the round. The man had admitted one thing. He obviously wanted to get away from the situation, and that was a good place to continue.

"Did you feel guilty when the verdict came in?"

"Um, well, I don't wanna say." The average citizen would have protested Joutsamo's style of questioning at this point, but Veikko Sandström wasn't one of those. Many times, Joutsamo had driven suspects to the point Sandström was at

now—where they felt they were also suspected in Raisa
Mäenpää's death.

"Are you guilty or not?"

"Yeah, yeah, I was guilty."

"A rapist?"

"Yeah."

"What?"

"A rapist. I already told you I did it."

Sandström wasn't a hardened professional criminal aware
of his rights. Like most common criminals, he was fairly
easily manipulated.

"Oh, you're guilty? Is that how the verdict made you
feel?"

Keeping his gaze on the table, Sandström said, "No... No,
it didn't feel like that."

"What did it feel like?"

"It didn't feel too bad. I got probation..."

"In other words, it kind of felt like a victory?"

"Not exactly. But I didn't end up in prison again."

Joutsamo kept a tight pace. She didn't want to give
Sandström a moment to think. Given a chance, he'd
immediately second-guess the situation.

"If you rape someone and don't end up in prison for it, it
feels good," she said.

"It doesn't feel good... Well, not having to go to prison is
okay."

"You raped Raisa Mäenpää," Joutsamo kept pressing.
"You didn't go to prison. How did Raisa feel?"

"I dunno."

"Did she feel good?"

"I dunno. Probably not."

"She certainly didn't," Joutsamo said. "Did you celebrate
when you heard the verdict?"

"I...um, I didn't. Well, I was relieved, you know."

"How did Raisa take it?"

"I don't..." Sandström began, but changed his answer. "She probably wasn't too happy about it."

"Probably?"

"Well, I guess she wasn't."

Joutsamo tapped the man's hand, and he raised his gaze from the table.

"Why wasn't Raisa happy about your probation?"

"Guess she expected me to go to prison."

"What did you do when you heard the verdict?" Joutsamo continued without a hitch.

"My lawyer called, and I was, well, pleased."

"You went to the bar with your buddies."

"Yeah, what else would I do?"

Joutsamo had gotten under his skin, but Sandström hadn't volunteered anything about Raisa. He didn't mention meeting with her or seeing her.

"What did your friends think about the verdict?"

"They didn't think anything."

"Don't give me that shit. You were probably throwing high fives."

Sandström was ashamed again.

"Well, nobody was sad about me not going to prison."

"You rape a woman and your friends celebrate. Is that what happened?"

"No, not quite..."

"You rape a woman," Joutsamo interrupted. "And you don't think anything of it?"

"I didn't have to go to prison."

Joutsamo wanted to give a sigh, but she kept her eyes on the man. The detective sergeant wouldn't let up for a second, but she was running out of options. The discussion was already becoming repetitive.

The man hadn't brought up anything that the detective could use. She would inevitably reach the point where she'd have to ask Sandström if he had met with Raisa, and he would have a chance to deny it. Up until now, Joutsamo had played the shame card, and she was winning. The facts would bring defeat.

"You only think of yourself."

"Well, not really…"

"What did Raisa think?"

"I guess she was…happy that they said I did it. I dunno."

Joutsamo was out of ammo. Sandström didn't have a wife or children and his parents were dead, so she couldn't refer to them. In the binder on the table was a photo of Raisa Mäenpää lying dead on her bed. Joutsamo pulled it out and set it down in front of Sandström.

"What do you think of this?"

"That's awful. Why…how did she die?"

"Were you there?" Joutsamo asked, grasping the last straw.

"No, no. I wasn't. I was at the Corner Pub. I didn't see her at all yesterday. How did this happen? Did someone kill her?"

Detective Sergeant Anna Joutsamo looked the man in the eye and was convinced that Veikko Sandström couldn't, in the eyes of criminal law, be considered to have caused Raisa Mäenpää's death. She couldn't get a homicide case out of this—it was about finding the cause of death. That's why it was important to keep all information confidential concerning Mäenpää's death—especially the photos.

"I have no more questions," Joutsamo said, putting the picture away. "You're free to go."

Sandström let out a sigh and asked, "How did Raisa die, and why? What's this all about?"

"We're done."

"I talked to you, now you tell me."

"I'm sorry, but it's confidential," Joutsamo said curtly and got up. "Someone will see you out of the building."

The detective gathered her papers. The cause of death of the woman who was raped would be recorded as suicide.

* * *

Suhonen took the elevator to the top floor. He glanced at Niina's door and waited a minute. Black scuff marks striped the beige walls—a sign of furniture getting moved in and out frequently.

The floor had three apartments. Out of habit, Suhonen read the other names on the mail slots: Hannula and Tuuri. It was quiet. For some reason he had expected to hear children squealing or dogs barking.

Suhonen started down the stairs. Between the floors of the old building was a small balcony for airing out rugs.

The hallway lights went out, and Suhonen hit the switch when he got to the third floor.

At the end of the hall, a laminated strip attached above the mail slot on the door explained the letters SaBG: Saramäki Bible Group, Assoc.

Suhonen wondered about the name. He knew what Saramäki was. When "Kakola," the old Turku Central Penitentiary, was closed down, a new modern building with maximum security sections was built in the Saramäki neighborhood in Turku. But a bible group? Was some religious community covering the rent of the apartment for released prisoners?

Jari Tanner didn't give the impression of a recovered criminal, but then again Suhonen hadn't met him yet.

Suhonen listened by the door for a moment before ringing the bell. It sounded like the television was on, but he couldn't be sure.

He could clearly hear the approaching steps, though. The peephole darkened, then the door opened.

The man had spikey hair and hard features. He was about five foot nine and weighed about two hundred twenty pounds. He looked healthy and muscular, the way some released prisoners did. Soon after their release, most well-trained physiques quickly got saggy from drug and alcohol use.

The man in a gray T-shirt had a quizzical look on his face.

"Who are you?" he asked in a slight Turku dialect.

His T-shirt had a screen print of a heart and a cross with a serpent wound around it. Below the picture were the letters SABG. The man's breath had no trace of booze or cigarettes, though it didn't smell like mouthwash, either.

Suhonen shifted his weight from one foot to the other, as if nervous, and said, "Hi, I'm Suikkanen. Sorry to disturb you."

He was speaking quickly, so Tanner wouldn't have a chance to shut the door.

"Well, um, I was upstairs to see my lady and then I thought..."

"You thought what?" Tanner asked with interest. But he folded his arms across his chest, as if warding the answer off.

"Well, I recognized the name Saramäki on the sign and thought maybe I could get some help on being saved."

Tanner squinted and said, "This isn't a drug hole."

"That's not what I meant. I've been making my rounds at the joints... Right now I'm sort of on leave from Sörkka, with permission that is...and I wondered if I could get some help, or advice."

"With what?"

"I thought I could start a similar group in Sörkka. How would I go about that, and could you maybe...?"

"You want money," Tanner remarked.

"Well, sometimes these groups have helped, and, um, Jesse is a friend of mine..."

Tanner was about to say something, but paused.

Suhonen kept jabbering, afraid Tanner would close the door.

"We're always short on dough. The old lady is pretty ornery."

"The lady upstairs with the baby?" Tanner asked with a grin.

Suhonen nodded and said, "We don't see each other much. They don't give me days off like the army does these days. But I'm thinking about starting a new life when I get out in a few months."

"That's always a good idea."

Suhonen put on a pensive look.

"Yeah, and for the baby, too. But could you help me out? I'll pay you back, of course, when I get done."

Suhonen was hoping Tanner would hand him something like a fifty euro bill. He could run it through the banknote register and maybe find out something about its origin. Finding a bill linked to a robbery would be a homerun.

"We do have assistance programs, but no cash register to dip into. You can write a letter. Or if you have access to a computer at prison, you can fill out a request form online. Our management will process it quickly."

Suhonen nodded, feigning disappointment and said, "Okay. I wanted to help my little lady with groceries, but that sounds fair, too. Um, what are the chances of getting the assistance?"

"Our own group has priority, of course. But others have a chance, too."

No they don't, Suhonen thought, but kept nodding.

"I'll have to apply for a transfer then," he said with a chuckle.

"Wait here," Tanner said and disappeared into the apartment. Looking in, Suhonen could see it was tidy. Coats were on hangers and shoes in a neat row. He saw no trash or beer cans on the floor. He couldn't see the whole apartment, of course—but who would only keep the entry clean.

Tanner returned, carrying a small book with a laminated cover.

"Here you go," he said.

Suhonen glanced at the black book the size of a paperback. The words "Old Testament" were on the cover.

"Read it when you're feeling down."

"Um, okay," Suhonen replied.

"And do the assistance application. Maybe we can save you, too. God bless."

"Yeah, same to you," Suhonen said as Tanner pulled the door shut.

Suhonen walked down the stairs. Either the façade was perfect or this was an authentic aid organization.

CHAPTER 12
WEDNESDAY, 7:50 P.M.
HELSINKI POLICE HEADQUARTERS

Joutsamo was eating a salad in the cafeteria of P-1, the remodeled police station Building One. During the day she could have put together her own from the salad bar, but in the evening only pre-made portions were available. The smoked reindeer in her salad tasted a bit like plastic.

The architect who designed the remodel must have been a fan of glass walls, because the cafeteria also had them. Luckily, no one had walked into one yet.

This late in the day, plenty of tables were available. Joutsamo sat alone. Uniformed patrol officers were laughing at something a couple of tables away. Takamäki had left to deal with insurance issues.

Joutsamo didn't envy her boss. A fire in one's own home had to be one of the most horrible nightmares, aside from the death of a loved one or a serious illness. Two of those things had now happened to Takamäki: his wife's death and the fire. Joutsamo wondered how her boss managed to cope. Maybe he was good at focusing on work and pushing depressing thoughts to the background.

Joutsamo was surprised to hear Takamäki had agreed to let the reporter, Römpötti, interview him about Raisa Mäenpää's case. Obviously, the television reporter had gotten the story from Nea Lind—no surprise, as Lind and Römpötti were friends.

"Okay if I sit down?"

The forty-year-old man was wearing a white dress shirt and a gray cardigan. Joutsamo recognized him as one of Financial Crimes detectives. The homicide unit rarely ran into the financial guys, but the man and Joutsamo had once been on the same team at a conference. Joutsamo remembered his last name as Oksa or Oksala. She wasn't sure if his first name was Jaakko or Jarmo.

She hated it when she was expected to know a name and couldn't remember it, or when she had to keep guessing afterwards. She thought it should be obvious in this day and age that nobody could possibly remember everyone's name.

"Go ahead," Joutsamo replied. She knew he was either a detective or detective sergeant.

"Thanks," the man said with a smile.

The dress shirt and the cardigan didn't match. The shirt called for a tie, and needed to be buttoned all the way up.

"Jarmo Oksa?" Joutsamo asked.

The man gave a small chuckle. He had a plate of microwaved lasagna, a green salad, and two glasses of milk in front of him on the table.

"You have a pretty good memory. I'm Jaakko Oksala."

"Anna Joutsamo," she said, ignoring her mistake.

"I remember you," the man said. "We saw each other a few days ago in the bar at Hotel Pasila. You seemed a little tipsy."

Joutsamo felt herself blush. She got completely wasted only once a year. Why did everyone have to remember it, and take pictures? Wasn't there a privacy law protecting those who got drunk? Or maybe it was reserved for those who did it every other day. Nobody ever talked about them.

"Your shirt and sweater don't match," Joutsamo said curtly.

The man realized his mistake. Some people didn't like to talk about getting drunk.

"I left my tie and suit coat upstairs. I had to wear them on this case."

"What case was that?"

"Insider trading. They'll talk more if they feel you're their equal. You know, look sharp."

I see, Joutsamo thought. So the police had to act on the suspect's terms? Maybe Sandström would've told her more if she had worn a mini skirt and a wet T-shirt when she questioned him.

"What have you got?" the man asked and took a bite of the lasagna.

Joutsamo ate a forkful of salad and a pineapple piece to cover up the reindeer's plastic taste.

"A routine case. A woman was raped, the man got probation. The man bragged about it, the woman killed herself. We're trying to find out if the chain of events has a connection from the criminal justice point of view."

"Interesting. And does it?"

Joutsamo looked sad and shook her head. She finished her bite of food before continuing.

"It was suicide. Though the rapist is the catalyst, he's getting off with no real punishment, for either the death or the rape."

The man was lifting a forkful of lasagna to his mouth, but stopped midway and set the fork down.

"You have this problem, too?" he asked.

"What?"

"Our criminal justice system with consequences that just don't work."

"The justice department is in charge of that. We just do the investigating."

"That's not exactly how it goes," the man said with probing eyes.

"What do you mean?"

113

"Well, take this case of yours. The man was convicted, and probably also fined?"

Joutsamo nodded.

Oksala continued, "In my opinion, the fines are part of the responsibility I mentioned. They need to be collected with the vigor of martial law in all its severity. Collection agencies, tax consequences, evictions, and so forth. And the non-prison part of consequences has to work."

"Non-prison part?" Joutsamo asked.

"We've been running tests on a trial basis. It's not official yet, but it probably will be soon because everyone is sick of these probations that are handed out due to the government's financial cutbacks. We can't afford the upkeep, so we just shake our fingers at the convicts."

"A good part of the financial crime cases end up in probation," Joutsamo said.

"That's one of the main reasons."

"Who's this *we*?"

"The police, the tax man, collectors, social workers, and in some cases also the Prison Department. We're working together, unofficially."

"Meaning?"

"The collection agency effectively takes their money and personal property. They are blacklisted with the credit reporting agencies and banks, and the word spreads quickly. Getting insurance and renting an apartment become impossible. The people will end up in last place in the city rental line. Because of their background, they won't be able to get financial assistance... Want me to go on?"

"Absolutely," Joutsamo said, staring at the man in awe.

"Rent deposits won't be returned, and any past deposits will be turned back into collections. Tax payments will be monitored in real time. Ankle bracelet surveillance and inspections, as well as Breathalyzer tests, will be increased. Children will be taken into custody. Mandatory mental health care will be considered, and might become necessary at this point."

Joutsamo could hardly believe her ears.

"So you'll turn these people into clients of the Violent Crimes Unit?"

"We won't—they'll do it themselves."

Joutsamo shook her head and said, "Depends on how you look at it."

She remembered pondering the philosophy behind punishment while dealing with her hangover. It had come to this: the judicial system wasn't able to dole out revenge, so the authorities did it themselves, outside of the letter of the law.

"Wouldn't you think it was right to get the rapist to sweat a little for what he did? Make him feel it in his hide?"

Joutsamo ate her salad without responding.

"The symbol for justice is a scale," Oksala continued. "Crime and punishment must be in balance. If the Justice Department can't do it, then we can. And it's all within the law. We don't turn a blind eye at the law."

Joutsamo didn't know what to say. The financial crime detectives had to feel stressed out by the constant probation verdicts. They might work for three years for cases that would then take another three years in court. The court would give out the probation sentences and for some odd reason the suspects' money and possessions would be gone offshore before the investigations would ever begin. That had to be frustrating.

"In other words, the authorities have to dole out revenge?" Joutsamo said. "With no concern for the individual? Hammurabi law style?"

"Hammurabi's law is overrated," Oksala said with a smile. "It says so in the second book of Moses in the Old Testament. An eye for an eye, tooth for a tooth, hand for a hand, foot for

115

a foot, burn for a burn, wound for a wound, bruise for a bruise."

Joutsamo didn't like what she was hearing and said, "So, with this logic, Sandström would first have to experience being raped and then commit suicide."

Oksala put his elbows on the table and leaned his jaw in his hands.

"Well, not quite, but he should have to feel the consequences. You said yourself that it bugs you to see Sandström walk free after raping and driving a person to suicide."

* * *

Juha Saarnikangas parked his old, rusty can by the front door. He had wanted an American van, such as a Chevy, but none of the car dealers had offered him more than nine hundred for his Ducato. Saarnikangas took that as an insult and wouldn't sell.

Juha thought his Italian beauty was worth at least two thousand. Regardless of the price, the car ran, which was the most important thing. However, his current status would've called for a better car.

Juha had had his long hair cut short a while ago, but his face was gaunt as before. The old surplus store army jacket he used to wear had been replaced by a brown leather jacket with some Thai word spelled on the back. The clerk had insisted it meant "dragon."

Juha pressed the buzzer at the front door. He considered Jari Tanner a strange fellow; last time he had shoved a copy of the Old Testament in Juha's hand.

The door buzzed, and Juha opened it.

He thought for a second between the elevator and the stairs, then chose the elevator since the apartment was on the third floor.

In a minute, Juha reached the Saramäki Bible Group's door. A muscular man whom Juha recognized opened the door and gave a small chuckle.

"What?" Juha didn't like surprises, and the chuckle made him uncomfortable.

"Nothing. I'm glad it's you."

"Who else would it be?" Juha asked.

Tanner stepped back, and Juha walked in and closed the door.

"Some guy came by, asking for money."

After a pause, Juha replied, "As long as it wasn't a man with dark, shoulder-length hair, wearing a black leather jacket."

"How'd you know?" Tanner said, turning sharply.

Juha cursed and asked, "Suikkanen?"

"Yep."

"What did he say?"

"He said he was just out of prison and seeing the woman upstairs."

"Oh yeah?" Juha asked, looking at Tanner firmly. "Well, let's go ask the woman."

"Not now. We've got to talk first."

* * *

Suhonen turned the Skoda from Beltway I onto Tuusula Street and was driving toward city center, when his cell phone rang. It was his own phone, not Suikkanen's.

"Speak," Suhonen said after he saw the number.

"What the hell is going on?"

The caller was Eero Salmela.

"I dunno. Elaborate," Suhonen said.

"Why did two of your detectives come in and take Veikko?"

"Who is Veikko?" Suhonen asked, puzzled. "And come in where?"

"He's my buddy Veikko Sandström, and they came in the Corner Pub. I'm outside now."

Suhonen could hear the tram clanking. Salmela was at least telling the truth about the location.

"Yeah," Suhonen said. "I dunno..."

"Shit, fuck," Salmela snapped. "Don't you goddam get it?"

"I gotta say I'm as confused as a fart in a fan factory."

Salmela drew a breath, then said, "And your pair of cops picked him up in public. Shit, from the back table in the Corner Pub. That could've been total chaos and even made the newspapers."

"Eero," Suhonen said calmly. "Settle down. What's the problem?"

Salmela huffed.

"Tell me the problem and we'll try to solve it."

"Don't you get it?"

"I don't have the game pieces at the moment," Suhonen said. He was starting to feel agitated, but kept his voice as calm as possible.

"Fuck. I gave you Jari Tanner's name, right?"

"Yeah."

"You demanded it. You pressured me like hell."

"I did," Suhonen replied. "Because I had reason to."

"Well, honorable detective sergeant," Salmela said, nervously, "What's it look like?"

"What's what look like?" Suhonen snapped now. "Gimme something I can understand."

"I'm talking about Tanner," Salmela said, sighing. "I heard it from Sandström. The cops picked him up. You can't fucking go anywhere near Tanner for a while. You got that? It's a damn explosive situation."

Suhonen was quiet for a moment. He had no idea who Sandström was.

"So you're saying we should just let them go ahead and burn down the lawyer's place in Espoo. And the wife and kids, too?"

"Don't play with hellfire," Salmela barked.

CHAPTER 13
WEDNESDAY, 9:45 P.M.
KALLIO, HELSINKI

Takamäki sat on Suhonen's couch—the one he'd slept on the previous night. He had put the couch back together and folded up the sheets.

His laptop hummed on the sofa table. He had gotten a loaner from work to replace the one that got burned. He'd been trying to think of and list everything destroyed in the fire. The fire inspector who stopped by the house had asked him to do that. Usually, the inspector was able to do the estimate, but this time the destruction was too severe.

It was easy to remember the television; he'd bought the Sony two years ago. But when did he buy the DVD player and what was the brand? The bookshelf had hundreds of books. How could he determine how much they were worth? The freezer and its contents. The refrigerator and the washer. Kaarina's clothes that still hung in the closet. How many Xbox games did the boys have? He had to remember the year he'd bought everything, so the insurance company could do the estimates. The task seemed impossible.

For a lot of items, like the CD and DVD collections, a rough estimate would have to do. The same went for the clothes—coats, pants, and socks. And how could one put a price on family photo albums? The burnt photographs were priceless, but from the insurance company's point of view they had no value.

Takamäki had told his boys about the fire. They were shocked.

He figured the insurance company had a system for estimating the value of various items. The paintings on the walls weren't worth much more than two hundred. Kaarina had bought them, and Takamäki had no idea how much she paid.

The townhouse association handled the actual fire insurance. The manager had told Takamäki he had talked with the Espoo police. According to the police, there were many unanswered questions, and with that the insurance company would freeze all the benefits until the investigation was completed. This worried the manager. Takamäki told him the situation was under control because the case had been handed to the NBI. The man wanted to know why, but got no reply.

Suhonen wasn't around. He had said he needed to check on some things and would be back later. Takamäki didn't like staying in someone else's apartment, but it was better than a hotel room in Espoo's Kilo neighborhood. He knew now why Suhonen had wanted him to stay. Suhonen had spent many Christmases with Takamäki's family in Leppävaara. It didn't feel good to be alone.

Since Kaarina's death, he hadn't realized how much he missed being able to say good morning to someone. He'd done that with the boys, but they had their own lives now and his family was falling apart.

Takamäki debated if he should get an apartment with one or two bedrooms in Töölö. With that he thought of Nea Lind's face.

The insurance money and the profit for selling the house after a renovation would probably be enough to buy a small apartment in Töölö. If anything was left, he could help the boys with rent or buy a one-bedroom in Vantaa.

Takamäki opened a can of Suhonen's *Kukko* beer. It might be nice to try apartment living after years in the townhouse.

He wouldn't have to shovel snow, and maybe he could sell the car or give it to one of the boys.

Previews for a horror movie based on nightmares came on television. It made Takamäki think of last night. He had woken up drenched in sweat after a nightmare about his father's death. He supposed the fire was causing shocking events of his life to resurface.

At the end of the television newscast was the clip about a woman who was raped and who had committed suicide. Takamäki wasn't particularly interested in seeing his own performance, but he wanted to know how Römpötti was handling the story. Had she found anything new to add to the case?

"The Helsinki Police are investigating an interesting chain of events that led to the death of a young woman," the serious news anchor stated. "Our crime reporter Sanna Römpötti will tell you more."

A picture of an apartment building in Kallio appeared on the screen.

"Twenty-five-year-old Raisa lived in this building. This morning she was found dead. It was most obviously suicide," Römpötti recounted.

She went on to say that about thirty young women in Finland commit suicide each year, generally by drug overdose or jumping from heights. The motive was often a result of depression or mental illness.

Attorney Lind appeared on the screen and said that Raisa had been a victim of rape last summer.

"The verdict was announced yesterday and the rapist got probation," she said.

"Probation," Römpötti repeated.

"In many cases, that's all rapists will get. It's wrong."

As the camera moved along the courthouse hallway, Römpötti added that about every other rapist got off with only probation.

"Why Raisa ended up committing suicide is not entirely clear."

Takamäki looked serious on the screen when he said, "In the case of the woman, we are investigating the cause of death. I can't comment one way or the other, because the investigation is confidential."

Watching the clip, the detective let out a light chuckle. Some statement, he thought. He had told the reporter he couldn't comment, but she still wanted to interview him on camera.

The story went on. Römpötti said the attorney had a strong theory.

"Raisa was bullied, and according to the information I have, the bully was in fact the rapist, who bragged about being able to rape Raisa without any consequences to himself."

Römpötti added that in Finland it wasn't illegal to provoke someone to commit suicide, because suicide wasn't against the law.

The reporter voiced her own comment to the camera in front of the courthouse.

"What the victim's attorney claims sounds harsh. But who is the rapist and bully? The name is in the public domain, of course. The man sentenced to probation for raping Raisa is thirty-six-year-old Veikko Sandström from Helsinki."

A picture of Sandström's face appeared on the screen and made Takamäki jump. The media didn't usually divulge the names of people convicted with suspended sentences unless they were public figures. Takamäki wondered how Römpötti got hold of the photo—it looked like one from the investigation files for the rape case.

Römpötti closed with Sandström's extensive criminal record.

Quite the story, Takamäki thought, and not kind toward Sandström. But the detective felt no sorrow for the rapist.

* * *

Suhonen sat in his car in the Niittykumpu Snacky diner's parking lot in Espoo. He was prepared with extra napkins for the mayonnaise dripping from his hamburger. Suhonen would've liked to eat at the Heikintori Ribis Grill in Tapiola, but it was closed at this late hour. He had tried to find information on Tanner, but only found confirmation of his geographical status: No one in the Helsinki area knew him, and there was no word on the street about any past or future arson. The NBI hadn't made any statements about the arson at Takamäki's home, so information on the streets was scarce on that, too.

It wouldn't be the first time Salmela's lead was less than waterproof, even if Salmela himself believed it. Information off the streets always came tainted with rumors.

Suhonen felt his cell phone vibrate before he heard it ring. It was the prepaid phone he used under his alias.

"Suikkanen," he said into the phone.

"What the hell kind of man are you?" a female voice snapped.

"Who is this?"

"Niina, remember?"

Suhonen remembered well the woman with the baby carriage from Tanner's building.

"Yeah, of course."

"What the hell did you do? And who the fuck are you?"

"You lost me," he said, baffled.

"Let me clue you in," the woman said sharply. "That night, after the walk, Teresa had just fallen asleep when the doorbell rang. It was the thug from the floor below and some friend of his in a leather jacket."

Suhonen became worried. Had Tanner gone over to check out Suhonen's story?

124

"They started asking about you. I didn't get it right away, but when they mentioned the black leather jacket, I figured it was you."

"Why the hell would you tell them that you live here and you're my husband?" she nearly shouted. "You got me tangled up in business I know nothing about."

Damn, Suhonen thought. He hadn't seen this coming.

"I, um…"

"Quit the humming around and explain," the woman went on.

"Maybe we should meet."

"Ha, they especially warned me about that. I'm not supposed to see you, and I have to move out. They called me a cop whore. What do you make of that?"

Oh no, Suhonen thought. This just got worse. Did Tanner somehow figure out Suikkanen's cover? Shit. Damn.

"Whatever you are, at least be a man," the woman continued. "You've gotta help me find a new place. I can't stay here with the baby, that's for sure."

"Calm down. I'll help you. I'm actually a cop."

"You're a cop?" the woman huffed. "Sure you are."

"Yeah, I'm telling the truth. My visit had to do with an operation in the building," Suhonen explained. He figured if his cover was blown with Tanner, he didn't need to hold on to it with Niina.

"What the hell. Some covert operation in my building."

Suhonen was glad the woman seemed to have calmed down.

"You said the spike-haired guy had someone with him. Who was it?"

"I dunno. He was skinny and narrow-faced, had short hair, and looked mean. He was wearing a leather jacket…"

"Did you hear names?"

"Well, I think the spike-haired guy called the other one Juha, as they were leaving."

"Juha?"

"The big guy said 'Let's go, Juha,' or something like that."

Except for the hair, the description matched a Juha Saarnikangas Suhonen knew. Years ago, Suhonen had saved the guy from the hands of a maniac. Saarnikangas had hit the bottom of the barrel. They had formed a friendship much like the one Suhonen had with Salmela. But it lacked mutual trust.

Saarnikangas was an opportunist who knew a lot and somehow got along with various parties. He had stayed away from the Helsinki circles for a while and spent time in Thailand. Rumor had it he'd gotten a big inheritance from America. Maybe he'd already spent his money in the Far East and had to return back to Finland.

"Niina, here's the plan. Pack some clothes for a few days for yourself and Teresa. I'll pick you up and drive you to a safe house. You won't have to worry about anything there. Then I'll help you find an apartment. Sound good?"

"Away from here?"

"You didn't seem so keen on the Malmi neighborhood when we met."

The woman thought for a minute and said, "Okay, let's do it. At least I won't have to sit at home, scared they'll come back."

"I'll be there in less than an hour."

They hung up, and Suhonen tossed the rest of his hamburger in the paper sack. He wasn't hungry anymore.

Suhonen started the car engine. What in the world was Saarnikangas doing in the Saramäki Bible Group's apartment? Suhonen didn't think Juha had ever done time in Turku, and he certainly didn't attend a bible group—though the former art student knew a thing or two about the subject.

First, he had to make sure it really was Juha. Suhonen decided to go to Pasila and get a photo of Saarnikangas, so Niina could identify him. It wouldn't be a problem to find a place for her in a safe house; one phone call to the director would do it.

THURSDAY,

NOVEMBER 29

CHAPTER 14
THURSDAY, 9:12 A.M.
KALLIO, HELSINKI

Veikko Sandström opened his eyes. It was a morning like any other: He had a headache, his eyelids felt heavy, and he had a bad taste in his mouth. His eyes had trouble focusing, but he could see the time on the clock radio on the nightstand: 9:12 A.M.

As long as he stayed in bed, he didn't feel too terrible. His white T-shirt was damp from sweat. He had to get up to use the toilet. The walls seemed to sway as he wobbled into the bathroom. Luckily, he didn't need to walk far in the small apartment. He tripped on his shoes and cursed.

Leaning on the wall, he took a piss. Then he splashed cold water on his face over the sink and avoided looking in the dirty mirror. He knew he wouldn't like what he saw. But it would get better, as always.

He'd gone back to the Corner Pub last night and stayed until closing. He hadn't mentioned the suicide there, but told people the trip to the police station had to do with an old burglary.

The whole police station episode was weird. Raisa had killed herself, and the cops thought he'd had something to do with it. It was crazy. The cops griped about budget cuts, but they seemed to have plenty of resources for this sort of thing.

Sandström found it interesting that the cops always had time to deal with his comings and goings. They were always in such a rush to get him into jail, but then he just ended up waiting there. He remembered many miserable nights on a thin plastic mattress, with pounding hangovers. But in jail at least he had a mattress, which wasn't always the case at home—sometimes he passed out on the floor.

He had a better set-up now. Society was taking care of him. In the city-owned rental he had a television he'd bought with the money he collected from welfare. He left it turned off on his way to the refrigerator because the morning shows were meant for rich people, not the working class. He saw it as a capitalist scheme. These days, no one pulled for the common man.

He hadn't read the newspaper for years. His internet was disconnected after he'd neglected to pay his bills. He sold his computer for thirty euros, having paid fifty for it a year ago.

The refrigerator had no beer. Cursing, he rinsed a dirty coffee cup and filled it with cold water from the tap.

He was in no hurry to go anywhere. He didn't have a job, and he had nothing else going on at the moment. But he'd have to come up with money somehow, so he could go to Thailand or the Canary Islands for a couple of weeks. Without a trip, the long Helsinki winter was too much for him. He needed to get a couple grand from somewhere. So far, he'd managed to get two hundred for some random gigs.

The doorbell rang.

Sandström jumped. Not the cops again? He didn't have any drug deals going on at the moment; they would've seen that yesterday at the police station. His buddies didn't do surprise visits—at least not at this hour.

The doorbell rang again. It sounded demanding.

Sandström weighed his options and grabbed a long-edged fillet knife from the kitchen.

He was sure his small debts wouldn't bring the debt collection agency to his door. He thought it best to open the door. At least then he wouldn't have to wonder and glance over his shoulder every time he went into town.

"Just a second," Sandström yelled. He put on a pair of gray sweatpants with white paint stains and dried blood on them. Sandström remembered wearing them last on a kitchen remodeling job last spring. He'd been paid in cash for the job, tax free. Later he'd heard something about the customer being displeased about the work quality.

Sandström regretted not having installed a peephole, but it did no good to whine about it now. He opened the door a crack, with the knife halfway behind his back.

The guy in the hallway was about Sandström's height, and muscular for a fifty-year-old. He oozed toughness and brawn. His short hair laid flat and his sideburns ran into a brown, full beard.

"Veikko Sandström?"

"Yeah, that's me. What is it?"

"I'm Pekka Asunta from the Collection Agency. You have unpaid bills."

Sandström now recognized the official-looking envelopes. He hadn't been able to afford to pay the fines he had received for some of his past crimes.

"I guess I do."

"Should we take care of it? Preferably not out here in the hall."

The man's tone of voice was demanding, and Sandström didn't want trouble. He opened the door all the way. They could talk as long as they wanted, but he didn't have any money. His buddies at the Corner Pub had said the collections people didn't take property these days, and the apartment belonged to the city.

Step right in, collections dude, he thought. Suddenly, he remembered some cash he had in a jar and wanted to get it out of sight.

Asunta walked in.

"What's that?" he asked, pointing to the knife in Sandström's hand.

"Uh, this?" Sandström said, pretending to be confused. "I was making breakfast."

He put the knife back in the kitchen alcove. He didn't have any bread out on the counter.

Asunta looked around the bare apartment. He'd done collections his whole career. The job had changed quite a bit in thirty years, and these types of home visits were quite rare nowadays. The clients were usually called into the collections office to draw up a report. Of interest were large personal property items, such as cars and homes, as well as income, of which the statutes allowed up to a third to be taken.

Now Asunta's boss had told him to visit Sandström in person and interpret the collections law by the old rules. Asunta did as he was told.

The men sat down at the wooden kitchen table and Asunta looked at the form on his laptop: Sandström owed in collections a total of 26,753 euros. Sandström said he had no assets, nor wages that could be garnished. Lying at this point would result in a conviction—likely probation—but Sandström was at no risk.

Sandström sat quietly in his chair as Asunta stood up without a word.

The agent walked around, attaching red Post-it notes to furniture and items to be counted as personal property. He would take with him the television, coffeemaker, microwave oven, the worn couch, and the bookshelf with its books. He considered the old clock radio, but marked it as a necessity, along with the mattress. The bedframe would go. The underwear, socks, and T-shirts could stay. He pulled a leather jacket out of the closet.

Normally, all of this would've been deemed worthless, but not this time. Asunta let the man keep the cell phone, which was necessary in order to get a job in construction.

Asunta typed the possessions in the computer and printed out the form on a small printer he'd brought with him. Sandström signed the form in silence.

"Wait a minute," Asunta said and walked to the coffee can in the kitchen alcove. "This is pure cash, and it'll do fine."

He counted the cash: three hundred forty-five euros.

"Don't take that. I won't have anything."

"You shouldn't have stared at the can the whole time. Besides, maybe you shouldn't commit crimes and ignore your bills."

Asunta printed another sheet of paper, deducting the cash from the debt. The new balance was 26,408 euros.

Sandström was mainly upset about losing the nest egg for the trip to Thailand.

Two burly men in coveralls came and carried the items out, and it was all over in half an hour.

An hour after Asunta had left, a man brought Sandström an eviction notice, on the grounds of unpaid rent and a rape that happened in the apartment. In the same stack of papers was a notice of discontinued rent assistance, which would have to be paid back.

"What are they taking it from?" Sandström wondered out loud. He glanced at the papers, but couldn't understand everything he was reading. According to the document, the eviction was an urgent temporary order given without hearing the party in question.

* * *

Takamäki was reading emails in his office. The police administration had sent an amendment to the instructions on mediation of crimes, and the Helsinki Police was forwarding it to all the officers. Takamäki wasn't interested; it was just another way for criminals to avoid real consequences for their crimes.

Suhonen's knock on the office door jamb interrupted Takamäki's thoughts.

"Anything from NBI?"

Takamäki shook his head and asked, "You mean the fire or the protection?"

"I'll protect you from anything," Suhonen said with a smile. "But I'm interested in the fire."

"You have something new on it?"

Takamäki and Suhonen had walked from the Kallio apartment to the Pasila Headquarters that morning. They could have taken the tram, but they both could use the exercise. It hadn't rained, despite the gray clouds.

Suhonen hadn't mentioned anything the night before or on the morning walk about having new information on the case. Had he found something now?

"Who's in charge of the investigation?" Suhonen asked.

"I don't know. I should probably ask Nykänen... I was looking at apartments for rent. The insurance company would give me some rent assistance."

"You don't like my free couch?"

"Sure, but I'll have to get my own place at some point. It'll take months to fix up my townhouse. My kid is on leave from the army this weekend, and he's staying at a friend's house."

"Will you be going back to the townhouse?"

"I don't think so. I'll have to talk to the insurance company. If they were somehow going to redeem it, I could get a two-bedroom in Töölö or something."

"You go look for an apartment, and I'll talk to the NBI."

Joutsamo came to the door and asked, "Got a minute?"

"Of course," Takamäki said.

Suhonen glanced at the woman. "I'll go..."

"No, stay," Joutsamo said, shaking her head.

"Oh," Suhonen replied.

"I want to hear your opinion, too," Joutsamo said and crinkled her nose.

Suhonen was about to make a clever remark, but realized it wouldn't help and swallowed his words.

Joutsamo stepped in and closed the door behind her, which piqued the men's interest and made them uncomfortable at the same time. They had no idea what this was about. Takamäki sat at his desk, Suhonen perched on the windowsill, and Joutsamo sat down across from Takamäki.

Joutsamo sensed the men's nervousness.

"Listen, I'm here on official business," she said with a chuckle.

"So, tell us," Takamäki said, relieved.

"It's about the man who bullied Raisa," Joutsamo said.

"What about him?"

"Last night, while I was having dinner downstairs, a financial crime detective came by. We talked about this and that and then he told me about a project the authorities have started for pressuring criminals."

Takamäki and Suhonen wondered what she meant and Joutsamo told them what Oksala had said. She stressed the fact that the detective claimed it was legal—it just wasn't the usual soft approach.

"Last night I received a text message," Joutsamo continued. "It came after the news bit from Römpötti. The message was short: *It's time to take action now*. I didn't recognize the number, but I found out it was the financial crime detective's."

"What's his name?" Suhonen asked.

"Jaakko Oksala."

Suhonen glanced at Takamäki, who shook his head and said, "I don't know him, either."

"That's not all. I saw the guy at the cafeteria this morning, and he told me how he had arranged for an eviction, collections, and welfare cuts for someone. The authorities would squeeze the guy dry today."

"Well, as long as the guy deserves it," Suhonen said.

"Nothing illegal about it, per se," Joutsamo said. "But…"

"But what?" Takamäki asked. He guessed what Joutsamo was thinking, but he wanted to hear it from her.

"Is that how the system is supposed to work? With the right target, the fences of bureaucracy mean nothing and suddenly the authorities work together seamlessly. I could see it with chasing a drug lord or a millionaire hustler. But Sandström is just a common loser."

"Sandström?" Suhonen asked, staring at Joutsamo. "Who is this Sandström?"

"You're completely lost?"

"Well, with no iPhone or Wikipedia with me…"

Joutsamo gave Suhonen the short version. The name Veikko Sandström made Suhonen think. He must have been the guy who told Salmela about Tanner. Salmela hung out at the Corner Pub, too.

"Was he here yesterday?"

"Just for questioning. How'd you know that?"

Suhonen didn't know; he just wanted to make sure they were talking about the same man.

"Somebody was talking in the hall, but it's not relevant," Suhonen said. "It sounded complicated."

Joutsamo shook her head, perplexed.

"I'm sure Sandström is getting what he deserves. I just wonder about the authorities' actions. Are we talking about an inside revenge organization making up for the court system's soft approach?"

"But they're acting within the law," Takamäki remarked.

"You could also ask," Suhonen joined in, "why the authorities shirk their duties in most cases."

"That's true in theory," Joutsamo replied. "But let's talk about what's really happening. Something has driven this group of authorities to take action."

"You mean arbitrary power?"

"These sorts of actions worry me."

"Are you concerned that the law pertains to everyone, or that it doesn't pertain to anyone?" Takamäki asked.

Suhonen wasn't interested in the speculation. He was thinking about Sandström, Tanner, and Juha Saarnikangas. Niina was safe now, at least.

"If the authorities are taking these measures, it's a wonder citizens haven't thought to take the law into their own hands," Joutsamo said. "Of course, one robbery will do it."

Joutsamo was referring to non-violent breaking and entering—with or without the residents at home.

"How do you mean?"

"If it happened to be the home of a celebrity or an authority figure, the media would make a big deal out of it. Then the residents of Westend, Kauniainen, and other high-end neighborhoods would hire home security companies to protect them when the police couldn't."

"The chief of Espoo Police would probably be glad," Suhonen said. "He wouldn't have to send patrols over there for nothing and he could keep them in Suvela, Leppävaara, Matinkylä, and Soukka."

Espoo was Helsinki's western suburb, and it had its share of problem areas.

"You guys don't see this is as a problem?" Joutsamo asked. She looked at Takamäki and Suhonen and continued, "I'm wondering whether we should do something about it or just watch."

"Find out who's involved, besides Oksala," Takamäki said. "Then we'll see what we can do."

CHAPTER 15
THURSDAY, 11:40 A.M.
KALLIO, HELSINKI

The chatter in the Corner Pub hushed as soon as Sandström stepped in the door.

He walked to the counter and greeted the bartender. Rane responded with an angry stare.

Sandström was confused. "What'd I do …?"

"Veikko, I hope you'll keep your distance for a while," Rane said, shaking his head.

"What's this? You're banning me from the bar? *Me?*"

"Haven't you read the newspaper or watched TV? Been on the internet?"

Sandström shook his head. The bartender grabbed an evening paper off the counter and opened it.

It was a full-page story. The large, double-line headline read: *A rapist bullied a young woman to suicide.*

The picture showed the front of the Corner Pub.

"This kind of publicity is totally unnecessary," the bartender said.

Sandström was reading the article and didn't hear the bartender. The story had been on television first. Raisa was referred to only by her first name, but his whole name was there.

Hell, he thought. Was this why the collection agent and the guy with the eviction notice had showed up that morning?

Shit, Sandström thought as he read on. This kind of reporting shouldn't be allowed. He had rights, too. He was getting livid.

Bullying her to commit suicide...that's a load of shit, Sandström thought. The whore cop had been after the same angle, but she hadn't succeeded.

"Gimme a pint," Sandström grunted.

"Okay, one," Rane said, feeling sorry for the guy. "But that's the first and the last."

"Can I go say hi to my buddies in the back?"

"Nobody's there," the bartender replied, shaking his head.

"Nobody?"

"They don't want to see you. Not Pile, not Eero. Nobody."

Sandström paid with change and took a long sip. The cold beer felt good, but his rage didn't cool down. He remembered the cop's name: Joutsamo. Anna Joutsamo. She had to be the one behind this. She couldn't trap him for the suicide, so she decided to get him good. The fucking reporters always ate out of the cops' hands. Sandström read the article again. There was an interview from Lind, Raisa's attorney. Sandström remembered the woman in the suit from the courtroom. She was also behind this.

Sandström was sure the TV news reporter was Sanna Römpötti. Shit. The three women conspired against him. Women. Of course. Fucking women.

Sandström decided he wouldn't take it sitting down.

* * *

Suhonen had been waiting in his white Golf for over an hour. He was in a parking lot by an apartment complex in the Pihlajanmäki neighborhood of Helsinki. It looked like rain, and he hoped he wouldn't have to use the windshield wipers and draw attention to himself.

Juha Saarnikangas's Red Fiat Ducato was parked twenty yards away. Suhonen didn't have electronic surveillance equipment, but he knew where Saarnikangas lived. He could've rung the doorbell, but decided not to. Someone else might be in the apartment, and he wanted to talk to Juha alone.

Suhonen considered what Niina had said about Juha and Tanner being together. Suhonen doubted Juha had turned religious, and he wanted to know what their affiliation was. He needed to take care of something else, too.

He had checked on the bible group online. Only one name came up: Jari Tanner. Suhonen had thought about calling the super in Malmi and asking about the apartment, but that might leak back to Tanner. He'd decided to call from his prepaid cell phone and pretend to be an interested buyer. The super had confirmed that a bible group owned the apartment.

Why would a group of prisoners from Turku want to burn down Takamäki's house? Suhonen couldn't come up with an answer. The Helsinki Penitentiary housed a number of criminals who held grudges. Maybe the group's operations weren't restricted to Saramäki, after all. Juha's involvement pointed to that possibility.

Suhonen had talked with the NBI investigator that morning. Kaunisto was the one who had entered Jari Tanner's address in the file, and he confirmed the information. They had no active investigation on Tanner, but because the address was linked to another case it was recorded for future reference. The investigator considered Tanner a professional criminal, but Tanner had served his latest sentence with no problems. The police hadn't heard of anything out of the ordinary.

The Turku investigator had no information on whether Tanner was involved with the Skulls motorcycle gang. The president of the Skulls was serving life in Saramäki prison. They still had a bounty out on Suhonen, as far as he knew. The biker gang and the police had faced off with each other in recent years, but Takamäki had never been under threat.

The detective from Turku had heard of the Saramäki Bible Group, but the name wasn't related to any of his cases.

Kaunisto didn't think it was a cover for a crime organization; if it was, there was no proof. The group had given assistance to released prisoners, and they were funded by donations. Kaunisto noted that the group's aid had diminished in the past few years.

Suhonen asked an acquaintance who worked in the tax department to check on the group for any information. He found out that the association had received two apartments as an inheritance gift. One of them was the apartment in Malmi, in use by the registered charitable organization. The other, a high-end apartment in downtown Turku, had been sold. The tax guy knew the name of the attorney in charge of the sale.

The attorney had denied having anything further to do with the bible group. A widowed woman, who died a couple of years earlier, had participated in the bible group and left the apartment to the organization in her will. The attorney, wanting to ensure that her will was followed to a tee, had also managed the taxes due on the sale.

Suhonen was confused. A gangster group wouldn't pay taxes. It was obvious that the bible group could afford to have their own T-shirts and Bibles printed.

Suhonen hadn't said anything to the NBI guy about the arson lead. He himself had wondered if it was legitimate. Salmela had heard about it from the rapist, Veikko Sandström, who had said Tanner was looking for someone to do it. Was Sandström just trying to make himself seem tougher than he was?

Sandström could have heard the Turku guy's name during one of his stints in prison and the rest could be bar talk. Those at his table would've gotten the impression that Sandström was in deep with an ex-con. Suhonen thought maybe he should run a cross-check on Sandström's and Tanner's prison records. Had they served time together at any point? Of course, that wouldn't prove they knew each other any more than lacking common prison time would rule it out.

At any rate, Tanner's name coming up in the Corner Pub in conjunction with a case like this meant that he was not big-time. Major criminals always used a shield-man to protect themselves.

Knowing that someone was looking for an outsider to commit arson made Suhonen think of two options: Either the person in charge wanted to make sure no one could connect him to the case in any way or the group was extremely few in numbers.

Suhonen had wondered if he should tell Joutsamo, Takamäki, and the NBI investigators about the lead. He didn't think it was necessary, for now. He wanted to protect Salmela, and sharing the information might cause the situation to get out of control.

He was glad he'd had to wait—it gave him time to think and connect the dots. He also considered what Joutsamo had said about the authorities' revenge group. He'd been involved in cases where authorities had torn to shreds the lives of hardened criminals. The men went to prison and their houses, cars, boats, summer cabins, and money went to the state. Their wives divorced them and their children were taken into custody. Those with the most to lose suffered the greatest. In financial crime cases, the pain might last as long as ten years.

The revenge group ended up shredding its target. Some were completely destroyed, others became bitter. The only ones seemingly unaffected by the consequences were those who committed suicide.

* * *

Veikko Sandström rang a button on the panel and opened the door when it buzzed. He was wearing a black beanie, pulled all the way down to his eyes.

In the entryway stood a female security guard in a dark blue uniform with the security company logo on the front. The woman smiled.

"How can I help you?"

"Listen, I'd like to see Sanna Römpötti," Sandström grunted. He kept his right hand in his pocket—he was holding a survival knife the collection agent had missed.

"Do you have an appointment?"

"No," Sandström said, shaking his head. "I've got a hot news lead for her."

She studied him. Some of crime reporter Römpötti's visitors resembled him in looks.

"Whom can I announce?" the woman asked in British butler style. "If she's in, that is."

"Leevi."

"And what's it about?"

"I already told you," Sandström said and glared at the guard. "A news lead. I'm not telling you what it is."

The security guard said something into the phone, but Sandström couldn't hear it.

"Römpötti is in, and she'll come down. It'll be a moment."

Normally she let the guests through the glass door into the waiting area, but she decided this guy could wait in the entryway. She glanced at a teargas bottle hidden from the guests' view behind the counter. She smiled at the surly man.

* * *

Suhonen was used to waiting. Over the course of his police career he had spent thousands of hours in stakeouts for drug nests and other places. The most important thing was to stay alert. His legs became tired, like when traveling on an airplane. He would get hungry. His thoughts wandered. He might have to take a piss.

But he had to be ready—either to take action or just to register things like the color or make of a passing car.

A stakeout usually involved two officers; one could relax while the other kept watch. But this time Suhonen was alone.

He had no idea when Saarnikangas would leave the apartment. A light was on, so somebody had to be in. The guy might play Xbox for hours. Suhonen knew Juha's phone number, but didn't want to call and give him a chance to think up a story. Juha's reaction would be telling and Suhonen wanted to see it.

The only things to note were the Ducato in the parking lot and the lights in the apartment. He didn't even spot anybody taking a dog out for a piss. He was getting sleepy.

Suhonen was in the middle of a yawn when he saw a broad-shouldered man step out of the front door. He recognized the guy immediately as Rane from the Corner Pub. His real name was Rauno Matalamäki. Suhonen remembered that the guy had done time in the Helsinki Penitentiary for a couple of drug deals as well as smuggling dope.

* * *

Sanna Römpötti left her office and walked down the stairs. A glass door with an ID card reader separated the news studio stairwell from the small lobby in front of the security guard's counter. The station didn't want any outsiders in the holy of holies. Reporters were constantly receiving threats of various levels, especially from the mentally unstable.

She saw a man dressed in a down coat and a beanie standing in the security guard's lobby, facing out. That the guard had refused to let him in told her something, but Römpötti was used to meeting all kinds of people. It went with her job; you never knew who might give you an important piece of information.

Sanna Römpötti unlocked the door with the ID card on a lanyard around her neck. She had on a black blouse and a lightweight, black jacket.

"Hello, Leevi," Römpötti said and introduced herself. "You wanted to see me."

Veikko Sandström turned around and grinned.

"I'm not Leevi, I'm Veikko Sandström," he said in a threatening tone.

He kept his hands in his pockets.

Römpötti noticed Sandström measuring her with his eyes. She didn't say anything. She had experience with threatening, violent situations; the small space and the locked door behind her were of concern. Fleeing was not an option. She couldn't show fear, and she needed to calm the man down.

"Nice to meet you. Should we sit down and talk?"

The lobby had a table and two chairs. Sandström's attack would be less quick if he was seated.

Sandström remained standing. He lifted his left hand to shake his finger, staring at the reporter.

"Why the hell did you go and tell all those lies in that story? What kind of fucking pile of shit are you? This will cost you."

The security guard was watching the situation. Römpötti was aware of the teargas canister behind the counter.

Römpötti didn't want to argue, and she knew she needed to appear amenable and calm. She kept her hands in plain sight and was careful to avoid sudden movements.

"I'm just a reporter."

"Just a reporter?" Sandström laughed. "You're a fucking pile of shit. The likes of you should be killed."

Sandström's violent speech was another sign of danger. He formed a fist with one hand and kept his other hand in his pocket. Römpötti wondered if he had a knife or a gun.

"I'm sorry if it's caused you trouble. Let's sit down."

"How much are you gonna pay me? Five grand, minimum."

Römpötti bypassed the comment. She didn't want to make things worse by declining.

"I could interview you on the subject right now. I'll call the cameraman."

She glanced at the security guard and said, "Leena, could you ask Kalle to come down."

The guard picked up the phone. Kalle would be helpful in case the situation became violent.

Sandström was taken aback. This wasn't how it was supposed to go. He was supposed to chew out the pile of shit, get some money, and teach the broad a lesson. But now she was offering him an interview and the cameraman was on his way down.

"Oh, so I would tell my side?"

Römpötti was glad for his reaction. The confusion had toned down his threats.

"Yeah. I'll do a part two to the story."

"Hell, no. I'm not doing that."

"It'll only take a couple of minutes. The questions are easy. What happened and why?"

Sandström took a step back.

"Will you do it?" she asked.

"You're a loon."

"But really, it'll just take a moment," Römpötti said. If Sandström had agreed to do the interview, she would've gone ahead with it. Raisa's cold fate was definitely the most popular story on the station's website.

Sandström shook his head. This wasn't how he had pictured it. He saw a broad-shouldered man approaching behind the glass door, holding a camera.

"I'm leaving, but remember: I didn't kill her."

Römpötti wanted to say she never claimed he did, but she thought it might make him angry again.

148

"Of course I'll remember," she said.

"And don't do anything like this again."

"I won't," she said, knowing it was a lie. "But the interview..."

Sandström disappeared through the front door.

Römpötti looked at the guard and the cameraman. With a chuckle she said, "He wouldn't agree to an interview."

"He's right," the guard said, looking serious.

"About what?" Römpötti asked, surprised.

"That you're crazy. I expected him to attack you, and I had the gas ready to go. And you were just talking about doing an interview."

"The television camera is mightier than tear gas," Römpötti quipped, and the cameraman smiled.

"We need to reconsider the safety precautions in this space," the reporter said, studying the lobby. "If he had attacked me, I would've had nowhere to go."

* * *

Suhonen saw Juha Saarnikangas step out the front door of his apartment building. Judging from his uncharacteristically brisk walk, he was in a hurry.

Suhonen got out of his car and marched toward the rusty Ducato. He would reach it at the same time as Juha. The side of the van shielded him from Juha's view.

Suhonen approached the van from the back just as Juha was inserting the key in the lock.

"Hello," Suhonen said with a cold tone.

"Well, if it isn't super cop Terence Suhonen," Juha replied.

Suhonen knew Saarnikangas was referring to an awkward movie made in 1980, in which the police officer played by Terence Hill gets superpowers from a nuclear explosion. The movie was unusually shoddy.

"God forgives—I don't," Suhonen said, making a reference to Hill's spaghetti Western. Terence Hill's and Bud Spencer's comical, tongue-in-cheek spaghetti Westerns had been hugely popular in Finland in the 1970s and '80s.

"I'll chat with you for a minute if you can tell me Terence Hill's real name and Bud Spencer's most remarkable sports performance," Saarnikangas said with a smile.

Suhonen looked at Juha. He'd had a haircut and gotten his rotten teeth fixed. His eyes, once dim, were now piercing. Even his skin looked better. The Thailand sun must have helped.

"You've come a long way from Alvar Aalto's architecture and Gallen-Kallela's art," Suhonen said, remembering Juha's ravings about the famous Finns when he had last met him in downtown Helsinki.

"Answer me or I'm off. Unless you plan to throw me in jail."

"Should I?"

Juha ignored the question and opened the van door.

"Terence Hill is easy: Mario Girotti, of course," Suhonen said. "Bud Spencer is a challenge. I know he was a swimmer who represented Italy in the Helsinki Olympics in 1952, but what was his biggest achievement?"

Suhonen rubbed his stubbly chin theatrically.

"Ten seconds, and no phoning a friend," Juha said.

"I'm taking a guess here, but I'll say Carlo Pedersoli was Italy's Tarzan, and the first Italian to swim the hundred free in under a minute."

"Correct answer," Juha said, genuinely surprised. "I always knew you watched spaghetti Westerns every night."

"Can't always judge a book by its cover. That goes for me as well as the three-hundred-thirty-pound Spencer. You've got a new look, too. What's new on the inside?"

"Is that why you've been waiting here for hours?" Juha asked with a shake of his head. "To ask me the color of my heart? What the hell, Suhonen."

Suhonen felt like Juha's heart had turned darker.

"When did you get back from Thailand? Did your American inheritance run out?"

"I just grew tired of laying around the pool, jumping off the diving board, hanging out at bars, and bonking picture-perfect women. It didn't fit my Lutheran work ethic where happiness has to be painfully earned through hard work. Are we done?"

Suhonen wondered if he should ask about Jari Tanner, but decided against it. Juha wouldn't tell him anything and Suhonen would only disclose his hand by asking. But he had to take care of one thing,

"The woman with the baby carriage in Malmi," Suhonen said.

"What about her?" Saarnikangas asked quickly.

"Nothing. She's got nothing to do with anything, so leave her alone."

"So you just stop by and screw her?" Saarnikangas said, laughing. "Is the kid yours?"

"No, that was just a white lie and a stupid move. Leave her be."

Saarnikangas gave Suhonen a measuring look and said, "It's hard to tell with you, but I think you might be telling the truth for once."

"I am."

"Okay, but it's probably best to get her out of the building anyway. Anything else?"

"No, as long as you know your return has been noted. I'm sure you remember that too much non-Lutheran activity here in the homeland will land you in jail."

Saarnikangas sat down on the front seat.

"I remember it as well as you remember the part of the oath where you promised to use police power the way the law intended."

"The ethical oath came into use years after my graduation," Suhonen said with a smile. "The hand of the law strikes like Spencer's fist, and takes you all the way down and hard."

"The sleuth at shady business," Juha said with a laugh and closed the van door. He rolled down the window as he started the clunky diesel engine.

"Don't worry. I'm not up to anything. I'll be going back to Thailand soon."

Juha backed his pile of rust out of the parking space.

Suhonen walked to his car. He had wanted to see Juha, and seeing him had confirmed the suspicion that the man was no longer a dime-a-dozen drug dealer but something completely different. Suhonen used to know how to handle Juha, but now he had no clue. The roles had become clear. But Niina would be safe from these criminals now. At least he had fixed that mistake.

His cell phone rang. It was Takamäki. He wanted Suhonen to come to the police station immediately.

CHAPTER 16
THURSDAY, 2:00 P.M.
HELSINKI POLICE HEADQUARTERS

The mustached NBI Head of Intelligence Nykänen and a tall lieutenant from the same bureau were sitting in Takamäki's office when Suhonen walked in. Suhonen knew Nykänen, of course, but wasn't familiar with the six-foot-two, slender-faced man. The forty-year-old had dark, short hair, and Suhonen thought about the hairstyles everyone from Jokiniemi seemed to sport. The lines on the man's face told of hard work. Perhaps he had a background in the financial crime unit.

He introduced himself as Keijo Partanen. Despite the man's effort to conceal his dialect, Suhonen detected a northern flavor from Oulu in his speech.

"We've been talking about the house fire," Takamäki said.

"What have you got?" Suhonen asked. It hadn't yet seemed necessary to mention the tips about Jari Tanner even to Takamäki.

"Revenge is certainly a strong motive," Partanen said. "We haven't yet discovered who might have done it."

Partanen explained that the NBI had gone through Takamäki's homicide unit's investigations from the past six months, but hadn't found an obvious, suitable candidate. There were several possible perpetrators, but according to the tips collected from the field and from prisons, no one had threatened Takamäki. That was to say, those friendly with the police had heard nothing.

"So we're SOL?" Suhonen asked.

"You could say that," Nykänen replied. "But it can't be considered real revenge if the victim doesn't know who did it. That would be missing the whole point."

"Maybe it was the wrong house, after all," Takamäki suggested.

Partanen looked like he disagreed.

"Based on the forensic investigation, the arsonist had parked a car at the corner of the woods behind the house. They found prints from size ten Nokia rain boots in the thicket. The arsonist didn't end up at your place by chance. He must've taken the canisters of flammable fluids with him since the team couldn't find any."

"What about tire tracks where the car was parked?"

"Unfortunately, they couldn't get any."

Suhonen thought about Takamäki's townhome. No one would come through the thicket behind the building by accident. It was obvious that the route had been planned beforehand.

Suhonen had tried to think of a possible motive Tanner and Saarnikangas would have for burning the house, if in fact they had anything to do with it. The homicide team had never investigated a case involving Tanner, and Takamäki had nothing to do with Saarnikangas.

"Are any of the candidates you've profiled doing time in Turku's Saramäki?"

"Why do you ask?" said Partanen.

Suhonen didn't want to divulge his information, yet. Partanen didn't ask again, but focused on his list instead. No one on the list was in Saramäki. Partanen said he would ask the Prison Department to give him a list from all the prisons, but he wouldn't limit the search to institutions alone. He would also get the names of all known criminal gang members. Takamäki could study them on his own and consider any possible candidates, if nothing more concrete popped up in the meantime.

Takamäki didn't think it was such a great idea; he might as well be looking through criminal records.

"Why did you mention Saramäki?" Takamäki asked.

"Well, for example, the president of the Skulls is doing life there for murder."

"That gang is so downtrodden right now," Nykänen inserted, "that I don't think they would have the energy for something like this."

The Skulls were a criminal motorcycle gang, and they and the Helsinki VCU had had a number of run-ins in recent years, some violent. The VCU had won the last few rounds, putting the key members in prison; the gang hadn't been very active recently.

"It only takes one crazy person."

"Sure, it's possible, but…"

"But you don't think so?" Suhonen asked.

"No."

"You know Rauno Matalamäki, right?" Suhonen asked Nykänen.

The name didn't ring a bell, but when Suhonen said Rane worked as the bartender at the Corner Pub, Nykänen remembered him.

"What's his connection to the Skulls these days?" Suhonen asked. "He used to be pretty friendly with them."

Nykänen thought for a minute and looked at Suhonen.

"I can't say for sure, but I don't think any members of the Skulls have been seen at the Corner Pub lately. Rane, with his powerlifting background, was providing steroids to them at one point. I think one of our units investigated him, but it was some years ago."

"We'll check out the Skulls again," Partanen said. "At least they'd have a clear motive."

The four men sat in silence in the room with glass walls. The view through the windows showed only the inside walls of the cup-shaped police station.

155

"I wonder if we should take the case public," Takamäki said. "Might start getting information that way."

"Not just yet," Nykänen said. "I'm sure we'd get info, but the majority of it would likely be false leads, or someone claiming credit for something they didn't even do. It would do more harm than good at this stage."

Suhonen wondered what harm it could do, considering the NBI had no clue at the moment.

"Just an idea," Takamäki said.

Nykänen stood up and Partanen followed.

"Keijo, wait for me outside," Nykänen said. "I have another matter for these gentlemen."

Partanen left and Nykänen waited for the door to close.

"Heads up, guys," he said, looking at Suhonen.

"What do you mean?" Takamäki asked.

"Suhonen's name is being mentioned in the halls of NBI."

"What's this?" Suhonen asked.

"The Viola Street gig. The NBI's narcotics unit has set up surveillance to run an operation in connection with the skinheads," Nykänen said and walked out.

Takamäki looked at Suhonen, perplexed.

"What Viola Street gig?"

Suhonen told Takamäki about his visit to the drug nest as Salmela's backup.

"Buying hash with a criminal. You can't be serious," Takamäki huffed.

"I had to do it to get the tip."

"What tip?" Takamäki asked.

Suhonen finally filled Takamäki in on the events of the last few days; how he had gotten a lead from Salmela about Tanner, and how Juha Saarnikangas was connected to it all. He also talked about the Saramäki Bible Group's apartment, and Takamäki now understood why Suhonen had asked about the prison.

"I get your point, but that won't help you. Nykänen said they had the apartment under surveillance. I wouldn't be surprised if your phone was tapped by now."

"I'll have to keep that in mind," Suhonen said.

Takamäki thought for a moment.

"About the tip. How did Salmela hear about someone looking for an arsonist?"

"Nothing mysterious there," Suhonen said. "He had heard mention of it at the Corner Pub."

"I thought Salmela had left that gang."

"He's not doing so great right now. Sandström is some kind of a link in this."

"On top of all the issues between NBI and us, you being involved in a drug deal is really serious," Takamäki said, shaking his head.

CHAPTER 17
THURSDAY, 8:50 P.M.
MECHELIN STREET, HELSINKI

Anna Joutsamo was running down the sandy, linden-lined park path in the middle of Mechelin Street, one of the major thoroughfares in western Helsinki, named after a nineteenth-century statesman and leader in the Finnish independence movement.

Dressed in a dark tracksuit, she had left her home near Töölö Square half an hour earlier, on a route taking her around Töölö Bay, continuing on Hesperia Street, through Hietaniemi, and back to Mechelin Street. In another five hundred yards, she'd turn onto Sibelius Street at the monument bearing the name of the great composer. Often when she passed the monument, she'd recall summer days when there'd more than a dozen buses lining the street and hordes of tourists with cameras.

Finally, to cool down, she'd walk up the short hill on Topelius Street back to Töölö Square. It would add up to about four miles. She enjoyed running, ever since Takamäki had raved about it a few years ago and she decided to give it a try. The gym might have been a better fit for a city girl like her, but running didn't cost anything. And the police station had a weight room for when she felt like pumping iron.

At first, Joutsamo had thought about work when she ran, but she soon realized she didn't need to think about anything. It gave her brain a nice break from all the negativity she constantly had to deal with on the job. Takamäki had stressed that.

Dripping with sweat, Joutsamo came to the intersection of Mechelin Street and South Hesperia Street, where the gravel path ended. There was no pedestrian crossing, but Joutsamo didn't care. She slowed down and looked both ways—no traffic. She picked up the pace again, but was starting to feel the miles in her legs.

The temperature hovered just above freezing. It was comfortable running weather, especially since it wasn't raining or sleeting.

The distance between South and North Hesperia Streets was only about a hundred yards. Joutsamo slowed down to a half-jog again. She didn't see any cars and started to cross the road. She took two fast steps and heard a car engine behind her on the right. The driver seemed to be speeding up instead of braking.

There was no time to make a conscious choice: only to react. Instinctively, she didn't try stopping; she knew it wouldn't have worked. Instead, she jumped to the left. The move saved her, as the car turning from Mechelin Street missed her by about two inches. Joutsamo felt a yank as the side mirror tore the pocket off her tracksuit.

Her immediate reaction was anger. Who would drive that way? She vowed to make sure they would lose their license.

Joutsamo watched the car. Instead of stopping, it continued down the street by the former military barracks' gray wall and toward the Taivallahti port. She couldn't make out the license plate, but thought the first letter might have been an X. The car was a dark blue, an older Toyota.

Joutsamo felt her pocket and remembered she had left her cell phone at home. All she had was her house key and a five-euro bill. She always kept cash with her, in case she twisted her ankle or something happened and she had to take the tram back.

Joutsamo watched the car turn right at the Taivallahti port intersection and north towards Restaurant Mestaritalli.

The detective stood frozen on the edge of the street. The closeness of the call caught up with her; she was scared and shivering. Damn, that was close.

Joutsamo couldn't tell if the traffic light had been red or green for the turning car. But the driver had to see her. Why didn't he stop? Was the driver drunk?

Joutsamo didn't feel like running anymore, and she walked across the street. The quickest way home was down the side of Hesperia Park onto Runeberg Street.

She couldn't shake the blue Toyota from her mind. Had the man, or woman for all she knew, tried to run her over on purpose? Now out of fear, she picked up her pace—Joutsamo wanted to get home.

FRIDAY,

NOVEMBER 30

CHAPTER 18
FRIDAY, 8:15 A.M.
HELSINKI POLICE HEADQUARTERS

Suhonen sat at his desk in the midst of the white bookcases. He was browsing through the tip database for any pieces to the puzzle, but couldn't find any threats against the police. No one had added leads during the night. He read through the Helsinki crime reports from the previous night. It was the typical metropolitan life: assaults, burglaries, vandalism, drunk drivers, vehicle thefts, and a rape. He was familiar with some of the suspects' names on the screen, but none piqued his interest.

Last night had been quiet at his apartment. Takamäki had gone out to dinner. After he had returned, Suhonen had pressed him. Takamäki finally relented; he had been out with Nea Lind. They had talked in the afternoon and planned to have dinner. Takamäki said both the food and the company were good and left it at that.

Suhonen had gone to the safe house to see Niina, and they had coffee together. Suhonen had then rented a couple of Terence Hill and Bud Spencer movies from a nearby video store and watched them at home. The films were just as poor as he remembered.

He ran into an announcement from the Kitee police department in Northern Karelia. At five in the morning a citizen had called in to report a herd of cattle in the Kitee city center. Eleven bulls were on the loose, making for an unpredictable and potentially dangerous situation. Eventually they were all rounded up and transported back to the farm.

Every police department had their problems, Suhonen thought. However, there was no lack of homicides in Northern Karelia. The number of killings per capita there was double that of Helsinki's.

"Suhonen?" said a male voice.

Suhonen turned around in his chair to see two men, each wearing a dark jacket and jeans. He knew them from the NBI narcotics unit. Behind them stood a uniformed man from the Helsinki Police. The officer had a crew cut, and the NBI men sported the typical Jokiniemi barber styles.

"Yes," Suhonen said.

"Let's go."

The man who spoke was the taller of the two, and Suhonen remembered his name to be Rahkonen.

"Where to?"

"To take care of something in Jokiniemi."

"Like what?"

"We'll tell you when we get there."

Kulta and Kohonen had stopped their work and were watching from behind their desks.

"Why not," Suhonen said. "I'll just turn off the computer."

He shut down the computer, pulled his second cell phone out of his pocket, slipped it into the drawer with his pistol, and locked the drawer.

* * *

Police interrogation rooms looked the same all over the world. It was no coincidence, but had psychological reasoning behind it. The point was to make the suspect as uncomfortable as possible. The bleak décor, lack of windows, gray walls, and soundproofing did the trick. The door was behind the interrogator. It was a psychological reference to the role of the detective-in- charge as doorkeeper. But it was also for safety; the interrogator could escape more easily in case the questioning went bad.

Dangerous situations weren't unheard of at NBI headquarters. Once, a nasty-tempered suspect had driven a pencil through an officer's hand. Since then, pencils were no longer given out in Jokiniemi.

Suhonen didn't usually conduct interrogations himself, but he knew the process.

The narrow-faced Rahkonen had left his jacket somewhere and was now sitting on the other side of the wooden table in his dress shirt. A computer sat on the table, but the NBI guy left it off.

A short, stocky NBI detective walked in the room carrying a shiny thermos. He, too, had taken off his jacket. Suhonen knew his name was Strömberg.

Suhonen, still wearing his leather jacket, leaned forward on his elbows. He hadn't gone through a security check or DNA testing, nor had his fingerprints or photo been taken. While this was routine for crime suspects, Suhonen didn't yet know why he was there. Naturally, he guessed it had to do with the events at the Viola Street apartment when he had been with Salmela.

"Coffee?" Strömberg asked and set three paper cups on the table. Without waiting for a reply, he poured coffee in all three.

Suhonen tried to look confident, but felt unsure. The interrogation room's ambience was getting to him, though nothing had been said yet. He figured the interrogators meant to give the impression that they were in no hurry. In the car they had talked about this and that—things like ice hockey and the weather. The NBI guys had obviously tried to find out what he was interested in. Suhonen had made short, meaningless comments. Being a fan of the local teams, he didn't really care how many games the Oulu Kärpät had lost in the Finnish Championship league.

Rahkonen slurped his coffee loudly. Suhonen tasted his—typical police coffee, made in a dirty coffeemaker and allowed to sit for too long.

"So, this is a preliminary questioning," Rahkonen said.

Suhonen had guessed that much.

The detective didn't choose to disclose whether Suhonen was a suspect or a witness in the case, or if they only wanted to talk to him. The difference was that if he was a crime suspect, he would be entitled by law to lie. Otherwise, being an officer, he would have to tell the truth. The goal was obvious: They wanted to use his story as a premise for suspicion of crime.

Suhonen said nothing.

"We have a video of you in an apartment with a man who bought dozens of grams of hash. Would you like to comment?"

A video. Nykänen hadn't mentioned anything about that. Shit, Suhonen thought, but tried to appear calm.

Suhonen looked Rahkonen in the eye. Despite the man's scrawny build, his eyes were sharp. He was serious.

"I'd better not comment at this point."

"What's that supposed to mean?" Strömberg inserted.

"Just what I said."

"Do you have something to hide?" Strömberg continued, a self-assured, crooked smile tugging at the corner of his mouth.

"I didn't say that."

"Then why won't you comment?"

"I'd like to know if I'm a suspect."

"That's what we're trying to find out," Rahkonen said, his eyes fixed on Suhonen. "And we need your cooperation."

Suhonen shrugged. He wouldn't be helping them along.

"You're playing with fire," Strömberg said, attempting a threatening tone. "You don't seem to realize how much trouble you're in."

On the contrary, Suhonen thought. He knew only too well the trouble he was in and how much worse it would be if he started explaining things now. As a policeman he wasn't in the position to lie, but telling the truth wouldn't help him, either, as the NBI and the Helsinki Police Department had been at odds for years.

The relationship had soured during a joint investigation by the NBI and the Ministry of Interior into the Helsinki Police narcotics unit's best men. The NBI had suspected a narcotics officer of using illegal means to confiscate large amounts of drugs. After a prolonged and painful trial, the men had been acquitted, but the mutual trust between the units was gone. Suhonen knew his case, with video proof, would have him fired—publicly, no less. The NBI had men who wanted to prove they were right in their suspicions of the Helsinki PD, and at this point any of its officers would do for a victim.

Suhonen kept his mouth shut. He imagined on the gray wall the philosopher Wittgenstein's words: *Whereof one cannot speak, thereof one must be silent*.

"You don't want to help us?" Rahkonen asked. "You'd be helping yourself in the process."

Suhonen disagreed. Some years ago, he had pretended to befriend a pedophile who dealt videos. Thus, he had to pretend to be interested in sickening child porn. It wasn't easy, but he had eventually managed to get into the ring, and several people involved in the international operation ended up in prison.

In the same vein, Joutsamo was able to feign sympathy toward a woman who had killed her husband. The detective would pretend to understand and comfort her, while the goal was to get a confession and send the killer behind bars for years to come.

"We know your job in the field isn't easy," Strömberg continued. "There's all kinds of gray area and all. Could you...?"

Playing on my sympathies, Suhonen thought. That's a basic interrogation technique. Remember Wittgenstein.

"Never mind," Rahkonen said. "Suhonen, wait here. We'll talk with the lead investigator for a minute. But remember that we gave you a chance. We're just trying to discover the truth."

CHAPTER 19
FRIDAY, 9:20 A.M.
HELSINKI POLICE HEADQUARTERS

Mikko Kulta sat at police headquarters with headphones on, listening to the interrogation minutes and typing the suspect's answers into the computer. In this case, the suspect was guilty and had confessed. The twenty-two-year-old Jaakko Pöntinen had punched a forty-six-year-old man in the head with his fist after the two men, both drunk, had argued in front of the train station.

The father of two teenaged daughters had fallen backwards and hit his head on the pavement, suffering severe injuries. It was obvious he was not capable of working, and it was possible he wouldn't be able to recognize his daughters.

The case was investigated as an assault and battery. It had come from Takamäki to Kulta's desk. The routine investigation team could have handled the simple case, but organizational changes never seemed to work out as planned.

Kulta typed up the words: "*I remember leaving the bar after the last call. I encountered a man outside and some kind of rumble started...*"

Kulta pictured the young, bald man. The detective had googled him and found information about the young man's background in mixed martial arts, which in Kulta's opinion made the assault even more serious. He had brought this up at the interrogation, wanting to make sure the prosecutor would see it and pursue a more severe punishment. When Kulta asked about steroids, the young man denied any use.

Kulta rewound the recording a bit, typed up the words, and continued listening. *"Some kind of rumble started, and I can't remember the reason because I was drunk."*

What Kulta typed wasn't exactly verbatim, but the point came across and Jaakko would have a chance to read it before signing.

Joutsamo walked into the room, and Kulta decided to take a break. He took off the headphones and dabbed the sweat in his ear with his pinky.

"How's it going?" Kulta asked Joutsamo.

"Okay," she replied.

"Have you found anything?"

Kulta knew about Joutsamo's close call with the car, and that she had been trying all morning to find information on the vehicle. She had looked for possible security camera footage along the car's route.

Joutsamo nodded.

"The car can be seen on the Taivallahti school security video. When we enlarged one of the frames, we could make out the letters XEH on the license plate, but no numbers were visible."

"That's a start. What about the driver?"

"The image shows a dark figure, but it's not clear enough to tell the sex of the person."

"That's not helpful."

"No, but a Toyota Corolla with license plate letters XEH was stolen last night from Pitkämäki Street in Paloheinä. The car is a 1998 model, and those older models don't have any anti-theft technology. The car was reported stolen this morning after the owner couldn't find it."

"What's the owner like?"

"A carpenter. No criminal history or links to anything."

"So it's a stolen car," Kulta said.

"Yep," Joutsamo replied. She had reported the vehicle to the patrol officers and they would let her know if the car was found.

"This is kind of strange," Kulta said.

"What do you mean?" Joutsamo asked.

"All this happening at the same time. Takamäki's house is burned down, someone tries to run you over, and Suhonen gets taken in for some weird interrogation."

"You mean these things might be interconnected?"

"Not necessarily. But it's a weird coincidence to have all this happening at once. I guess Kohonen and I are next," Kulta said with a forced chuckle.

* * *

Suhonen had been waiting for an hour in the Jokiniemi interrogation room, and he could feel his stomach rumbling with hunger. He'd had a small breakfast, and for his morning snack he only got the coffee, no sweet roll. His cell phone was in his pocket, but he didn't know whom he would text. If he had a Facebook page, he might have posted, *I'm having a light gray Wittgenstein Zen moment in Vantaa*, or some other vague phrase. Hell no, Suhonen thought.

In his downtime he tried to focus on Takamäki's arson, but it was difficult. The interrogation room was genuinely depressing.

The door clanked, and Rahkonen stepped in. Strömberg followed him. Both smiled as they sat down.

"You should've talked while you had the chance," Strömberg sneered.

Suhonen had no reason to reply.

Rahkonen coughed and said, "We have discussed the matter with Special Prosecutor Härkälä and he agrees with us."

Rahkonen switched on the desk computer.

"We clearly have reason to suspect you of a narcotics crime. Härkälä is still weighing the possibility of a gross narcotics crime, considering it's about a police officer's insolent behavior. But at this point it's a narcotics offense. Do you understand?"

Suhonen shrugged. The visit to Viola Street with Salmela was a mistake, but he was perplexed by the NBI's actions. The police had the apartment under surveillance, and they could see all of their drug deals. Salmela had walked out with fifty grams of hash. Was one of the dealers an undercover cop? Suhonen thought about the men in the apartment. He hadn't recognized any of them and couldn't think of who they were. Who was more guilty—Suhonen or the NBI guys who were standing aside watching several obvious drug deals take place?

Rahkonen's computer was running now, and he pulled a microphone out of the drawer and set it in front of Suhonen.

"We'll take care of the initial interrogation right now. It's also being recorded on video," the detective said, pointing to the camera by the ceiling in the corner of the room.

"We need your name first, of course."

"Are you joking?" Suhonen asked.

"No. First and last name."

Suhonen pulled his police ID card out of his pocket and set it down in front of Rahkonen.

Filling out the information required for the preliminary investigation file took a moment. Suhonen said his address and phone number were confidential, and they were not noted.

The recording started, and Rahkonen stated that Suhonen was suspected of a narcotics crime. Suhonen was informed that he had the right to an attorney, but he declined. The interrogation could be held without one.

Rahkonen recorded the starting time, the place, his name as the interrogator, and the name of Strömberg who was also in the room.

It was a hell of a bureaucracy, but it served a purpose. The walls were eating away at the suspects in every windowless interrogation room all over Finland.

Rahkonen shifted his sharp gaze from the computer screen to Suhonen.

"You were in an apartment where hashish was sold. Are you guilty of a narcotics crime?"

"No comment."

"Do you deny having been in the apartment?"

"No comment."

"Why did you go into the apartment?"

"No comment."

"Who else was there?"

"No comment."

"Why don't you want to talk about it?"

"No comment," Suhonen kept repeating.

"What's the matter? Why don't you want to answer?"

"No comment."

Rahkonen didn't type the answers into the computer, he would transcribe the recording later. He glanced at Strömberg, who had a faint smile on his face. The Helsinki detective seemed to be fishing for a conviction by acting like a professional criminal. His answers would look extremely unfavorable in the file that the prosecutor and the court would see.

Rahkonen remained serious, but was irritated by the Helsinki detective's behavior. How could a police officer act this way—take part in a drug deal?

If convicted, Suhonen would get a fine, or at most a short suspended sentence of two months for his involvement in buying fifty grams of hashish. But at the very least, he would be fired.

Rahkonen hadn't planned on asking, but his desire to show the arrogant cop who was boss made him say it.

"One more question. Eero Salmela, who was with you in the apartment, said you led him there. Do you have any comment on that?"

Suhonen jumped. Salmela had told the detectives that Suhonen led him there? Shit.

Suhonen wanted to let out a heavy sigh, but remembered that the interrogation was being recorded. An investigator from the NBI would examine every microscopic facial expression and write a report about it.

"No comment," Suhonen said, keeping his previous tone.

Rahkonen felt victorious. This guy was obviously involved, and maybe in more than one drug deal. The police force needed to be rid of abscesses like him. It was pointless to continue the interrogation when the suspect refused to comment on anything.

"At the moment you're being held as a suspect for a narcotics crime. Prosecutor Härkälä will decide on your possible arrest within twenty-four hours. We will search your home and your place of work. The prosecutor will inform the Helsinki Police Department headquarters of the investigation so they can make the appropriate administrative decisions."

Suhonen still had no comment. The shit was finally hitting the fan.

Rahkonen stopped the recording. Strömberg asked Suhonen to empty his pockets onto the table. Next, he would have his photo, DNA sample, and fingerprints taken for the file.

"You must be some kind of an idiot," Strömberg snorted. "And you're a cop. We don't need the likes of you in this field. Since we're busy at the moment and your home won't be searched for a couple of days, you'll get to find yourself at home in the Vantaa police station's holding cell. And since you refuse to talk, I think Härkälä might have grounds for your arrest.

Suhonen lamented his dilemma—he was screwed either way. By talking he'd give the NBI more evidence that would definitely be used against him down the road, since the NBI wouldn't believe his story. But by being silent, he'd end up in a gray jail cell immediately.

Suhonen contemplated Rahkonen's comment about Salmela. Why had Salmela claimed Suhonen led him to the apartment? Suhonen knew Salmela couldn't stomach sitting in the cell, and wondered if the guy was trying to talk himself off the hook.

CHAPTER 20
FRIDAY 10:00 A.M.
HELSINKI POLICE HEADQUARTERS

Joutsamo was sitting in Takamäki's office with him. She had recounted Kulta's suspicion of a connection between the experiences of the three detectives.

Takamäki shook his head doubtfully, but listened.

"It's not impossible," Joutsamo said.

"It would take quite a bit of organizing. The arson and your incident with the car would be easy, but how would anyone get the NBI to go along with something like that? I don't believe they hate us enough to burn my house down or attempt to run you over."

Joutsamo didn't have a reply. They hadn't heard from Suhonen since he had been taken from the police station two hours earlier.

"If we leave Suhonen out of this, we can see similarities in the things that happened to you and me," she suggested.

Takamäki nodded, then said, "But there's no information in the field of anyone who might be out for revenge. I talked to Nykänen yesterday, and he said the NBI has made no progress in the arson investigation. By the way, did you file a report about your incident?"

"No."

"Why not?" Takamäki asked.

"The case would be transferred to a different unit, and I wouldn't be able to gather the information myself."

Joutsamo had told Takamäki about the security camera footage and the stolen car. She had also found out that a

Toyota Corolla had been discovered freshly torched on a remote road in Kirkkonummi. The car was a late-1990s model with no license plates. The West Uusimaa police were in no great rush to investigate the case because it was only about a burnt piece of junk.

"You probably should."

"I'll take care of it. This way I'll have more information to give the investigators, and they won't have to file it away in the unsolved cases binder."

"We need to let Nykänen know, too," Takamäki said. "Suhonen had information about the fire, with a lead to Saramäki prison."

"We need Suhonen for this. He has the best contacts for rustling up details."

Takamäki's computer sounded a soft alert for a new email and he glanced at the screen. The sender was the Helsinki Police Commissioner.

The detective opened the email and read it quickly.

"Looks like we won't be getting Suhonen to help us for a while," he said.

"What do you mean?"

The question on the subject line was short: *What is this about?*

The original email was from Special Prosecutor Härkälä in the West Uusimaa prosecutor's office. He mentioned the preliminary investigation concerning a Helsinki police VCU detective. According to Härkälä, Suhonen was a suspect for a narcotics crime and was being held at NBI. A decision about his arrest would be made in the next few days.

"Shit," Joutsamo said. "This sort of thing translates to a police kick in the ass."

"Yep," Takamäki said quietly.

* * *

The head of the Helsinki narcotics unit was picking chunks of meat from his pita bread with a plastic fork. Karhu was fifty, slightly pudgy, and had a receding hairline; but his most obvious feature was the pirate-like eye patch over one eye.

"This is the city's best gyro," Karhu declared, a drop of reddish-brown sauce in the corner of his mouth.

Takamäki had his own plate of food. The men were sitting at a fast food restaurant on the second floor of the Pasila train station. Karhu had promptly agreed to Takamäki's lunch invitation when he heard Takamäki was paying for the gyros.

"Ever thought that these gyro joints would be excellent venues for drug deals?" Takamäki asked. "The strong ethnic background, transportation ready to go, and distribution all over the country."

Karhu's fork froze midway and he asked, "How do you know about the investigation?"

"I, um, well..." Takamäki stuttered, confused.

"I'm kidding," Karhu said with a chuckle. "The pizza and gyro business is run by decent folk. They might evade taxes and employment laws, but they won't mess with drugs. And they're excellent cooks."

"Guess so," Takamäki said, unsure if Karhu was being serious or not.

"But you probably had something you wanted to talk about," Karhu said and kept eating. He had asked for double jalapeños.

"Did you hear about Suhonen?"

Karhu nodded somberly.

"What do you think?"

"The NBI hasn't let go of old grudges. They seem to be after us constantly, and apparently after you, too. The video surveillance was set up in an apartment on Viola Street. I knew about it and warned all my detectives not to go there. Guess Suhonen didn't get the memo."

"Was it a trap for the police?"

"Not intentionally," Karhu said, shaking his head. "This was part of an operation to go after neo-Nazis. The surveillance was to see who goes in and out of the apartment and who their contacts are."

"But they're dealing drugs?"

"One of the guys in the apartment; it's not part of the police operation."

"Is the guy in on the NBI operation?"

"The seller isn't, but they needed someone there to set up the surveillance."

"So the NBI overlooks the hash deals?"

"The small amounts, yes," Karhu said, nodding, and still eating. "Up to a hundred grams, the possession of hashish for someone's own use is a matter of a fine. It's not worth it to be constantly arresting them. We'll let possession of a few grams go, if it can help with another investigation. I'm sad to say it's legal to possess small amounts of hash in Finland these days. It takes a kilo of hash to land a dealer in prison and be slapped with more than fines or probation."

"How long have they been running the deals out of the apartment?"

"As far as I know, it's been active for a few weeks. The NBI also wants to find out where the neo-Nazis are buying the stuff from. I'm not surprised they don't know yet, considering it's the NBI after all."

Takamäki noted the bitterness toward the NBI that ran deep in the Helsinki police drug unit.

"So you've got nothing going as far as the Nazis?"

"No," Karhu said, shaking his head. "They're small-time dealers. We're after the guys with hundreds or thousands of kilos."

Takamäki worked on his gyro, but didn't think it was very good. Karhu had already devoured his and crumbled the wrapper onto the tray.

"Delicious."

"Well," Takamäki started, with a hint of hesitation at bringing up the matter. "How do we get Suhonen off the hook?"

"We?" Karhu said.

"Yeah, or me," Takamäki specified, embarrassed.

"Or am *I* supposed to get involved in a prosecutor's investigation of an undercover cop, who is caught on video in the middle of a drug deal?" Karhu asked with a chuckle.

"Of course not."

"Should *you*?" Karhu asked. "If anything goes wrong, it might be a sizable commotion."

"I doubt Suhonen went there knowingly to buy hash."

"Have you talked with him?" Karhu asked, alert.

"Not today. But he told me about it yesterday. The informant promised him details on my house fire if Suhonen went there."

"Okay. And you feel guilty…"

Takamäki didn't reply. He hadn't thought about it from that angle, but Karhu might be right.

"Your house fire is weird, alright. I've heard nothing about it in the field, and no rumors are circulating about threats against you. That's unusual."

The snitch had needed Suhonen as a back-up, and in his greed for information Suhonen had complied.

"But this is from yesterday?" Karhu's question was more a statement.

"Yeah."

"So you don't know what he said in the interrogation?"

"No, he's in Jokiniemi now."

Takamäki set the rest of his gyro on the tray.

"I'll be honest with you."

"That's nice," Karhu said, grinning.

"Last night, a car tried to run over Joutsamo while she was jogging. Something's up, but we don't know yet what it is."

"Yeah," Karhu said in a solemn tone.

"First of all, I need Suhonen in the field to investigate. To get him out of Jokiniemi I'm going to need a foolproof reason for his visit to the apartment."

"And you need me for that?"

It was Takamäki's turn to nod.

* * *

Römpötti's desk phone rang and the small screen showed an unknown number.

It was quiet at the office, with only two or three supervisors present. They're probably playing Tetris, Römpötti thought to herself as she answered the phone.

"I've got a tip for you."

Römpötti thought the caller with a low voice was trying to sound hoarse.

"Yes, what is it? We always welcome tips."

"This is a hell of a case. A Helsinki cop is a suspect in a drug crime."

"Oh? Tell me more."

"I can't. You look into it yourself. The NBI is investigating the case."

"Is it an old case?" Römpötti asked, guessing the call would end soon, and she wanted to get as many details as she could.

"Nope, it's fresh. And that's all I'll say," the caller added and hung up.

Römpötti set the receiver down. The lead was definitely worth a look. Investigations into cops were always serious matters that reporters needed to stay on top of, considering the power of the police in society. Römpötti wished she had gotten more details.

These callers somehow imagined that reporters had magical powers to gain newsworthy information based on whatever little tips they were given. It was obvious the caller

181

knew more about the lead, but didn't want to tell. Römpötti would have to dig for hard-to-get facts. It would've been a lot easier to confirm existing information.

Even so, Römpötti greatly appreciated the tip. There were never too many.

CHAPTER 21
FRIDAY, 1:10 P.M.
KILO
COURTHOUSE, ESPOO

Special Prosecutor Härkälä from West Uusimaa had immediately agreed to meet with Takamäki and Karhu, head of Narcotics. Takamäki knew most of the Helsinki prosecutors, but he couldn't remember what Härkälä looked like. His homicide unit rarely dealt with the Espoo guys.

Takamäki parked his unmarked VW Golf in the Kilo courthouse lot. The combination police station and courthouse, built in an industrial area, had recently been remodeled. Takamäki didn't think it looked much improved. One end of the cereal box-shaped building housed the Espoo Police Department.

Karhu walked in right behind Takamäki. Bringing a colleague with him added to Takamäki's credibility, and he could use some of that now.

The metal detector beeped as the detectives passed through, but the pair was cleared by presenting their badges. Takamäki thought his phone was the culprit, but then realized that Karhu, a long-time Narcotics detective, probably was carrying a gun.

Takamäki had brought a stack of documents, hoping they would help.

The men rode up the elevator and called from the phone outside the office. Härkälä quickly came to open the heavy security door. The West Uusimaa prosecutor's office looked like any other police station: small rooms, narrow hallways, and piles of documents.

Jorma Härkälä led them through the hallways to his office. The forty-year-old, slender, athletic man with gray sideburns and skinny-rimmed glasses was wearing a gray suit and a blue tie.

Härkälä's desk lined the long wall, as his office was too narrow to fit a desk in sideways. By the door was a small, round table with two chairs. Binders were stacked on the shelves and on the floor.

"So, how can I help?" Härkälä asked as he sat down at his desk. The detectives were seated side by side three or four feet away.

After the friendly opener, Härkälä crossed his arms. Takamäki took it as a bad sign.

"As I said on the phone, we're here to talk about Suhonen," Takamäki began. "He reports to me, but he also works a lot with the Narcotics unit's cases."

"Undercover work," Karhu added.

"But it seems he's gone astray this time," Härkälä pointed out.

"No," Takamäki said, shaking his head.

"No?" Härkälä asked in surprise.

Karhu coughed and asked, "Do you know the backstory to the apartment that NBI has under surveillance?"

"Not really."

"Then we'd better shed some light on it," Karhu said and looked at Takamäki.

"You're not supposed to know this," Takamäki pointed out quickly. "But we trust you'll keep it confidential."

"You can count on that."

Takamäki was pleased at Härkälä's reaction. They had passed the first hurdle in winning his trust; he hadn't chided them for spreading confidential information.

"Great," Takamäki said. "The NBI is running an operation concerning neo-Nazis."

"Okay."

"That's why they put a camera in the Viola Street apartment. The NBI wants to find out about the neo-Nazis' contacts and drug deals."

Härkälä nodded.

"We think a case of ours might be connected to them," Takamäki said, pulling documents from his pocket. Among them was a photo of a tough-looking bald man. Takamäki handed the photo to Härkälä, who peered at it with interest.

"That's a picture of Jaakko Pöntinen. A few days ago the twenty-two-year-old got into an argument with a middle-aged man at the Helsinki train station, and hit the man once in the head. The man fell, hit his head on the pavement, and now lies as a half-vegetable in Meilahti Hospital. It sounds like a routine case, but there are some interesting details."

"Like what?" Härkälä asked.

"Pöntinen is a mixed martial arts competitor. Other fighters like him have been found guilty of assault in Helsinki—usually when drunk."

Takamäki handed Härkälä the interrogation notes. He had underlined the part where Pöntinen denied using steroids.

"Besides drugs, the Helsinki Narcotics unit targets illegal steroids," Karhu joined in. "They've discovered them during various raids on biker gangs, for example. We now have leads pointing to sizable quantities."

Karhu wasn't making it up. Tips on large amounts of steroids on the streets were always circulating.

"At any rate," Takamäki continued, "based on these leads, we at the Helsinki VCU are worried about people in the martial arts circles mixing steroids and alcohol, leading to violent behavior. Naturally, we've been working with the Narcotics unit from the start. Suhonen's job was to find information on the mixed martial arts and kickboxing circles."

"Do you have minutes from the planning meeting?" Härkälä asked.

"No," said Takamäki.

"And can you document the decision to send him in undercover?"

"No. We were not yet conducting an official investigation, but were only at the intelligence-gathering phase. A possible connection between the fighters and the neo-Nazis would be cause for serious alarm. Naturally, we had no idea of an ongoing NBI investigation; no one mentioned it in our meetings with other departments, the customs officials, or the border patrol."

Extensive investigations concerning organized crime were handled as teamwork among the three departments to avoid duplication.

"That sounds like something we should look into," Härkälä said after a pause, "but it doesn't explain why Suhonen was in the apartment and bought fifty grams of hash."

"He was there with his informant, Salmela," Takamäki explained. "I don't know why the drug purchase took place, but his immediate intervention would have spoiled our chance of getting information on the connection between the martial arts guys and the neo-Nazis."

"Makes sense," Härkälä said.

Takamäki was glad Härkälä understood, and he was relieved to see the prosecutor uncross his arms and lean forward.

The detective started to feel hopeful about the outcome. It was time for the last spike. He glanced at Karhu.

"Yes," Karhu began. "I also want to mention that Suhonen immediately informed me of Salmela's hash purchase."

"Informed you?" Härkälä said in surprise.

Karhu nodded and continued. "We were on another case at the time and couldn't go to confiscate the drugs. We later saw on the Narcotics database that the NBI had already arrested Suhonen. And frankly, for us fifty grams isn't even worth a phone call. We search for hundreds or thousands of kilos."

"Always kinks in communication," Härkälä noted.

"Especially with the NBI," Karhu said with a nod.

"Yeah, I'm aware of that," Härkälä said. "But why didn't Suhonen mention anything about this in the preliminary questioning today? The investigators called me two hours ago and said the man clammed up completely. 'No comment' was all he'd say."

"He's afraid of compromising the steroid investigation with any potential leaks in the system," Takamäki said. The detective was glad to hear Suhonen had kept quiet; it fit Takamäki's story.

"Besides, his key informant is involved," Takamäki went on, "and you never say anything on paper that would risk your informant. You never know where papers end up. And, if anyone in the underworld got even a whiff of Salmela talking to the police, he'd be as good as dead."

Härkälä remembered well an investigation one of his prosecutor colleagues had conducted on a police officer, who had tried to access the NBI's informant database. As a result, the police wanted a new lead investigator. It reflected not only the power of the police when one of their own was a suspect, but also their desire to protect the informants. In that sense, Härkälä could see why Suhonen had refrained from comments.

"You're giving him a good explanation for his actions," Härkälä said, rubbing his hands together. "Sounds good, but…"

"But what?" Takamäki asked.

"I still want to hear it from Suhonen—with no contact from either of you."

"I doubt he'll talk to you without my permission," Takamäki said.

"Fine, you'll go with me and give our man in the cell permission to spill the beans. If his story matches yours, Suhonen's preliminary investigation is over. There have been no statements to the public or media, so we have no pressure from there.

"Let's do it," Takamäki said with a nod.

He only had one problem: Suhonen had no idea about who Jaakko Pöntinen was or any connection to steroids and the neo-Nazis.

* * *

Sanna Römpötti had little success with the couple dozen phone calls she placed to her best contacts in several police departments and the administration. She was making no progress. At one point she wondered if the whole purpose of the tip might have been to get her to contact her sources and expose her network to the competition. She had switched to her prepaid cellphone number so the calls couldn't be linked to her.

The caller who gave her the lead had only mentioned four facts: the tip was about a Helsinki police officer, the crime was drug-related, the case was fresh, and the NBI was investigating it. That was all she could get out of him.

She had written down the key words in the notebook on her desk. During the phone call she had scribbled question marks and police logos with its famous sword on the paper.

Römpötti couldn't even be sure it was about anyone in the Helsinki PD; an officer who lived in Helsinki might work in Vantaa, roughly ten miles away.

She was surprised to hear the NBI was heading the investigation. The reporter knew that police crime was always investigated by a special prosecutor. However, detectives from other departments could be used in aiding the investigation, and maybe that was the case here.

Making a wide range of calls came with risk. No doubt the officers she contacted would be interested in the case and want additional information. Rumors would circulate in the hallways, and the material might end up in the hands of someone else working for a different media outlet. But with the use of the internet, the significance of scoops had diminished; newspapers used to be able to sell their headlines for an entire day before television channels would get onboard. In the age of digital media, however, stories were ripped off by other media at ruthless speed. Usually, the article would mention the original source, but that meant nothing to the reader.

Römpötti also considered the possibility that the tip was false, or that the caller had misunderstood something. It was likely, however, that a sensitive piece of information had been kept in closed circles.

The reporter refused to give up. She would make as many phone calls as necessary to get to the story. Next, she would contact various chiefs within the police organization, then the Ministry of the Interior. It would ultimately get to the minister, who would undoubtedly be interested in the crime reporter's suspicion and order an investigation from the police administration. The police commissioner would get the info from the Helsinki chief of police, who would in turn get it from his subordinates. As the memos came together, the number of people with the information would rise dramatically. It would be easy to send an email to a friend or colleague and mark it "FYI." No one would intentionally spread confidential content, but forwarding it was worth the effort because the friend or colleague could then send the facts to the informant for future reference.

The minister of the interior would probably not talk, but, considering all the dissonance and mistrust in the police administration, someone eventually would.

Römpötti knew she might not get the information today, but she would tomorrow, or the day after. This piece of news had no expiration date.

CHAPTER 22
FRIDAY, 2:20 P.M.
NBI HEADQUARTERS, VANTAA

The massive, gray stone structure of Jokiniemi prison rose up in a former wheat field; it seemed out of place in the otherwise pastoral countryside. The design of the five-story building purposefully induced feelings of aversion, focusing on security. Its appearance would become even more menacing once the planned annex was completed; including the parking garage, doubling its current million square feet.

Takamäki had parked by the end of the building in the visitors' lot, and Härkälä had arrived a few minutes later. Takamäki made good use of the few minutes he had. Narcotics head Karhu was no longer needed and had gone back to his office in Pasila.

The men walked about a hundred yards along the sidewalk toward the main door. Takamäki remembered reading somewhere that in the ancient Comb Ceramic culture, about five thousand years ago, people living in this area were right on the seashore. Now the sea was six miles away.

Takamäki opened the front door and let the prosecutor into the majestic, high-ceilinged lobby. A security guard sat in his booth on the right. Härkälä said something to him and they waited.

In a moment, a tall, narrow-faced man opened the side door to the lobby. Takamäki knew the interrogation rooms were there. Outsiders were usually not admitted into the building.

The man introduced himself as Rahkonen and said his colleague would soon bring Suhonen.

Takamäki said he'd make a stop in the restroom. When he returned a moment later, Rahkonen had opened the door to one of the interrogation rooms. Takamäki thought that the room, with a metal-barred window, must have been used mainly for questioning plaintiffs and informants.

There was enough space for three people in the small room. Takamäki didn't follow Härkälä in, but waited by the door.

Suhonen appeared from around the corner, followed by a slight-framed police officer. He was surprised to see his boss. Härkälä had heard the men approaching and stepped in the hallway.

"No talking," the prosecutor ordered.

Suhonen was taken aback by Takamäki's handshake—especially the wet palm.

C'mon, get the hint, Takamäki thought.

Härkälä took the reins and said, "Here's what we'll do. Rahkonen and Strömberg, you wait in the hall while Takamäki, Suhonen, and I have a chat in the room."

Takamäki bore his eyes into Suhonen's. He couldn't use any gestures; Härkälä was likely watching their every move, and he was afraid even the stare might have been too much.

"Sounds good," Takamäki said with a nod.

Härkälä let Suhonen into the room and followed, with Takamäki behind them.

Things were going down the crapper fast. Takamäki tried to think of another way to get the story to Suhonen, but had no chance. He had no Plan B.

Suhonen was about to sit down in a beige plastic chair, but changed his mind.

"Um, maybe I could take a leak first," he said. "The NBI is violating my human rights: there is no toilet in the holding cell."

"Go ahead," Härkälä said.

Takamäki could barely conceal a sigh of relief.

Suhonen walked to the restroom between the two NBI officers and closed the door. He thought about Takamäki's wet palm. Was he trying to say there was something in the bathroom? Suhonen glanced around the small washroom and the toilets, but didn't notice anything special. He checked the trash can, but only saw used paper towels.

He looked at the paper towel dispenser and decided to lift the sloppily closed top.

A knock on the door made him jump. Strömberg yelled, "Hurry, up, we don't have all day!"

"Yeah, I'll be right out."

Suhonen found a folded piece of paper and read it. The handwriting was small, but neat. *The reason for going to the drug nest: a drunk, 22-year-old kickboxer, Jaakko Pöntinen, assaulted a man by the train station. We suspect steroid use has messed him up. Tip: Large quantities of steroids on the streets. Investigating with Narcotics. You were looking for information on Pöntinen's connection with neo-Nazis. You told Karhu about Salmela's hash deal.*

Wow, Suhonen thought to himself. This was how it was going down. Corrupt cops accused of drug crimes had often attempted this type of information exchange in prison, but that sort of activity wasn't expected of on-duty officers.

Suhonen read the note once more, then ripped it to shreds, wrapped it in toilet tissue, and flushed it. No trace of evidence remained. He washed his hands.

* * *

Veikko Sandström looked at the coins in his hand. He counted three euros and seventy cents; the sum total of his earthly possessions.

He could buy one three-euro pint at the bar.

A small pub with seats for maybe twenty people was located near the Itäkeskus shopping mall, in eastern Helsinki. The clientele was much like those at the Corner Pub.

Sandström had taken the metro there after he was kicked out of the Corner Pub. He didn't feel like sitting in the other bars in Kallio. All the patrons seemed to be reading the afternoon papers, but at least people here didn't know him, or hadn't recognized him from the pictures in the paper.

It had only taken him ten minutes to get there from the Sörnäinen station.

Sandström remembered that the small bar was one of the places a guy called Sludge frequented. The nickname had stuck after he had neglected a fungal infection in his ear until the pain became so severe he had to be transferred to the prison hospital. The man had the same distaste for his nickname as Veikko did for "Zipper."

Sandström had hoped the guy could give him a gig, but hadn't seen him around, and he didn't have the guy's number.

He had hoped the reporter would've panicked and handed him some cash, but the devil woman had pressed him for an interview instead. Shit, wasn't the media required to pay for personal insults?

He had nothing left to sell after the collections visit and his eviction.

He could always get beer money from a quick burglary, but he wasn't worried about that yet—he still had enough to get another pint, with still half a pint left in the mug.

After a gulp there was only a quarter pint. Sandström glanced at the other customers. Nobody's pocket seemed worth picking. He wondered if he should go find unattended jackets and purses in the library or a café. That was one option.

But street robberies and kiosk hold-ups were for fools; the risk of getting thrown in jail was too high. He'd leave that to those who were deep in drug debts. Sandström had been in a debt cycle himself and didn't want to end up there again. The collections methods were harsh—he could still remember the pain from the vise tightened around his finger joint.

Sandström had tried the social security office after the collections man had left, but they had nothing for him. The clerk told him a freeze had been placed on all his benefits.

Should he get a job? No way in hell. He'd rather try stealing cameras or tools from stores. He could always sell them; a tenth of the retail price meant he'd get ten euros for a drill. He could steal packages of tenderloin if he could find some restaurant to buy them.

Sandström thought of the old Toyota he had picked up in Paloheinä. That was an easy gig; but stealing an old Saab would be even easier: bust the lock and start the car with a screwdriver.

He wondered if Sludge needed more cars—or anything else. He was annoyed he had let the car go for such a low price. He only made two hundred on the deal, and he knew the guy could afford more. Maybe he could ask. Sandström tried to think of what the car might have been used for. A robbery? There was nothing in the news about it, though.

Hell, the guy simply needed to shell out more dough. Four or five hundred would have been more in line with market price. Sandström wanted to get two hundred more. He recalled another gig he had done for the same guy; being flat broke he'd done it for dirt cheap.

He finished his beer. He didn't want to make the phone call in the bar. You never knew who might overhear it.

* * *

Suhonen walked out first and held the heavy iron door open for Takamäki.

"Rahkonen and Strömberg didn't look happy," Suhonen said.

"Nope. They didn't."

The men stepped out of the NBI building into the gray weather. They turned left and headed for the parking lot.

"Thanks," Suhonen said.

"I promised Karhu you'd do ten free stakeouts for the Narcotics unit on your days off."

"Was it hard?" Suhonen asked with a small chuckle.

"You mean to talk Karhu into it?" Takamäki said, turning to Suhonen.

"Yeah."

It was another fifty yards to the parking lot.

"Not really. Karhu doesn't like the NBI, but he likes you. He knew about their surveillance operation and had warned his men. Guess you didn't hear about it?"

"No. Salmela wanted to go there and specifically asked me to be his backup."

"Careless."

"Yep, it was," Suhonen agreed with a nod. "But at least this time I didn't have to pay for my stupidity."

"Right."

Takamäki spotted his car and pulled out the keys.

"I have to go find Salmela," Suhonen said. "We have stuff to talk about. Serious stuff."

The car lights flashed as Takamäki unlocked the doors with the key fob.

"Such as?"

"I'm interested in why he wanted me in the apartment with him."

"You think he knew about the cameras?"

"I don't think so. He would've been busted for buying the hash. Fifty grams for his own use means a pretty big fine— two months' pay basically."

Takamäki thought about it. That was the same as the fine for reckless driving, assault, or shoplifting. Fifty grams was a sizeable amount.

"Are you in a hurry?" Suhonen asked.

"No, why?"

"I thought I'd go look for him now."

"Fine with me," Takamäki said.

Suhonen looked at the detective and said, "Well, give me the keys, and I'll drop you off at the Tikkurila train station. You can catch a local to Pasila from there."

Takamäki smiled as he tossed Suhonen the keys. On the way, he told Suhonen how someone had tried to run over Joutsamo.

* * *

Sandström stood on the sidewalk. He waited for the blue bus to take off and pressed the green call button on his cell phone.

There was a reply at the other end.

"Whaddya want?" the man grunted.

"It's Veikko…"

"I know. Don't use names, remember?"

"Yeah, sorry."

"What is it?" the man asked in a demanding tone.

"I was wondering if you had a gig for me… I need some cash."

"Nope," came the blunt reply.

"Well, would you have some cash then?"

"What do you mean?"

"I've got nothing but bottoms in my pockets. I'm broke."

"That's your problem," the man said, chuckling.

The sneering annoyed Sandström.

"It's your problem, too," he snarled.

"How so?" the man asked, hardness returning to his voice.

"I got you the car. You probably need it for something. So you'll wanna keep me happy."

"Is that a threat?"

"I'm asking for more cash. That's allowed, right?"

"Not after the fact. We had a deal. You took care of business, and I paid you what we agreed to."

"But not enough. Two hundred's a low-ball."

After pausing, the man asked, "And watcha gonna do if I don't give you cash?"

"I dunno. I gotta think about it. Someone's bound to be interested."

"And just who might that be, I wonder," the man said rhetorically.

"I'll have to think. Somebody, for sure. But you could throw a little extra my way—insurance money, so to speak. Or a bonus for a job well done. Then if you ever needed my help, I'd surely take your phone call."

"So that's your proposal," the man said after a pause. "How much are we talking about?"

"A few hundred, maybe five. Sounds fair, right?"

"I suppose," the man agreed. "Meet me at nine by the concrete statue between Helsinki Street and Linnanmäki amusement park. You'll get your bonus."

"Um, isn't the statue up on the hill?"

"It's easy enough to get to. It's just a precaution—best we don't get seen together," the man said in a low tone. "Nine o'clock sharp, don't be late. I'm not waiting."

"I'll be there," Sandström said.

He felt the coins in his pocket and counted them. It was still three euros and seventy cents. Soon it would be more. With his current cash situation, he could afford to buy three beer cans from the store, but only one pint at the pub. Only bums drank on the street, though, and Sandström wasn't one of them.

A man walking by shoved a twenty euro bill in his hand.

"What?" Sandström asked, surprised.

"You look so down," said the fifty-year-old in a ball cap. "I just won sixteen hundred euros on sports bets. Happy to share, thanks to the German soccer league."

"Thanks," Sandström said, and thought about how easy it would be to rob this guy. Sixteen hundred was a lot of dough.

He watched the man walk away. What a loser to be doling out money like that—not that Sandström minded.

He returned to the pub. The day wasn't a total waste after all.

* * *

Prosecutor Härkälä placed a Bluetooth piece around his ear and pressed the small button. Driving with a handheld device was illegal in Finland, and he wanted to avoid any tickets.

He drove his Nissan Micra west on Beltway III and saw the exit sign for the airport on the right. The Jumbo Mall was on the left.

"Härkälä," he answered.

He couldn't hear anything, and adjusted the Bluetooth. It felt uncomfortable.

"Hello, it's Härkälä. I'm having trouble hearing you."

"Hi, it's Sanna Römpötti from TV news."

The prosecutor remembered the crime reporter well. A while back, she had done a story about one of his drug cases. Having a reporter sitting in the back of the courtroom made everyone mind their Ps and Qs. He might have been a little nervous at first, too. Especially after the court session, when she had talked with him alongside a cameraman with his camera running. He had planned on declining the interview, but knew he would have looked like an idiot with the camera in his face and the microphone pointed to his mouth. The reporter would have used the reaction in her report, no doubt.

A more experienced colleague had later advised Härkälä to always agree to interviews, especially on difficult cases, such as organized crime. If a prosecutor declined an interview, it would be even more challenging than it already was to get normal citizens to testify. The prosecutor could never show fear, not even in the face of publicity or its consequences.

Härkälä wondered what the reporter wanted now. He recalled attending a lecture that Römpötti had given on how to interact with media. In it, she had listed three key points: Do not lie; do not lie; do not lie.

He considered pulling over in order to focus on the conversation, but it was impossible on the busy beltway. He just had to try to pay attention to the phone, and not get into an accident.

"Can you hear me?" Römpötti asked.

"Yeah, yeah," Härkälä replied. Of course the reporter never asked if this was a good time to talk—that would have given the other party a chance to escape the conversation.

"I'm looking into a case I believe is under your jurisdiction," Römpötti said. "It's about a crime committed by a police officer."

Härkälä thought about the police crimes he had under investigation. There were two or three arrests where the detained accused an officer of using excessive force. He had a couple of financial crime cases with alleged problems on collections, and some DUIs with off-duty police officers acting like idiots. It was no use wondering which one Römpötti was referring to. And, there was Suhonen's case, but the reporter couldn't possibly know about it.

"Okay, which one." he said.

"The one about a Helsinki detective accused of being involved in a narcotics crime. Do you know anything about it?"

Härkälä told himself he should be honest.

"There's no such case," he said.

"No such case?" the reporter asked in surprise. "What do you mean?"

"I mean we have no such case."

Härkälä wanted to add "anymore," but he didn't.

"You don't have it or no one does?"

"I don't know about anyone else."

"Then how can you say that?" Römpötti asked, and then realized something. "You *had* a case like that?"

"Sort of."

"What does that mean?"

The question irritated the prosecutor, though he had often used it himself when interrogating suspects who denied the charges. However, he always had to keep his tone formal and polite.

"We investigated the suspicion of a crime, but it turned out to be nothing."

"I see," Römpötti said. "When was this?"

"It was cleared up today."

"Today?"

"How did you hear about it?" Härkälä inserted.

"An anonymous caller," Römpötti said.

Härkälä wondered if the reporter was telling the truth, though it wasn't his business unless someone had broken a vow of confidence.

"So have you closed the case yet?" Römpötti continued without giving the prosecutor a chance to speak.

She knew that cases of suspected crimes that were not forwarded on to a prosecutor were closed, with all their related documents then becoming public information.

The matter had been addressed in the Jokiniemi interrogation room, and Takamäki and Suhonen had agreed with Härkälä's decision. NBI detectives Rahkonen and Strömberg had protested vehemently.

Härkälä hadn't written a report on the allegation, so technically the crime didn't exist and there was no reason to close the case.

"No need for formal reports," Härkälä said. "I received an allegation, but upon further investigation we found that the police officer committed no crime."

"What was it about?" Römpötti asked.

"I can't comment on that."

"Why not?"

"It's confidential. I can't talk about information learned during the course of my investigation, especially if it's a false allegation."

"With no crime, you have nothing to keep confidential, right?"

The reporter made an annoyingly valid point.

"The confidentiality has to do with official police operations."

"So it was an undercover operation?"

"I can't comment," Härkälä said. He was upset that he had already divulged too much.

"You can't?"

"No. Sorry."

"Don't be sorry," the reporter said. "It sounds interesting. I'll be in touch."

Härkälä wondered if he had made a mistake. Römpötti was known for her persistence. She wouldn't leave things unresolved. Of course, according to Takamäki, Karhu, and Suhonen, there was no crime. Suhonen had been caught in a lurch when searching for information on a serious offense, and he couldn't disclose his identity as a police officer. Suhonen's friend had bought hash and would be convicted, but Suhonen had reported the purchase. The detective had done nothing wrong.

Härkälä took the exit for the Turku expressway towards the Kilo courthouse. He'd have to email the Helsinki police commissioner and let him know that the allegation on the police officer suspected of a crime had been withdrawn. Härkälä would call it what it was—a misunderstanding.

CHAPTER 23
FRIDAY, 5:10 P.M.
KOIVUKYLÄ, VANTAA

Suhonen sniffed the air in the stairwell and recognized the faint, sickly sweet smell. He could tell someone was smoking hash in one of the apartments.

The scent grew stronger as Suhonen climbed the stairs to the next floor. He walked to the end of the hall on the right and saw the name Koivunen on the door. He cracked open the mail slot. The smell was definitely wafting into the hall from that apartment.

It had taken Suhonen three phone calls to find out where Salmela lived. His apartment was a one-bedroom in the concrete jungle of Koivukylä in the eastern suburb of Vantaa. The neighborhood near the commuter rail station was one of the most restless in the Helsinki metropolitan area.

Suhonen didn't know if Salmela was at home, but someone was smoking in the apartment. The lock on the door seemed loose. He pulled a six-inch piece of wire from his sleeve and twisted it into a loop.

The stairwell was quiet and Suhonen was glad the neighbors had no dogs to bark at the strange rustling.

Suhonen thought for a minute and decided to pull out his Glock and make a powerful entrance; scaring Salmela would be a good move.

He felt for the pistol, but it wasn't there. Shit, he thought. He had left it in the drawer at the police station that morning.

Suhonen hesitated for a moment. Someone in there was likely smoking the stuff from Viola Street. It was possible Salmela had drugs in the apartment, which might have lured others there as well. It was unlikely, however, as Salmela had just had to pick up his personal load. Whatever was being smoked in there was probably from the Viola Street apartment.

He quit wondering and pressed the wire around the lock tongue. He smelled the potent tang from the hash. Suhonen closed the door quickly behind him to keep the stench from spreading into the stairwell and causing everyone in the building to float away

The apartment had a narrow entryway. Coats hung on the rack and an old rag rug lay on the floor. On the left was a bedroom, and a living room on the right.

Suhonen walked in carefully and peered into the living room. The décor was minimal, to say the least. No bookcase, no pictures on the wall. By the window was a kitchenette, and in front of it a folding card table and a red chair, probably snatched from a dumpster after an office had moved and put their old furnishings in the trash. A small, outdated television sat on a plastic table in the living room. Salmela was slouching on a brown, worn-out couch with a bong on a low, wooden coffee table. His eyes were closed and he looked scraggly. He was wearing a tank top and briefs. The tattoos on his arms looked faded.

Suhonen backed up and quietly checked the bedroom. Clothes were scattered on the floor and a thin, bare mattress and a blanket sprawled in the back corner. Lumped next to the mattress were two yellow Alepa grocery sacks and a shoulder bag.

Suhonen was glad to realize that he and Salmela were the only two in the apartment. His head was spinning from the hash vapors.

He walked into the living room and opened the balcony door. The fresh air felt good.

"Hello," Salmela said from the couch. He smiled stupidly and his eyes were bloodshot. Suhonen recognized the signs; his friend was wasted.

Suhonen grabbed the glass bong off the table. It worked by a simple principle: the drug burned in the lower port and the smoke cooled off as it flowed into the breathing tube through water, making it easier to inhale. The bong was for the experienced; occasional users preferred the drug in a cigarette.

Suhonen poured the water down the sink in the kitchenette and rinsed the bong under the tap. He was tempted to break the device, but decided against it.

"Didn't the NBI take your stuff?" Suhonen asked.

"They don't know how to look for it," Salmela said, his face snarled into a grimace.

"You got more hash in here?"

"No," Salmela said, but Suhonen could see he was lying.

"Fuck," Suhonen hissed.

"Not happy?"

"No."

"Me neither, though I can't stop laughing. That's the only humorous thing about my life."

"Yeah," Suhonen replied. He walked into the kitchen and found a red plastic IKEA mug on the shelf. He filled it with cold water which he poured on Salmela's face. The couch got wet and water dripped onto the floor.

"That felt good," Salmela said with a smile.

Suhonen was drawn between feeling sorry for his old chum and being angry with him.

"Listen, Eero," he said. "Can you answer a couple of questions?"

"Of course. The purpose of life is suffering... The Lord giveth and taketh away, blessed be the name of the Lord... What else would you like to know?"

Suhonen glanced outside and thought for a minute. Dusk was settling in, and the lights were on in the neighboring buildings. He wondered if he should haul Salmela to the hospital, the drug rehab, or the police station. Nobody had ever died of cannabis overdose, so there was no big risk.

"Why did we go get the hash?"

"Look at me," Salmela said with a smile. "This is why."

"Why did you have to bring me?"

"I didn't know what those fellows were like."

"Don't gimme that shit," Suhonen said, raising his voice. With the balcony door open, the room was starting to feel cool, but in his leather jacket Suhonen didn't mind.

"Nothin' more to it."

"Eero, we go way back, but I'm only so patient. You got me into deep shit, for which I now owe my bosses. I definitely didn't want that, and it's your fault. I wanna know why."

Salmela's smile turned into a desperate grin.

"I, um…"

"Quit stuttering and tell me."

"I can't," Salmela said, agonizingly.

"Eero," Suhonen snapped. At this point, he didn't want to mention the interrogation notes where Salmela claimed it was Suhonen who suggested they go to the apartment. He would bring it up later, if the need arose. "Who do you fear more?"

Salmela looked up at Suhonen.

"Should I fear you?" Salmela asked, and continued, "Behold, to fear the Lord is wisdom, and to shirk from evil is understanding."

"I won't listen to this for long."

"Then leave. Nobody asked you to come here."

"Why?"

"That was an unfortunate thing," Salmela said. "I didn't wanna do it. He said I could have the hash at no cost if you were with me."

"Who?"

"Sandström," Salmela replied. "When I heard you fellas had picked him up, I got sand in my shoes—get it?"

"I'm not amused."

"He knows more about it. I was just a pawn."

Suhonen looked at the squeaking Salmela. Sandström was behind it.

206

"Where is he?"

"Dunno. Maybe at his place."

* * *

Takamäki leafed through stacks of papers on the desk. Preliminary investigation reports to be sent to the prosecutor were being prepared. He was familiar with the cases, having taken part in the investigations, but he was having trouble focusing now. On the top was the interrogation of Jaakko Pöntinen, who had assaulted a man by the train station. Takamäki had shown it to Prosecutor Härkälä.

Takamäki knew he had used questionable means in Suhonen's case, and he felt bad about it. On the other hand, Suhonen hadn't gone into the drug nest with a hash purchase in mind. He had just been careless and foolish.

Takamäki had been careless, too, leaving the note in the NBI restroom. It could have ended in the hands of Rahkonen or Strömberg, which would have, at the very least, made him accountable for dereliction of duty.

Karhu from Narcotics had played a pivotal role. He was probably the only detective Takamäki could approach with something like this. Now Takamäki owed Karhu a big favor. The time would come sooner or later, and he wouldn't be able to decline. He hoped it wouldn't mean having to dance in a grass skirt or wear a Santa suit and a beard at the Narcotics' Christmas party.

Takamäki read through Pöntinen's interrogation once more. The man had confessed and chalked it off to being drunk. Takamäki grabbed a yellow Post-it note and wrote on it neatly: *Question Pöntinen again, asking specifically about steroids. Has he used them? How common are they in his circles? Which gyms? Who sells them? Etc. Look for a motive for going nuts. We're helping Narcotics unravel a steroid case.*

If Pöntinen was abusing steroids, this would give him a chance to explain. He might disclose that in a second interrogation. And Takamäki wouldn't mind having a more thorough questioning in the files, just in case he ever had to explain his actions during the Suhonen investigation.

Takamäki glanced at the clock. It was getting late. He had planned to look for an apartment today, but it had turned out to be a busy day. He couldn't stay at Suhonen's place forever, even if he was welcome. He'd do some apartment shopping tomorrow—then again, that's what he had said yesterday.

Takamäki thought of Nea Lind. He had seen her now and again since the summer. They had gone to the theater, movies, and out for dinner. He wondered if the attorney would like to go for a nightcap at one of the Töölö pubs, and decided to give her a call.

CHAPTER 24
FRIDAY, 8:50 P.M.
HELSINKI STREET

Veikko Sandström walked down the sidewalk on Helsinki Street. It was a surprisingly long stretch when not sitting in a car or a tram. A commuter train loudly changed tracks on the bridge ahead of him, and then clanked on. A car or two speeding down Helsinki Street passed him. On the left, the lights were on in the Deaconess Institute, which housed people with substance abuse or other social problems. The hill toward Linnanmäki amusement park on the right looked dark and menacing.

The pavement was still wet, although the rain had stopped a while ago. Traffic lights hung on a wire stretched between poles over the six-lane street. Two of the center lanes had tram tracks.

The area had been used as hunting grounds in the 1870s, especially for foxes. The amusement park, built in 1950 upon the massive bedrock, took its name from the castle-like water tower in the center of the park. The amusement park had expanded gradually, but not toward the rock-covered hill near the train tracks.

Half-way up the hill, behind the sloping bedrock, stood an odd, thirty-foot tall concrete statue. It resembled an open book on a pedestal. One of two lamps lit up half the statue, the second was broken.

Sandström had no idea what the structure was supposed to portray. Judging by the age of the concrete, it was from the '60s or '70s. It was ugly as hell.

No stairs led to the statue, but with the majestic view of Töölö Bay and the city skyline, the area was a popular drinking spot in the summertime.

Sandström walked up the worn path, illuminated by the streetlights below, and reached the top of the hill in less than a hundred feet. The ground was rocky and bare around the statue. Small shrubs dotted the surroundings, fighting for their lives in the rocky ground. Sandström didn't see any beer cans, but there were cardboard pieces of six-packs, along with shards of glass and plastic bags. He also spotted an old disposable grill.

He could hear the din of the cars below on Helsinki Street. He chose the dark side of the statue and felt a cool breeze. The soft rain resumed.

Sandström wondered about the strange location for the meeting. The man was right: nobody would see them here. He was late, after all the fuss he'd made about Sandström staying on schedule.

Sandström noticed a plaque at the foot of the sculpture. He could just make out the inscription: *Finland's Construction Union donated this statue to the City of Helsinki on its fiftieth anniversary. Sculptor Kain Tapper 1973.*

Huh, Sandström thought. Suddenly, a rustling sound startled him.

"Back here."

Pebbles scrunched under his feet as Sandström rounded the statue. He could only make out a figure.

"It's avant-garde."

"Huh?" Sandström uttered.

"He crossed the line in the seventies. Back then all the public sculptures were bronze, stone, or steel. Tapper designed this one out of concrete, probably to mock the people who financed the project."

"Who cares," Sandström said. "You got cash for me?"

"Yeah, but show me your phone first."

"Why?"

"I wanna see who you called."

Sandström hadn't made any calls, and calmly handed over the phone.

"And your wallet."

"What's this?"

"You want the cash or not?" the man asked in a cold tone.

"What do you need my wallet for?" Sandström protested, but pulled out the lean leather billfold from his coat pocket and placed it in the hand holding his phone.

"I wanna make sure you're telling the truth. Damn snitch," the man hissed and swiftly drew his right hand out of his pocket.

The quick move of the fillet knife slashed deep into Sandström's throat. He tried to say something, but could only lift his hand to his throat. He was too late, and he fell on the ground. Blood was pumping onto the concrete.

The guy with the fillet knife looked at his gloves. No blood stains. No one was around. He went back the same way he'd come, on the north side of the bedrock, and pulled his black beanie tighter on his head.

The drizzle turned to sleet. The man welcomed the sleet so it would hide his traces, and walked briskly on.

SATURDAY,

DECEMBER 1

CHAPTER 25
SATURDAY, 6:23 A.M.
KALLIO, HELSINKI

Takamäki woke up to a phone ringing. The ringtone wasn't his and came from farther away—he realized it must be Suhonen's.

Lying on the couch, Takamäki grabbed his phone and glanced at the screen: 6:23 A.M.

What the hell, he thought. It was Saturday, and he wasn't on duty today. Why did the phone have to go off at this hour?

The ringing stopped, and Takamäki closed his eyes again. It was still dark outside, but the street lamp cast a dim, yellow light into the living room. Rather than darken the room, Suhonen's curtains just provided privacy from the apartments across the street.

Takamäki heard Suhonen use the bathroom. Then he loaded the coffeemaker and walked into the living room.

"You awake?" Suhonen asked, but it was more of a statement.

Takamäki sat up on the pullout couch and yawned. Suhonen was wearing boxers and a white T-shirt.

"Yeah. The phone woke me up."

"We get to go to work."

"Yeah?"

"We won't even need a car; we can walk to the crime scene from here."

"What's up now?"

"Sandström was found stabbed to death in Alppi Park," Suhonen said.

"That Sandström?" Takamäki said.

"Shit. We should've done a stakeout at his place last night, or something."

* * *

The men were hit by the biting wind as they walked down the hill on Helsinki Street. A half inch of slush covered the pavement, but fortunately the sleet had stopped sometime during the night. Even though the slush would melt by the end of the day, winter was on its way.

Takamäki and Suhonen studied the ground to see if they could spot anything unusual—anything to help them solve the crime. They wondered if the surrounding buildings had security cameras, or if any of the apartments offered a view to the crime scene.

It didn't look good. The crime scene at the foot of a decades-old statue was in the center of Helsinki, yet removed from it. The twenty yards from the street to the rocky area made a big difference.

Takamäki kept thinking of one question: Why would someone want Veikko Sandström dead?

He knew they wouldn't be able to get statements from many witnesses. If the crime was committed in the early morning hours, it was likely nobody was around. If the victim and the killer had used the same route as the detectives did just now, someone driving by might have seen them. But it was impossible to see anything essential from a moving car. A nurse or a resident at the Deaconess Institute might have been looking out the window at just the right time, but it seemed like wishful thinking. In crime investigations, wishful thinking was code for upcoming hard work, which was only occasionally rewarded.

Suhonen and Takamäki reached the point where the path wound from the edge of the grass to the concrete statue. The detectives knew no one had walked through there recently, as no footprints were visible in the slush.

Takamäki stopped.

"Let's walk around to the Linnanmäki entrance. The Forensics guys can rake through here first."

The Forensics team had only one shot at it. If it was botched, the homicide investigation would become much more difficult. The past few years had provided many examples of this.

Takamäki picked up his phone and dialed Dispatch. He needed a team of patrol officers to isolate the area to keep any curious folks—especially the media and their photographers—from reaching the hill and stomping on potential evidence.

Suhonen and Takamäki walked back up the hill from the other side; the detour to the statue took almost ten minutes. A staircase from the top of Sture Street led to the amusement park and forked first into dirt paths, then a paved walk to the left toward the railroad. The paved path ended about sixty feet from the statue, the same as on the Helsinki Street side.

A police van and an unmarked Forensics van were parked on the street.

A uniformed officer was about to stop Takamäki and Suhonen, but then recognized the detective lieutenant.

"Have you been here from the start?" Takamäki asked.

The bald, stout officer nodded. He was surprised to see the detective lieutenant at a crime scene—the higher-ups usually stuck to paperwork at Pasila, wearing in their comfortable moccasins.

"The call came from a dog owner. They had walked here around five this morning. I think the owner might let his German shepherd hunt foxes or city rabbits, but that's irrelevant now, right?"

"Right," Takamäki said.

The patrol officer handed Takamäki a note with a name, address, and phone number, and said, "This is the guy. He said his dog was loose and started barking at the foot of the statue. The man went to take a look, and when he saw the body, he called his dog away and immediately called the police."

"And you?"

"I was just about to finish my nightshift, but Dispatch gave me the gig anyway. I'm working overtime now."

"Congratulations," Suhonen said. "Not many officers get any nowadays."

The patrol officer looked embarrassed. He figured the other guy was also with the homicide unit, though he didn't much look like a cop.

"What did you do when you got here?"

"I already told the Forensics guys."

Takamäki saw two men in coveralls around the statue.

"Fill me in, too," he said.

"We drove the van up here, using approximately the same route as you. The K-9 officer waited here. My partner and I went to look, but the man was already dead. That was obvious right away."

"Did you see any other prints in the slush?"

"Only the dog owner's footprints," the officer said.

The slush made it hard to investigate the crime scene. Takamäki wondered if they should have a tent built around the area to help the Forensics team do their job. They could then increase the temperature enough to melt the slush and reveal any hidden clues.

"Go on."

"We didn't call an ambulance, just reported the homicide to Dispatch. We've been making sure nobody goes over there."

"Has anyone been there?"

"No," the bald officer said, shaking his head. "Only Forensics."

"If the media finds out about a dead body by the statue," Takamäki said, giving the officer a stern look, "how do you think they'll get over there?"

Realizing his mistake, the officer said, "From the Helsinki Street side, of course."

"The Forensics team could get some prints from the grass over there."

"I'll go right now. The van's stuck up there anyway—the path ends at the stairs to Alppi Park."

"Okay," Takamäki said.

The other patrol officer stepped out of the van as the bald one hurried down the hill.

"Is there a problem?"

"No," Takamäki said, shaking his head. "VCU is here."

The brunette female officer glanced at her watch, chewing her gum.

"You were quick; it only took you a little over an hour."

"What?" Takamäki said. "Didn't the homicide nightshift show up right away?"

The woman shook her head.

"We recognized the guy as the rapist they showed on TV. Dispatch saw on the computer that we were supposed to notify Suhonen about this guy. The nightshift at the VCU said Suhonen would take over.

Takamäki and Suhonen followed the route the patrol officers had used to take a closer look at the victim.

* * *

Joutsamo left her bicycle by the corner of the police station. It was only a fifteen-minute ride, but if she pedaled hard enough she could work up a good sweat. Takamäki had called and asked her to meet him at nine-thirty. Sandström's death was an unfortunate turn of events, but she felt no grief over him.

If anyone asked, she would tell them she didn't feel anything for other victims, either. But each violent death took its toll over time.

She locked her bike and picked up her helmet. Unlike those who rode in from farther away, she didn't commute in sports clothing.

Joutsamo walked to the door and noticed Jaakko Oksala— the financial crime detective from the cafeteria the other night. He was heading to the door at the same time from the opposite direction.

Oksala greeted her and unlocked the front door with his ID card. She suddenly realized she had forgotten Takamäki's request to find out who all were involved in Oksala's pressure group of authorities.

"What are you doing here on a Saturday?" Oksala asked.

"Homicide pays no mind to time or place," she replied with a smile. "What about you?"

"A financial crime case only requires time. I'm getting ready for an interrogation scheduled for tomorrow: a suspect in a real estate deal. We've heard the guy is returning to Finland from Moscow on an afternoon flight. We'll meet him at the airport."

Oksala held the inside door open for Joutsamo.

"That Sandström guy got what he deserved, by the way," he said.

"Oh," Joutsamo uttered, and looked at the man, confused.

"We put the screws on him," he added with a chuckle.

Oksala wished Joutsamo a good day and started up the stairs. Joutsamo took the elevator.

Suhonen, Kulta, and Kohonen joined Takamäki and Joutsamo in the conference room. Kannas from Forensics had also arrived. Each held a steaming cup of coffee.

It was usually Joutsamo's job to run these meetings, as she was the most familiar with the case details. This time, only Takamäki and Suhonen had been to the crime scene, so Takamäki took the lead.

"The case looks complicated," he began. "At 5:53 A.M., a guy named Jari Vuorenpää alerted the police about a dead body he found by the statue in Alppi Park. The crime scene is on the bedrock up the hill from Helsinki Street towards Linnanmäki. The patrol officers who responded recognized the body as Veikko Sandström. We heard about the case because Suhonen had made a note in the system to have him alerted if anyone saw Sandström. But we'll talk more about that later."

Takamäki turned to Kannas, who was to give the forensic report from the crime scene. He handed out photos.

"The man was identified as Sandström by his fingerprints. The cause of death can be clearly seen in the photos: one deep slash to the throat. We found no other injuries; there were no signs of struggle on his hands, so it had to have been done by surprise. The upward angle of the slash tells us it probably came from the front."

Each detective looked at the photos of Sandström lying on his stomach, his head turned to the side. Even though a thick layer of slush covered him, the body was still clearly visible.

"I'm estimating the time of death to be between eight and eleven last night," Kannas said. "But that's just a guess. We'll get the pathologist's report later."

Kannas was very experienced, and the detectives knew his estimate was going to be accurate.

"We haven't found the knife, and evidence is pretty sparse. Sure there are beer cans, cigarette butts, and used condoms—just nothing fresh."

"Footprints?"

Kannas shook his head and said, "The slush isn't helping in the search. The ground is mostly bedrock. We found a print matching Sandström's shoe in the gravel at the base of the statue. It's likely he ascended from the Helsinki Street side. The other side of the statue is rock. We'll revisit the scene this afternoon, after the slush has a chance to melt."

Takamäki had brought up the idea earlier of using a tent to help with the investigation, but Kannas didn't deem it necessary.

"Why would anyone go there?" Kulta inserted. "It's a good place for drinking beer at sunset in the summertime, but I wouldn't think anyone would want to sit there for fun this time of year. Especially in the sleet."

"He must have planned to meet someone," Kohonen said with a nod. "The killer, more than likely."

"Someone wanted revenge when Sandström didn't get sent to prison for the rape. Someone from Raisa's circles."

"Raisa didn't really have her own circles," Joutsamo pointed out.

"Someone who kept up with the news...a vigilante?" Kulta suggested.

"What about the people in the Corner Pub?" Kohonen continued. "Maybe they rejected him after she killed herself."

"Who else might be upset with Sandström?"

The conversation died down because nobody wanted to mention Nea Lind's name out loud. They knew Takamäki and the lawyer were close.

Kannas drew the attention back to his findings and pointed to the Ziploc bag on the table.

"Sandström didn't have a wallet or phone on him. In his pockets we found a key, twenty cents, some receipts, and a note with an address on it."

"Robbery?" Kulta asked.

"For a wallet and a cell phone? It's possible. Judging by the victim's position, they were taken before he was stabbed—if he had them in the first place."

Joutsamo had been listening quietly, then said, "We've got motive, but we need to find a reason for Sandström's visit to the statue. I'd like to get back to the beginning: Why was Suhonen interested in Sandström?"

Takamäki looked at the undercover officer and said, "That's a long, complicated story."

Suhonen considered telling the long version, but opted for the short one.

"It has to do with the arson of Takamäki's townhouse. I'm not sure how Sandström is connected to it, and he can't tell us anymore. I'm pretty sure he knew something about it."

"Is that why he was killed?" Joutsamo asked.

"I don't know," Suhonen replied. "We should see what Tanner from that bible group and Saarnikangas have been up to."

"Let's keep all lines open for investigation," Takamäki inserted. "Mikko and Kirsi, you go question the residents and nursing staff at the Deaconess Institute and see if anyone saw anything. Then check Sandström's apartment and the Corner Pub. His buddies should know something about his comings and goings. Anna, you look through the databases and check the internet. I'll go through his phone records, as soon as we can find the provider."

"I have a cell phone number for him from around the time of Raisa's death," Joutsamo said. "I can check it out."

"Good," Takamäki said and glanced at Suhonen. "You keep digging, too."

Suhonen sipped his coffee. Damn sure he would. He hadn't come into the office so he could go back home and take the rest of the day off.

"I'll send out a press release. We definitely need the public's help," Takamäki continued.

"Seems complicated," Kulta said.

"Yeah," Takamäki said, nodding. "But we'll solve this. It doesn't exactly look like a professional hit, or we wouldn't have the body."

The meeting was over. Joutsamo approached Takamäki, as the others left the room.

"Another thing is puzzling me," she said.

"What?"

Joutsamo told Takamäki she had just bumped into financial crime investigator Oksala and he had told her Sandström got what he deserved. She wondered if Oksala's people were involved, but she doubted it. She didn't want to mention it in the meeting and clog other lines of investigation.

Takamäki agreed with her. They needed to look into it.

* * *

Joutsamo walked down a flight of stairs to the financial crimes department. The homicide unit's walls were painted red, but one floor below they were moss green. She wasn't sure which room was his, so she checked all the nameplates by the glass-walled offices. She could see from the hallway that the rooms were unoccupied—financial crimes weren't solved on Saturdays.

Oksala's room was the second to the last before the hallway took a ninety-degree turn. The door was open.

The forty-year-old was wearing a white dress shirt and the same gray cardigan as before. Binders were stacked on the shelves and on the floor, and a couple of them were open on his desk. A hanger with a dark gray suit coat and a blue tie draped over it hung on one end of a shelf.

Joutsamo knocked on the door.

"Hello," she said.

"Hi," the man replied, turning from his computer.

"You busy?"

"Not terribly. How can I help?"

Joutsamo sat down in the chair by the door. She pushed the door shut.

"Something secret?" Oksala asked.

"Not really," Joutsamo said with a small chuckle. "Just a couple of questions."

She had decided to start with a question about the group—otherwise the man might not answer any of them.

"So, who is involved in this group of yours?"

"Our group of investigators here in Financial Crimes?"

"No, I mean the group who puts on the pressure."

"Why do you want to know?"

224

Joutsamo felt like saying she was the one asking the questions, but she realized it wasn't an interrogation.

"I'm interested. Do you have something to hide?"

"Leikas and Liimatainen from the Tax Department, Hippeläinen and Kaisko from Collections, Saarinen from the Prison Department, and Francke from Social Services. We've got others, but those are the key guys. There's nothing to hide. We got the idea while we all went to a conference in Tallinn. That was some trip!"

Joutsamo committed the names to memory. She didn't want to write them down in front of Oksala, so she memorized the first few letters of each name: Lei-Li-Hi-Ka-Sa-Fra.

"Okay, I have another question: Where were you last night?"

"What's this about?" the man asked with a chuckle.

"Just answer the question."

Oksala stared at Joutsamo, now clearly irritated.

"I was at home. I took my son to soccer practice and picked him up. Then I watched TV and sipped a couple of glasses of red wine. What's this…?"

"What time was the practice?" Joutsamo interrupted.

"It started at six and ended at seven-thirty. Out in Kauklahti, Espoo."

"And your wife was at home?"

"No wife. I'm divorced. We have the boy two weeks at a time and it was my turn."

"And he watched TV with you?"

"Yep, CSI at nine. Then I put the boy to bed and watched the ten o'clock news. Do you want to hear me regurgitate highlights from both?"

Joutsamo didn't, because it wouldn't prove anything; the news was available anytime on the internet. But the man had an obvious alibi.

"What is this about?" Oksala asked.

"Sandström," Joutsamo said, looking Oksala in the eye. She wanted to see his reaction. "He was found murdered this morning."

"What?" Oksala said, astounded. "Sandström, murdered? ...And you thought that I..."

"Think about what you told me this morning."

"What did I say?"

"You said Sandström got what he deserved."

"Oh, hell," the man said, exhaling sharply. "I can see why you'd come here."

Joutsamo felt the man was genuinely surprised.

"Did I have reason to?"

"Definitely not. Wow, I'll have to be careful with what I say. We wouldn't do that. We put the screws on, but we don't kill or do anything else illegal."

"Yep," Joutsamo replied.

"Why was he killed? And who did it?"

"If I knew that, I wouldn't be here."

Joutsamo stood up and walked into the hallway. She pulled a notebook from her pocket and wrote down the names Oksala had listed.

Something bothered her. It was an unpleasant feeling of forgetting something. She was headed back to the stairs, when a nameplate caught her attention: Pitkämäki.

That was it. Of course! Joutsamo suddenly knew what had been bugging her.

CHAPTER 26
SATURDAY, 10:45 A.M.
SARAMÄKI PRISON, TURKU

The prisoner was lying on the bed when the guard walked in.

"Be quick about it."

The fifty-year-old, stout inmate sat up. He had a receding hairline, high cheekbones, and sharp eyes.

The guard handed him a phone, the man took it, and said, "The Lord thanks you."

"As long as he makes up for it, too," Vesterinen, the guard, said.

"The Lord doesn't leave good deeds unrewarded," the prisoner said.

"Five minutes, maximum."

The guard left the cell, which resembled all the other prison cells in Finland. They all were rectangular and had an iron door, a small window, a bunk, and a table. This one was luxurious: the prisoner didn't have to share it with another inmate.

The inmate looked at the old and cheap Nokia phone; it had no internet connection. He could've also sent a text message, but they stayed in the phone's memory. He didn't want to risk it at this point. He was better off making a call. He was allowed to make calls from the prison phone, but they were monitored. He figured his calls were probably taped.

The man stood up and punched in the number.

"Safe line?" came the quick reply.

"Fairly," the prisoner said.

"Okay."

"What's the scoop?"

"Small snags, but they're being taken care of," said the voice on the other end.

"Such as?"

"One person became a security risk, but we dealt with it."

The answer was adequate for the prisoner.

"You've failed. Those bastards were on TV again."

"It's not an easy task."

The view out of the window was of gray-green firs behind the prison buildings.

"It's time for the final wrath. Do you get me?" the prisoner said.

After a moment's silence, the voice at the other end said, "I understand."

"Today. The consequence of sin is death."

"We're still in the middle of some things."

"Quit complaining and think of something... At the perfect moment."

"At the perfect moment... Yep, will do."

"Bless you," the prisoner said.

"Thanks," the voice said, after a pause. "Um..."

"Speak."

"I know our reward is great in heaven, but..."

"Take the money."

"Sounds good."

The prisoner ended the call, removed the number from the phone's memory, and knocked on the door. The guard took the phone and quickly shoved it in his pocket.

* * *

The press release had been issued ten minutes ago. The third caller was Sanna Römpötti.

"What's the body by the statue?"

"A dead man," Takamäki said.

"Um, I heard it might be the same Sandström I did the news report about."

"Do you promise not to let the name leak until I publicly disclose it? That might become necessary pretty soon; we're in the dark with the case."

"Yeah, I promise," Römpötti agreed.

"It was the same Sandström."

"Shit," Römpötti grunted.

"Why?"

"I'm just wondering if this is revenge for the rape. Looks pretty bad."

Takamäki paused, then said, "And you'd feel guilty for disclosing his name in your news story?"

"Yeah. Although, I'm just doing my job."

"We have no clue as to the motive, since we don't even have the killer."

"Okay. FYI, he stopped by here yesterday to yell at me."

"About what?"

"The TV bit, of course. You can use that for a timeline about his whereabouts. We've got him in our security feed, if you need to know what he was wearing."

"Email me a picture."

"Okay."

"And remember what you promised."

"Of course," Römpötti said. "I won't be the first to disclose the name."

Takamäki set the phone down and thought for a minute. Then he called Nykänen at the NBI. They needed to work together and share all their information.

CHAPTER 27
SATURDAY, 12:00 NOON
KOIVUKYLÄ, VANTAA

Suhonen rang the doorbell to the apartment. The sickly-sweet smell was gone out of the stairwell. He heard noises from the apartment and figured Salmela was at home.

"Who is it?"

"It's me," Suhonen said.

"Oh, you."

"Open the door, and damn fast, or I'll come in wearing the doorframe."

Suhonen heard the clinking of the security chain and the door opened.

Salmela looked tired, and said, "I decided to use the chain; last time you came in unannounced."

Suhonen walked in. As Salmela backed up, Suhonen pulled the door shut sharply.

"Come in," Salmela said in a mocking tone.

"The shit stops here. Sit down!"

Salmela did as he was told. Suhonen grabbed a plastic chair from the kitchen and set it three feet away from Salmela.

Salmela's cheeks were sunken in and his eyes were bloodshot. He was wearing a T-shirt and gray sweatpants and his hair was disheveled.

It would have been easy to feel sorry for Salmela, but Suhonen decided to bypass his feelings.

"What brings you here this time?"

"Why did we go into the apartment?"

"Don't…" Salmela said, turning to the window. But he had no way out.

"It's time to finally quit the shit. Why?"

"Well, I went to get the hash…"

"Who told you about the place?"

Salmela didn't answer.

"Who told you to bring me along?"

Salmela was quiet.

"Who do you fear so much that you won't talk?"

"Didn't Sandström say anything?"

Suhonen looked Salmela in the eye and said, "Sandström is on the medical examiner's metal table."

"What happened to him?"

"He got his throat slashed last night. I saw the body in Alppi Park."

Salmela jumped at the news of Sandström's fate.

"Shit. This is the devil's doing."

"What do you mean?"

"Nothing."

"I'm the tempter now; should we head for the mountain, the desert, or the police station?" Suhonen said. "This is no game."

"It never was," Salmela said.

"Or do you think it's an Xbox game you can restart over and over?"

"No."

Salmela buried his face in his hands, and, in a desperate voice, said, "Damn, you've got me in deep shit."

"Speak," Suhonen barked.

"I can't."

"You don't have a choice."

"Fuck."

"You get what you ask for. Let's go to Pasila and have you officially questioned about Sandström's murder."

"I didn't do nothing to him," Salmela cried.

"Convince Takamäki and Joutsamo," Suhonen said, getting up. "But I guarantee it'll take you weeks. You have no alibi for last night."

"I was here alone, smoking hash. You saw me."

"Not at the time Sandström was killed."

"I'll be dead if I talk."

"Get up. They won't be able to get to you in the holding cell."

Salmela shook his head.

"I don't wanna go in the joint again. I spent too much time there. I wasted so many fuckin' years. I can't even sleep in the bedroom anymore—I just nap on the couch. Without the hash I can't even fall asleep. Dammit, I'll go crazy."

Suhonen looked at his old buddy. Pity was about to take over, but he had to stay strong.

"You already are. Let's go," Suhonen said and pulled out the handcuffs he had purposefully brought with him.

"Shit," Salmela groaned. "Shit."

"I'll get you an extra outing in the yard. That way you'll only have to stay in for twenty-two and a half hours at a time."

Salmela looked up. His eyes were wet.

"What do you wanna know?"

Suhonen felt bad.

"The gig at the Vallila apartment. What for?"

Salmela looked out the window again.

"I'm sorry I hustled you. They gave me the free hash for bringing you with me. I had no dough; I had to do it. But I had a feeling it would blow."

"You had to get me into the apartment?"

"Yeah. I didn't know why then, but…"

Salmela stopped mid-sentence.

"Why did you tell the NBI it was me who took you there?"

Salmela couldn't bear to look at his childhood friend, so he stared into the kitchen.

"That was part of the deal; I had to say that, in case I got caught."

"You had to say that?"

"Yeah. I'm truly sorry I got you in trouble."

"Last question: Who told you to do all this?"

Pleading, Salmela asked, "No prison?"

"No prison," Suhonen said and shook his head.

"And you promise to protect me?"

"Of course," Suhonen replied with a nod.

"It was Juha."

"Juha Saarnikangas?" Suhonen asked in surprise.

"He's changed since his time in Thailand. He hangs out with a much tougher crowd these days."

"Who?"

"I dunno for sure. But there was talk of it at the pub. Sandström might have been able to tell you, but not anymore. Jari Tanner is involved, but that's all I know."

Juha Saarnikangas and a trap, Suhonen thought. But how the hell did Saarnikangas know about the NBI cameras in the skinheads' drug nest?

* * *

The conference room at the Pasila Police Headquarters could seat twenty people, but there were only four there now: Takamäki, Joutsamo, Suhonen, and the NBI's Nykänen with his handlebar mustache.

They hadn't made any coffee.

Joutsamo drew three circles on the whiteboard. She titled them *Takamäki's fire*; *Attempted run-over of Joutsamo*; *Framing Suhonen*. An arrow from Takamäki pointed at Sandström's name, and above it were the words *Tip for arsonist search*. Likewise, an arrow went from Joutsamo's name to Sandström, with the note *Connection to stolen car.* The name Pitkämäki, which Joutsamo saw in the financial crime unit's hallway, connected Sandström to the car likely used in the attempt to run over Joutsamo. According to the crime report, the Toyota had been stolen from Pitkämäki Street—and that address was written on the note found in Sandström's pocket.

A line was drawn from Suhonen to Salmela, and on it were the words: *Hired for a job*. The line continued from there to Saarnikangas's name. Another line connected the fire to Saarnikangas and Jari Tanner. The attempted hit and run was the only thing not connected to Saarnikangas and Tanner, whose names were linked with the words *Saramäki Bible Group*.

"Looks bad," Nykänen said.

"What have you guys found in your investigation?" Takamäki asked.

"We've only had the arson. Before coming here, I spoke with Partanen, who's in charge of the case. Frankly, they're still at square one, but these things are never quick to solve. Forensics is completed at Kari's house, and they have the boot prints, but since we have no leads on the threats, we haven't really gotten anywhere. The Skulls were a wash, by the way. We have an informant in Riihimäki, who said the bikers weren't involved."

"Do you believe it?"

"Yeah. It's inside information; the Skulls aren't involved."

Suhonen remembered seeing Rane walk out the door from Saarnikangas's building in Pihlajanmäki. Perhaps the guy was there by chance, and hadn't met with Juha. Or they might have had other business. At any rate, Suhonen was glad they could rule out the Skulls.

"Will that sketch do?" Joutsamo asked.

"It's a good start, anyway. But who's behind Tanner and Saarnikangas? Draw another circle there. Suhonen knows Juha, of course, but Tanner is from Turku and has no connection to you guys.

Joutsamo was about to stand up, but Suhonen beat her to it. He drew the last line, then a circle with a question mark inside. He also drew a line down from the arrow between Salmela and Saarnikangas, and added a circle with the letters *NBI* in it.

"Jaakko, what's the connection here? If and when I was framed, how did Saarnikangas know the apartment was under surveillance?"

Nykänen looked uncomfortable and didn't say anything.

"The way I see it, we only have two choices. First, the whole neo-Nazi thing is a trap for the Helsinki Police—mainly revenge against our Narcotics for old grudges. I don't necessarily buy that, but it's possible. The other option is that a genuine investigation is underway…"

Nykänen joined in and said, "It's a real investigation, and not a trap."

"Good," Suhonen said. "But it doesn't change the fact that Juha Saarnikangas knew about the cameras."

"No."

"That only leaves one option: Juha is one of your informants. Or should I say, snitches."

"I can't really comment on that…"

"Goddamn, Nykänen," Suhonen interrupted. "You guys have been bamboozled. Some dime-a-dozen snitch took you for a spin and your socks are still in a bunch."

"Saarnikangas is no dime-a-dozen snitch," Nykänen said.

"I helped him get on his feet a few years back. He was a heroine-addict art student. Shit. He was a total loser then. After he got on his feet, he ended up hanging out with the Skulls. Now he's playing you guys for fools."

"That's not exactly accurate," Nykänen inserted, shaking his head.

"Then tell us how it is," Suhonen said.

"This is for your ears only. It can't be used in the investigation, or anywhere else."

Takamäki looked at his ex-subordinate. This type of talk gave him bad vibes.

"Suhonen knows that Juha took a trip to the States a couple of years ago."

Suhonen nodded. It was news to the others.

"He got an inheritance from his American aunt and met a relative by the name of Mathias Rein in Minneapolis. Mathias didn't stick to the straight and narrow. But the inheritance story checks out."

"Didn't Saarnikangas serve time for drug deals?" Joutsamo asked. "He couldn't have gone to the States, then."

Nykänen chuckled and said, "The Americans can't get to our criminal records—not yet, anyway. That's just one you check yourself in the immigration papers. But the point is, Saarnikangas and the American conned a Finnish-born gangster in an art deal and something caught the FBI's attention. The body of a professional hit man was found by the Canadian border and the cops suspected Saarnikangas, and Rein might have had something to do with it. Relieved that the hit man was dead, the FBI was interested in Juha. However, they couldn't find any direct link."

The homicide unit's detectives listened closely.

"Juha went to Canada, and flew from Toronto to Bangkok where he stayed for a little over a year. He was loaded, and naturally our contact over there heard about a newly rich guy. We also received an FBI background check on him and a report of the events. The Americans had nothing to go on, so we couldn't make it official."

"Bangkok must be a pretty wild place," Suhonen remarked.

"You'd be a good contact in that corner of the world. A lot of Finnish criminals enjoy the climate, and you could ride your motorcycle year-round."

"Are you hiring?" Suhonen asked.

"Let me know if you're interested."

"But when did Juha get back to Finland?" Joutsamo cut in.

"Based on the information our contact found, Juha was planning to stay in Thailand.

"He was in the hotel business with local gangsters. We're not sure what happened, but we think one of them might have swindled him out of money. Maybe the sand got too hot under

236

his feet, and he had to return to our snowy scenery," Nykänen said.

Suhonen chuckled.

"He arrived here in September, and we had a talk with him. We pressured him on what happened in the States, but with little success. We couldn't get much for the FBI, but I had the impression that the FBI was more interested in knowing the hit man was off the market. They were ready to give Juha and Rein medals for doing away with him. Anyway, after we made contact with Juha, he became our informant. His leads usually held water. Then he told us about the neo-Nazis, and we checked it with the Security Intelligence Service. His information seemed reliable."

"Juha is a skilled schemer, obviously," Takamäki said.

"Yep," Nykänen agreed with a nod. "Anyway, that's how the operation got started. We wanted to know who the neo-Nazis dealt with, and set up surveillance in the apartment."

"Did Juha take it there?"

Nykänen nodded again.

"But this isn't easy for us, either. The situation is volatile. Compromising Juha's role as our informant would mean we'd never be able to recruit anyone else."

"You don't mean Saarnikangas has immunity, do you?" Joutsamo snarled.

"No, of course not. He'll have to pay for his crimes, but his connection to the NBI can't be disclosed, no matter what."

Takamäki looked at Nykänen. He was calm. Takamäki wondered how Römpötti would react, if she found out one of the NBI's informants had most likely been involved in a murder in the States.

"His role can't be disclosed in court, either," Nykänen continued. "We need to make sure the case is handled confidentially, so reporters don't have a chance to listen to his stories. It wouldn't be to his benefit to speak out, but Juha is unpredictable these days."

"And you're using him as an informant?" Joutsamo remarked.

"Well-balanced, clear-thinking people are scarce in the criminal underworld. People like that wouldn't contact the police."

"Juha isn't the principal part of the case," Suhonen inserted. He wanted to get on with the discussion.

"No, he's not," Nykänen agreed.

"Who's he working for?" Joutsamo asked.

"I don't know. We've viewed him a freelancer, doing gigs for whoever's paying."

"The NBI paid him?"

"Yes. He knows a lot of people, and had made new contacts in Thailand. That's a hell of a place for informants, by the way. But I don't think he's on anyone's payroll."

Joutsamo read between the lines that the NBI wasn't too interested in Saarnikangas and his deals, as long as he kept the leads coming about others.

"That's the background on Saarnikangas," Nykänen said.

"He's no common junkie; he's an operator. And if the information from America is correct, he may also be capable of murder."

"You think he might have killed Sandström?"

"I think it's possible," Nykänen replied.

"Why?" Joutsamo asked.

Nykänen looked at the drawings on the board and the lines pointing to and from Sandström's name.

"Multiple reasons, of course, but if Sandström had something to do with this scheme—if he stole the car, for example—someone could've wanted him dead to remove any connections. Sandström's publicity of late has been pretty…how should I put it, overwhelming, and you had him here for questioning, too."

"Not about this, but Raisa Mäenpää's suicide."

"Who knows what suspects are saying at the police station and why they are brought here," Nykänen said. "But let's not get stuck here."

"Right," Takamäki agreed.

"Saramäki prison was brought up earlier. Up until now, we've been searching for someone wanting revenge. We are looking just on what we can remember and look up on prisoner records. Partanen and his guys have focused on the Skulls, but we can rule them out now. Let's flip this over. Partanen gave me the most recent lists of inmates of the maximum security prisons. He got them from the Prison Department yesterday."

Nykänen pulled out stacks of documents from his briefcase at his feet and handed them out.

"On that list of prisons are Sörkka, Saramäki, Kylmäkoski, and Riihimäki. Initially, I was just going to go over these with Kari. But now, looking at the board, I think you should go through these and mark your initials next to the names of anyone who might hold a grudge against you. And we should focus on the Saramäki prison at this point."

Suhonen glanced at the list from Riihimäki. Next to each name was the inmate's nationality, social security number, their date of entry to prison, the estimated date of release, and the crime. Each of the ten pages held about thirty names. This would take a while, Suhonen thought.

"If we can't find anything from these, I have lists from the rest of the prisons, as well as all the registered members of organized crime gangs. Some of the names will be duplicates, but we can use them if the prison lists don't produce anything."

"And if we still don't find anything," Suhonen smirked, looking at Nykänen, "my desk has the Helsinki metro area phonebook."

Joutsamo took the list of Sörkka's inmates and exhaled sharply.

"Take your time," Nykänen said and stood up. "I'll make some coffee."

CHAPTER 28
SATURDAY, 2:20 P.M.
TURKU EXPRESSWAY, NEAR LOHJA

The expressway plunged into the tunnel. Suhonen was driving the Helsinki PD's unmarked Skoda, and Nykänen was sitting next to him. The speed limit was 50 mph in the tunnel, but Suhonen drove 70.

The Karnainen tunnel was the longest on the highway. Along with the other seven tunnels, it was built to keep traffic from disrupting the endangered flying squirrels' nesting habits. The construction of the Helsinki-Turku freeway took fifty-three years.

The radio was off, and the men sat in silence. The meeting at the station had ended forty-five minutes earlier.

Takamäki, Suhonen, and Joutsamo had perused Nykänen's inmate lists and found one name of interest in the Saramäki prison. It became even more interesting when the phone call to the warden had revealed the person's affinity to religious matters. Suhonen had thought of the many Bible quotes from Salmela. Had he tried to hint something about the significance of the bible groups? Suhonen had classified the quotes as nonsense.

The name was Kimmo Aarnio.

Suhonen wondered why he hadn't thought of the guy earlier. The case was a year old, and he hadn't heard anything about Aarnio. The guy hadn't threatened anyone, nor had he left any leads. He hadn't sent letters or made any phone calls.

Aarnio had been sentenced to life in prison for two murders last winter. Both victims were young women. The third victim was a close call—Aarnio had raped Nea Lind while she was on a work assignment, but she had made it out alive.

The man met the criteria: Takamäki's unit had arrested him; he was doing time in Saramäki, and his interest in religion made him an excellent candidate.

Joutsamo had pulled out Aarnio's psychiatric evaluation, and Takamäki leafed through the document. Aarnio had been deemed to have full mental capacity at the time of the crimes. In other words, he was mentally sound and fully aware of his actions.

The man had pleaded not guilty, but the forensic evidence was indisputable. The police hadn't been able to find other homicides to pin on him. Other young women had gone missing over the years, but Aarnio couldn't be linked to them. He had also spent long periods of time abroad. The NBI had tried to work with Europol to find out if Aarnio could be connected to any unsolved murders in other countries, but despite DNA samples they couldn't get any hits.

Prior to the murders, Aarnio had been convicted of two rapes. The first resulted in probation, and the second sent him to prison. His method was always the same: he drugged the women and then raped them. In the second rape, he had used aggravated violence—that, combined with being a repeat offender, put him away. Then, he had graduated to killing his next two known victims before Lind.

Takamäki wasn't interested in Aarnio's past crimes, but he wanted to find out what the man was about, and if he was capable of such a revenge operation.

The psychiatrist had tried to discuss Aarnio's crimes with him, but Aarnio declined the evaluation and had refused to be interviewed, so the analysis only scratched the surface. Usually, criminals wanted to cooperate with the doctors, so as to help themselves get rid of the burden of guilt. The doctors would often find reasons elsewhere—abuse in childhood, incest, personal traumas, or psychiatric illnesses.

Based on the psychiatrist's report, Aarnio didn't just have one personality, but he was a collection of various characters, which he alternated as needed. He might be charming and pleasant one moment, and suddenly be filled with hatred and lechery.

Had there been something out of the ordinary in his childhood? The doctors assumed so, though they couldn't find anything specific. His mother had died not long after giving birth to him, and his father, a priest, had been a tough and callous parent. Aarnio seemed emotionally thwarted; he lacked the ability to feel empathy. The results of the evaluation suggested his personality was shattered.

Based on how the murders took place, the doctors concluded that Aarnio's intention was to gain power over his victims. The evaluation quoted an American research report, which claimed that these types of killers typically had been abused or abandoned as children and, as such, felt powerless and inadequate.

CHAPTER 29
SATURDAY, 4:15 P.M.
SARAMÄKI PRISON, TURKU

Maire Ronkainen, the prison's assistant warden, led Nykänen and Suhonen to her office. Ronkainen gave an impression of toughness. The fifty-year-old woman's black suit coat and skirt matched her hair, which she had pulled into a tight bun. Her lips taut, she had a serious look in her eye.

Ronkainen's office had a desk and a round, white conference table with a thermos, three coffee cups, and three cinnamon rolls. Ronkainen poured coffee without asking.

"The warden is on vacation, but I think we can manage," she said and sat down.

She got straight to the point.

"Go ahead. You wanted to know about Kimmo Aarnio."

"Yes," Nykänen said. He had given her a quick overview on the phone. "We also want to meet him."

"We can't force him unless it's an official interrogation, so it'll be up to Aarnio to decide."

Suhonen didn't like how Ronkainen immediately took the prisoner's side and refused flat out to set a meeting with him. He needed information about the man.

"What kind of a prisoner is Aarnio?"

"He's got an unusual background, and in a different prison he would probably be in solitary at his own request. However, our facility is new and the cell blocks are small, so he's been treated like a normal inmate."

"A normal inmate?"

"Naturally, we've had to think about who to place in the same cell block with him, but it hasn't been too difficult.

Aarnio gets along with the other inmates as well as with the guards. We haven't had any problems until about two months ago."

"What happened then?" Nykänen asked and grabbed a cinnamon roll. He had skipped lunch.

"The guy became a religious fanatic."

"What do you mean?"

"His behavior became unusual. We have a few born-again Christian inmates, but they're usually quiet and reserved. With Aarnio, it went the opposite way. He began to preach his message—at times, in a pretty aggressive tone."

"How do you mean?"

"He displayed emotional violence, if not physical. One inmate asked for a transfer, and many others have downright refused to go into his block. Aarnio sees himself as the leader of a congregation."

"Is he?"

"He's got some followers, and some of them have been released."

"Is Jari Tanner one of them?"

"Yes," Ronkainen said, looking surprised.

"Have you heard of the Saramäki Bible Group?"

"Yes. The group was fairly active around here at one time, but lately hasn't organized any events. An elderly widow used to be an active member, but she fell ill and quit about five years ago."

"Go on," Nykänen said.

"Where was I?"

"He was leading a congregation."

"Yes," Ronkainen said, collecting her thoughts. "Typically, religious behavior in prison is about searching for forgiveness for one's deeds. Repentance, change of direction, show of mercy and compassion. But with Aarnio, it's different; he's clearly drawing examples from the violent verses of the Old Testament. To him, God and Jesus aren't merciful—his God is full of revenge and unforgiving, like in the Books of Moses."

Ronkainen stood up and picked up her laptop, which was already on.

"I'll show you a video, and you'll see."

She set the laptop on the desk, in view of both detectives. On it, a man was standing in a hallway with three men sitting in chairs in front of him. The corner of the screen showed the date and time, along with the camera number.

Ronkainen clicked on the video.

In a booming tone and large, lively gestures, Aarnio said, *"The Lord is my shepherd, and I shall not want. He who calls on the Lord is saved."*

He was almost shouting as he continued, *"He is a God of vengeance; He will repay... For I, the Lord, am a vengeful God who will visit the iniquity of the fathers on their children to the third and fourth generations of those who hate me... The Lord is a warrior."*

Ronkainen stopped the video and said, "Now, you see... We can't have that sort of preaching in prison. We sent Aarnio to solitary for a couple of weeks to cool off. The prison doctor went in and talked with him, but to no avail."

"When was this?"

"About a month ago. He's also spoken degradingly about women—and considering his crimes, that's worrisome... We have more clips, if you'd like to see them."

Nykänen and Suhonen nodded, and Ronkainen clicked on the next clip.

"In this one, Aarnio quotes the Bible about burnt offerings."

The video clip started. It was taken with the same camera as the previous one.

"If your offering to the Lord is a burnt offering of birds... You shall choose your offering from turtledoves or pigeons."

After the calm beginning, Aarnio's tone of voice hardened.

"The priest shall bring it to the altar and wring off its head, and turn it into smoke on the altar and its blood shall be drained out against the side of the altar. He shall remove its crop with its contents and throw it at the east side of the altar, in the place for ashes.

"He shall tear it open by its wings without severing it. Then the priest shall turn it into smoke on the altar, on the wood that is on the fire; it is a burnt offering, an offering by fire of pleasing odor to the Lord."

Suhonen felt a chill in his spine as he listened to Aarnio talk about the scented and pleasing burnt offering.

Ronkainen stopped the video.

"That's disgusting," Nykänen said.

"I checked the wording. It's verbatim from the Old Testament. We have to let a prisoner quote the Bible, or we'll hear about it from the Prison Department. Freedom of religion is a basic human right."

"Mental hospitals are full of folks who went crazy from religion."

"But Aarnio isn't crazy. His daily behavior is relatively normal. He only gets ecstatic like that when he's preaching. If he agrees to meet with you, you'll see for yourself."

"Agrees to meet with us, huh?" Nykänen huffed.

There was a knock on the door and a uniformed guard entered.

"I talked with Aarnio," he said, tentatively. "I asked him about meeting with you. He said he was focused on the Bible right now and couldn't break away, but he will meet with you at seven."

Suhonen glanced at his watch. "Two hours."

"Could we get something to eat around here?" Nykänen asked.

* * *

Takamäki's cell phone rang. The caller's number wasn't listed.

"Hello," he said.

"Takamäki?"

"Who's asking?"

"A friend," said a hoarse male voice. "I've got info on Sandström's stabbing."

"Tell me," Takamäki said with interest. The bulletin hadn't mentioned the method of killing, so the caller must have known something.

"Not here."

"What do you mean?"

"The phone's not safe."

"Should we meet?"

"Fine. Come to Restaurant Mamma Rosa at seven."

"How will I recognize you?"

"I'll get a table under 'Virtanen.' Ask for it, and don't be late. And bring that female sergeant with you."

"Why?" Takamäki asked, perplexed.

"So I won't have to go over things twice."

Takamäki considered it a rare request, but not completely impossible.

He stood up and walked to his unit's office. Joutsamo was the only one there. Kulta and Kohonen were out in the field, trying to dig up information on Sandström. The Deaconess Institute had taken longer than expected, because their nightshift staff had already left and Kulta and Kohonen had tried to catch them by phone.

Joutsamo was sitting at her computer. Looking into Mäenpää's death, she had already found out Sandström didn't have a Facebook account, and neither did Aarnio, Tanner, or Saarnikangas. Joutsamo found some Google entries about the men, but none of them were helpful. She was looking at a public website that posted news about various homicides to see what was mentioned about the case. The site sometimes had good leads.

"Listen, you wanna get some pizza tonight?"

"What?" Joutsamo said, surprised.

"At Mamma Rosa."

"What's this?"

Takamäki told her about the phone call, and she was ready to go.

CHAPTER 30
SATURDAY, 5:15 P.M.
KALLIO, HELSINKI

"I remember the apartment," Kulta said.

As the detectives climbed the stairs in the apartment complex on Third Street in Kallio, he pulled out the key they had found on Sandström.

"I was here last summer, investigating the rape case. We took pictures and looked for evidence."

The detectives reached the door.

Kulta cracked the mail slot open and listened. Kohonen stood back, holding the crime investigation bag. The apartment was quiet, although Sandström could have had a roommate.

Kulta rang the doorbell, but nobody answered. He put the key in and turned.

They stepped in and closed the door.

"A pretty bleak place," Kulta grunted. The only things in sight were a mattress and a pile of clothes.

"I wonder if someone's been here before us and picked up stuff."

Kulta grabbed a couple of official-looking documents off the floor and read them.

"Yep, the collection agent's been here recently," Kulta said and showed Kohonen the papers. The redhead quickly leafed through them.

"He was evicted, too. Sandström wasn't doing too great."

"Right, and then he got his throat cut… Let's check the place. It won't take long."

Kohonen started with the living room, and Kulta looked in the closets. They weren't looking for anything specific, but everything was of interest. Notes with phone numbers or dates for meeting someone; store receipts linking his comings and goings to times and places. Photos would show people he knew, and the phone SIM card would list calls. Phone bills would reveal his cell phone numbers and providers, and they could start phone taps and obtain phone records.

All Kohonen found in the living room was dust. The paint on one of the walls was lighter than the rest—probably where a bookshelf used to be. Two stacks of paperback detective novels sat on the floor. The collection agent must not have wanted them.

Kohonen thought the television had probably been in the now-empty corner. She wondered if an Xbox or a PlayStation console had stood there. In the lab, Forensics could find out a lot from all the messages and chat sessions that were stored in internet-based games.

Kohonen checked the list of collected items, but unfortunately no game consoles or computers were on it. Any that had been confiscated could have been picked up from the collection agency.

"Come here and look at this," Kulta hollered.

Kohonen finished rummaging through the pile of dirty clothes. Kulta was kneeling in the entryway, his head in the wardrobe.

"There's a secret door in here. Could you hand me the screwdriver from the top shelf."

Kohonen found the tool and handed it to Kulta.

"My basketball player's knees aren't made for this," Kulta said and took the screwdriver.

"I can do it…"

Kulta grunted for a minute, then pulled out a piece of white-painted particle board.

"It was attached with only one screw."

He shined a flashlight into the cabinet and said, "Will you look at that."

The compartment held four brown tubes.

"Looks like dynamite."

"A bomb?"

"No, these are separate tubes."

"Should I call the bomb squad?"

The Helsinki bomb squad usually took care of any dangerous explosives. But with large quantities, they called in experts from the army.

"No need. These are fresh, and there's no detonator."

Kulta moved back and Kohonen took some pictures. Kulta then carefully placed the tubes in a plastic bag and Kohonen snapped a few more photos.

"I'd guess these are from a robbery of a road construction site. I wonder if Sandström did a gig like that," Kulta pondered.

"Why would he keep them in here? He didn't blow up any bank safes, did he?"

"No," Kulta said, shaking his head. "And these types of explosives can't be used to blow up a safe. You need something that goes off quicker."

"What should we do with them? We can't take them to headquarters," Kohonen said.

"I know an army explosives guy in Santahamina. We'll drive there. But let's finish checking out the apartment first."

Kohonen nodded. "We still have to stop by the Corner Pub."

"Yep. And evening's the best time for the ambiance."

"Let's see if we can do it without drama this time."

Kulta let out a light chuckle.

In fifteen minutes, they had looked through the apartment. Though the dynamite was not armed with a detonator, Kulta carried the bag very cautiously.

CHAPTER 31
SATURDAY, 6:40 P.M.
SARAMÄKI PRISON, TURKU

Nykänen and Suhonen were offered cream of cauliflower soup for dinner. When Suhonen got a whiff of the aroma at the prison cafeteria door, he felt like driving to the nearest gas station for a burger with fries.

The watery soup was far from creamy, and the cauliflower was leathery. The only thing worse Suhonen could think of was a milk-based vegetable soup. But he was hungry and couldn't go all day on oatmeal and cinnamon rolls.

Suhonen and Nykänen had sat down at a corner table to talk with Vesterinen, a guard from Aarnio's block. The guard wanted to know their reason for their visit, but didn't get an answer.

Vesterinen didn't have anything bad to say about Aarnio. He thought the guy was strange, but easy to get along with, which was important to a guard. He suspected that the fervent religious views were just a way to add some action to the boring prison routine. The preaching gave Aarnio a chance to receive praise from supposedly like-minded inmates. The guard didn't deem him aggressive or dangerous, and considered plenty of inmates in Saramäki worse than Aarnio.

Vesterinen readily explained how nine out of ten inmates came in with a drug problem. Many of them were diagnosed with ADHD or dyslexia after they were sent to prison. Prisoners were provided free health care, employment, safety, and a warm room with a television. Tax payers shelled out nearly two hundred euros per inmate per day, which added up to more than sixty thousand euros a year—enough to buy a small apartment in most Finnish cities.

Criminal politics didn't interest Suhonen or Nykänen, so the conversation died down. Nykänen went back for another cup of coffee.

After Vesterinen left, the detectives discussed their plan concerning Aarnio. They had initially come here to find out if Aarnio was capable of carrying out a revenge attack, and whether he had a motive. According to Assistant Warden Ronkainen and the guard, the man didn't seem bitter. On the other hand, they worried about Aarnio's fixation on the vengeance theme from the Old Testament. Ronkainen had told them Jari Tanner had been a disciple of sorts when he was doing time in the same cell block as Aarnio.

How would they open the meeting with Aarnio? One option was to bring up an old rape or homicide charge from the murder investigation and watch Aarnio's reaction toward the police. They also could set up a video camera, so they could later analyze his behavior.

Bringing up Tanner would expose their suspicions. Aarnio wasn't stupid, and he would start guarding his words. It would then be difficult, maybe impossible, to find any connection to the fire, the attempt to run over Joutsamo, or the framing of Suhonen.

Nykänen had pointed out that their investigation was unnecessary, because Aarnio had already been convicted of two murders and had only served a year of his sentence. He would continue to serve time for at least fifteen more years. Any additional convictions wouldn't add that much to his sentence.

Suhonen reminded his colleague that Tanner and Saarnikangas were roaming free.

According to the clock on the cafeteria wall, it was 6:45 P.M., when the guard came and asked them to go to the visitors' lobby.

* * *

Takamäki led the way into Mamma Rosa. The restaurant was located on Runeberg Street in the basement of a six-story building constructed just before World War II. It had only been a ten-minute drive from the police station, and they parked the car by Töölö Square.

Takamäki in his dark blue pea coat and Joutsamo in a black trench coat looked like the perfect customers for the Italian pizzeria—a middle-aged couple coming for dinner just before seven.

Coincidentally, Joutsamo lived only twenty yards from the restaurant and had grown tired of their pizzas—you could only eat so much salami.

Takamäki told the host that they had a reservation under the name Virtanen, which was the most common surname in Finland. He thought the caller might have been messing with them and half-expected the reservation to be bogus. But the man seemed to know how Sandström was killed. Takamäki felt nervous.

The host glanced at his list and smiled, raising his eyes. "Welcome."

The staircase in front of them led to the basement, but the host led the detectives to a table by the window on street level. The covered summer terrace outside the window had been closed for the season. The cars parked in the street partially blocked any view of the square, but there was nothing to see anyway—the several-acre Töölö Square, which was surrounded by gray apartment buildings, was deserted. Mamma Rosa was a pizzeria, not a tourist spot.

"Anything to drink?" the server asked after Takamäki and Joutsamo hung their coats on a nearby coat hook and sat down.

The restaurant had plenty of room; only ten other customers were there.

"Sparkling water," Takamäki said.

"Same for me."

The server looked disappointed. He had expected cocktails and a bottle of wine.

Takamäki wondered why the table was set for four people.

"Kind of an odd place to meet an informant," Joutsamo said. "Of course, even our national leaders have exchanged information here."

She was referring to the exchange of information between opposition leaders and cabinet members that had caused a scandal a few years back. Those meetings had taken place in this very restaurant.

"Well, we'll see what happens. He'll show up if he wants to. If not, the pizza's on me."

Joutsamo chuckled and instinctively tucked a strand of her dark hair behind her ear.

"And you think someone who knows something is coming? This isn't some ploy to take me out on a date?"

"No, of course not. I'd ask you directly."

They were seated opposite each other, with Takamäki facing the door.

The sparkling water arrived quickly.

"There you are," the server said. "Would you like to wait for the others to arrive before ordering?"

"The reservation is for four, right?"

"Yes," the server said, confused. "Is there a problem?"

"No," Takamäki replied. "Just checking."

The server shook his head, perplexed.

The menus were on the table, pizzeria style.

Takamäki took a sip of his water. He felt nervous. This type of a meeting was more like Suhonen's thing. On the other hand, it wasn't an undercover operation, and Takamäki could be himself, and not pretend to be someone else. If the caller decided to show up, they would be able to ask him questions.

One of only a few cars on the street had been parked right in front of their window. The wet asphalt and pavement on the square gleamed under the street lights.

Takamäki glanced at his watch. It was 6:54 P.M.

* * *

A long, white table with chairs along each side split the room in half. Bulletproof glass reached to the ceiling in the center of the table. Six-foot high divider walls separated the chairs. Nykänen and Suhonen chose the middle booth because it had two phones.

Two minutes before seven, the door opened on the other side. A man dressed in gray sweatpants and a black-collared shirt walked in. A guard followed him, and promptly walked over to his chair in the corner of the room and sat down.

Kimmo Aarnio sat down and picked up the phone.

"Hello, I hear you're the cops—devils in disguise."

He spoke with an even tone and appeared calm. His hair was combed neatly.

Suhonen had asked Ronkainen to record the discussion on the security camera in the corner.

"That's right, except we're not devils, but Nykänen from the NBI and Suhonen from the Helsinki Violent Crimes Unit."

"Suhonen!" Aarnio exclaimed. "We haven't met."

"No," Suhonen replied.

"It's a pleasure—but a shame, in a way."

"What do you mean?"

"Joy, laughter... We cast away our burdens, break the bonds of slavery. He who reigns in the heavens is laughing. The Lord mocks them."

Suhonen saw Aarnio glance at the clock on the white wall. It was one minute to seven.

"How long will you, holy and true almighty, stay your hand and keep our blood from those who live on Earth? Why did you unrighteous tempters want to see me?"

Takamäki was taken aback when he saw the woman walk to the host stand. He knew her; it was Sanna Römpötti.

Römpötti also looked surprised to see Takamäki and Joutsamo seated at the table where the host was leading her.

"What are you two doing here?" the reporter asked and stopped at the end of the table.

"I was going to ask you the same thing."

"Table reservation for Virtanen?"

"Yes," Takamäki said. "A man with a hoarse voice called you, too?"

"Yeah. Weird," Römpötti replied.

She took off her coat.

Takamäki glanced at Joutsamo. He wondered if this was one of Römpötti's plots, but didn't think so.

* * *

Aarnio took another look at the clock.

"What's with the clock?" Suhonen asked.

"Seven is the perfect number, and seven o'clock marks the perfect moment," Aarnio said with a smile and lowered his gaze on the table.

"What have you got against the police? Why do you think we're devils? We're the good guys after all," Nykänen added.

Aarnio laughed.

"Good guys? You men, how long will you mock my glory? How long will you love vanity and search for lies?"

"We search for the truth," Nykänen inserted.

"Woe is the city, covered in bloodshed, full of deceit, spoils, and an undying thirst for savaging."

Aarnio's speech started as a mutter, difficult to cipher. Suhonen and Nykänen sat in silence. Then his tone grew louder.

"Fall on us and hide us from the face of the one seated on the throne, and from the wrath of the Lamb; for the great day of their wrath has come, and who is able to stand?"

Aarnio's voice kept rising as he stared into space past Nykänen and Suhonen.

"The first angel blew his trumpet, and there came hail and fire, mixed with blood, and they were hurled to the earth...When they have finished their testimony, the beast that comes up from the bottomless pit will make war on them and conquer them and kill them..."

Nykänen looked at Suhonen and said, "I think these are quotes from the Book of Revelation."

Aarnio went on, now shouting, *"Then I heard a loud voice from the temple telling the seven angels: Go and pour out on the earth the seven bowls of the wrath of God."*

Suhonen looked at the man preaching in ecstasy. He was totally nuts. Suhonen was worried about the tone of voice and the clock, and he thought he should call Takamäki.

"Then Death and Hades were thrown into the lake of fire...the lake that burns with fire and sulphur, which is the second death."

Aarnio stood up and lifted his arms toward the ceiling.

"But as for the cowardly, the faithless...the murderers, the idolaters, and all the liars...their place will be in the lake that burns with fire and sulphur...

"Surely I am coming soon. Amen," Aarnio said and turned around.

The guard looked at the detectives and shook his head as he opened the visitors' lobby door for Aarnio. Suhonen pulled out his cell phone.

* * *

Römpötti was still standing by the table, hanging up her coat, when Nea Lind walked into the dining room in her dark blue trench coat.

"What's this?" she asked, when she saw the three.

"I don't know," Takamäki replied. "The man with a hoarse voice called you, too?"

"Yeah," Lind said, creasing her forehead.

"There's something fishy about this. Why would someone want to talk to the police, a reporter, and an attorney at the same time?"

"Maybe he wants protection and witnesses," Römpötti suggested. She took a chair and sat down next to Takamäki.

Takamäki's eyes quickly swept around the room.

"I don't believe anyone's coming," Lind said and took off her coat. "I think it's a joke. But I'm starving, so could we…?"

Everything looked in place in the restaurant. Takamäki's nervousness had rubbed off on Joutsamo, who was also looking around the room.

Takamäki shifted his gaze outside. A man leaning against a street lamp at the far end of the square caught his attention. The man had something strange on his face. Takamäki's phone rang in his pocket, but he couldn't answer it now. The man was far away, but Takamäki noticed he was holding binoculars. He was watching the restaurant.

Suddenly, the man dropped the binoculars and lifted his right hand. He was holding something. Shit, Takamäki thought.

"Get down!" Takamäki yelled, knocking down Römpötti in the chair next to him as he dove down.

The flash of light blinded him, and the boom from the explosion was deafening. Before passing out, Takamäki managed to realize that something had exploded outside. Then the pain subsided.

* * *

Suhonen was standing in the beige prison hallway, holding his phone.

"It rang at first, but now it goes straight to voice mail."

"Maybe the battery died," Nykänen suggested.

"I dunno."

"Aarnio is creepy."

"Think about what he's done. It's hard to face yourself after that," Suhonen said. He called Joutsamo's phone, but the call went straight to voice mail, too.

"Did you listen to what he said?"

"That's what worries me. The great day of wrath, the angel blowing the trumpet, revenge, killer beast, fiery lake," Suhonen listed. "And seven o'clock is the perfect moment."

"And he said it was a pleasure to meet you, but a shame, too. What did that mean?"

"He said he'd get back to us," Suhonen said, attempting a grin. But worry shadowed his expression.

"He's clearly insane," Nykänen said.

Suddenly, his cell phone beeped.

The text message came from the state emergency services department. Nykänen was on the list of contacts due to his position at NBI.

Nykänen read the message and didn't say anything. With a shaking hand, he gave Suhonen the phone. The message was to the point: *A large explosion at Töölö Square in Helsinki. No information on casualties, but assume there are some. Local hospitals have been alerted to receive a large number of victims.*

"Shit," Suhonen said.

"Guess that explains the day of wrath and brimstone," said Nykänen, his voice low.

"Fucking Aarnio kept us here until seven."

Suhonen had a bad feeling that something had happened to Kari and Anna.

Firefighter Erkki Rajala sat in the cab of the fire truck. The alarm for Töölö Square had sounded in the middle of their floor hockey match at the fire station, but they left immediately. The truck was on its way within one minute, as required—maybe even a bit quicker.

The siren was blaring as the truck had sped between the sports complex and the opera house, across Mannerheim Street, and onto Runeberg Street. Rajala had first wondered if a propane tank had exploded in the grill joint near the square, but preliminary information on the radio hinted at something more serious.

A minute earlier the fire chief had arrived, first on the scene. His initial assessment was grim: "We'll need many units and a lot of ambulances."

Traffic was at a standstill heading up to Töölö Square, forcing Rajala's fire truck to drive on the tram tracks to get around them.

Concerned onlookers had gathered on the street to watch and snap cellphone photos.

Rajala and the other firefighters got off the truck and pulled out the hose. A car fire about twenty yards away was spreading thick, black smoke. Not much was left of the vehicle, but the fire was spreading to a badly damaged car in front of it.

Seeing this immediate threat to the public, the chief barked an order to extinguish the car fires.

With only the fire, car headlights, and flashing blue lights illuminating the scene, it was eerily dark. The explosion had either broken all the streetlights or cut off electricity in the area.

Sidewalks were covered in shattered glass and debris from the explosion. Windows were broken in the apartment buildings surrounding the square. Rajala saw paramedics move a limp body away from the fire. At least one dead, and probably more to be found.

Rajala figured it had to be a bomb, probably placed in the car parked in front of the restaurant—no propane tank or other household items could cause the magnitude of this explosion. The smell of the explosives lingered in the air.

Rajala and the other firemen pulled the hose closer. Rajala put on a gas mask to fight the toxic car smoke.

He grabbed the hose and moved alongside the burning car. Immediately the flames died down and the smoke turned a lighter color. Nevertheless, the fireman kept spraying water on the dying flames.

With sirens on and lights flashing, more emergency vehicles showed up at the scene.

The center of action seemed to be the restaurant, and they suspected they'd find the majority of casualties there. The impact of the explosion had shattered the large windows toward the interior of the pizzeria, wreaking havoc on the diners and staff.

The car fire was almost out, but Rajala kept spraying.

He hoped it had been a quiet evening at the restaurant. Now, men and women in white coats were rushing to the scene from the nearby Töölö hospital.

CHAPTER 33
SATURDAY, 7:45 P.M.
TURKU EXPRESSWAY

Suhonen was driving, flooring the accelerator; the speedometer read 118 mph. He had to focus on driving, but was listening to Nykänen give orders to his crew on the phone.

"Get a team to the Saramäki Bible Group's apartment on Malminraitti Street...full search... Same with Saarnikangas's apartment in Pihlajanmäki...and tell Narcotics to go find fucking Saarnikangas; chase the rat out of his hole, pronto. It goes without saying we need to watch the borders. Yeah, call... Aw, hell, that's bad."

Nykänen hung up and Suhonen asked, "What's bad?"

He had to brake hard, as a bus was passing a semi-truck ahead. The bus moved back to the right, and Suhonen floored the gas again.

"The place is like a war zone. At least four are dead and dozens injured, some critically."

Suhonen's white knuckles gripped the steering wheel. "No information on names?" he asked.

"No. They don't even know the ages and sex of the dead yet."

Suhonen was quiet.

The car radio was spewing a description of the scene.

"I'm standing right in the square, in front of Sandels cultural center. Shards of glass are strewn around. The police have isolated the whole area surrounding Töölö Square. Dozens of emergency vehicles and flashing lights are making the scene look unreal. There are no street lights, and the

apartments are dark. Smoke is lingering in the air. The only sounds we hear are car engines and the sirens of the emergency vehicles arriving and leaving.

It seems that the restaurant Mamma Rosa, on the corner of the square, and the area in front of it, have taken the biggest hit. The police haven't confirmed yet if it was a bomb, but that's what it had to have been. Mrs. Nylund, you live nearby. What did you see?"

An elderly woman replied, *"There was a boom. I was watching the news on television and the windows rattled. It scared me to death..."*

Suhonen turned off the radio. He didn't want to hear it.

"Let's think about it rationally, and try to hold our emotions in check."

"Yep," Nykänen replied. He used to work for Takamäki in Helsinki VCU, and, at one time, Joutsamo worked on Nykänen's team in the Espoo narcotics unit.

"How did Aarnio arrange it?"

"With the help of Saarnikangas and Tanner, of course."

"But we saw Aarnio's visitor list. Nobody went there for the last few weeks, and before that it was only cops."

"Someone get time off?" Nykänen wondered. Before they were paroled, Finnish prisoners were often given short releases to help get their affairs on the outside in order.

"No one from Aarnio's block has been out in the last two weeks. He couldn't have planned this so far ahead. How did he know about the seven o'clock time?"

"Either he has a phone in his cell, or it's one of the guards."

"That guard, Vesterinen, asked us at least twice why we were there. I didn't think anything of it at the time, but now it seems suspicious."

Nykänen agreed. He called the NBI's unit in Turku and told them to get a team to the prison, especially Aarnio's block, and run a background check on Vesterinen. At moments like this, acting was better than thinking.

Aarnio had been isolated even before Suhonen and Nykänen left Saramäki.

"This wasn't done without money," Suhonen pondered aloud. "Tanner may be one of Aarnio's born-again fools, but Saarnikangas would want a big reward for this. I think he's missing the Thailand sun and saw a great opportunity here."

"The airports have already been…"

"That's not what I mean," Suhonen said. "Where did Aarnio get the money? Has he been hoarding it somewhere, or is the association some kind of a front?"

"Aarnio's name doesn't appear in the association's documents."

"Someone has had to use their accounts or get cash. It was probably Tanner."

Nykänen made another phone call.

"Get the financial crime unit to check out the bible group's accounts. Find all the account transfers over the last three months—what they had to do with and who was paid—plus how the money has moved from there. How the hell should I know who the lead investigator is? There's no time for bureaucracy now. Put my name down, I'll sign it all… We have to catch these assholes. We can decide later who gets to talk to the media—all the same to me… What the hell do I care that it's seven-thirty on a Saturday night. Pull a Glock on the bankers and tell them we need the information, like fucking now!"

"Damn financial crime guys, and their fucking business hours," Nykänen huffed as he hung up.

The Skoda dove into one tunnel after another in Lohjanharju. Suhonen had slowed down to 95 as more traffic piled up ahead.

"Why Töölö Square? What's there?" Nykänen wondered out loud.

"Joutsamo lives by Mamma Rosa. The radio said that building was worst hit," Suhonen said. Flashbacks of bringing his inebriated colleague home a few days ago came to him; he had to squeeze his eyes shut to stem the tears.

"You think they might have been watching her?"

"Maybe. I hope not."

"That's a pretty outlandish way to attempt to kill one detective."

Suhonen kept his eyes on the road.

"Kari isn't answering his phone, either."

"If they were together, or if Joutsamo was the lone target, someone would've had to watch the place. A timer works on a place, not on a specific person."

Suhonen's phone rang. It was Mikko Kulta.

"Hi," Suhonen said.

"Yeah, you have any info on Takamäki or Joutsamo?"

"No. I was just about to call and ask you the same thing."

"I can't reach either one," Kulta said after a pause.

"Do you know if either one of them was in the restaurant?"

"I'm afraid so. A note on Joutsamo's desk says *Mamma Rosa, 7 P.M.*"

"Did she have a date?" Suhonen wondered.

"With Takamäki, maybe. A colleague in the hall said they had left here together at twenty to seven. He said it looked like they were going on a job. They took one of the department's cars."

"Someone must have lured them there," Suhonen said. "Can't we get a list of names for the injured and the dead from the hospital?"

"No. In cases like this, they rescue first and ID later."

"Go to Töölö hospital and find the ones who are less injured. See if you can get something out of them. I'll be there in half an hour."

"Suhonen," Kulta said in a melancholy tone. "This is beginning to look like it'll have a terrible ending."

"We'll work first and grieve later. Keep your phone on," Suhonen said and ended the call.

"What the hell went wrong here?" Suhonen said, hitting the steering wheel. "Other than every fucking thing."

Suhonen told Nykänen about Joutsamo's note.

"Nobody could predict something like this."

"That's the problem; we only react, and never predict."

* * *

The nurse's lips moved, but Sanna Römpötti couldn't hear anything. Her head was still buzzing and she was dizzy. Best to lie still.

She had lost all sense of time and had no idea how long she'd been lying in a bed. Maybe it wasn't that long, since she was still wearing her own clothes. She hadn't lost consciousness in the explosion.

"You can probably talk to police officers who are here to see you," the nurse yelled.

Römpötti nodded, despite the pain.

A tall, blond man and a short, red-haired woman walked in. Römpötti recognized them as VCU detectives, but at the moment couldn't recall their names.

She saw the man's lips moving, but she couldn't hear him. People had a strange habit of whispering in a hospital.

"My ears are buzzing, I can't hear. Speak up, please," Römpötti said. She couldn't tell how loud her voice was; she was probably yelling. Her head ached.

"It's Kulta and Kohonen from homicide," Kulta said loudly, exaggerating the pronunciation. "We saw your name on the hospital list. What happened?"

That's what Römpötti had tried to figure out, but her thoughts were blurry. She was getting flashbacks.

"I, um, we were sitting at the table."

"Sorry," Kulta interrupted. "Who's 'we'?"

"Joutsamo and Takamäki were there first. Then I came in, and then Lind, and then..."

"You were all there?" Kulta asked, frowning. "Did you have a meeting?"

"No. I was there to get a tip on the Sandström homicide case."

"I don't get it. Did someone ask you all to come there at the same time?"

"Yeah, but we didn't know about each other. A man with a hoarse voice called me that afternoon..."

Römpötti stopped talking. Her throat was dry. She tried to sit up and reach for a glass of water, but her hand was shaking.

Kohonen grabbed a straw from the side table and took the glass. She supported Römpötti's head with her hand so the reporter could take a sip.

Römpötti tried to smile and said, "Thanks, I feel a bit weak."

"You were saying, about the hoarse voice," Kulta urged.

"Yeah, he called me, and apparently the others, too. He said he'd talk about Sandström's case at seven in Mamma Rosa. The table had been reserved under the name Virtanen."

Römpötti didn't need to tell the detectives that was not the caller's real name.

"And he had called everyone?"

"I guess so. We didn't have a chance to talk much before..."

"What happened?"

"Nea arrived last, and she said she figured the caller wasn't going to show up. Takamäki stared out the window, and suddenly yelled for us to get down."

Römpötti paused.

"He threw himself on me...made me fall down... I hit my head on the floor...at the same time...a hell of a flash, and a booming noise... That's why I can't hear much."

Römpötti's eyes were wet.

"Kari saved me. But he caught shards of glass. He was on top of me, bleeding... I thought of the scene in *The Unknown*

Soldier, where the Russians shoot Hietanen in the eye, and he bleeds on top of the soldier lying in the foxhole."

"Did Takamäki hurt his eyes?" Kulta asked.

"I don't know. His head was bleeding. The glass shards were everywhere, and tables and chairs were scattered... People screaming at the top of their lungs were running up from the basement, but it was quiet upstairs. Nobody could even yell. I was conscious and stood up. Takamäki, Joutsamo, and Lind were lying on the floor in a pool of blood. I think I tried to find their pulse... I'm not sure what I did...I don't know what good it would have done, with an explosion like that right next to you.... Next, I remember being outside... It was quiet. Somebody asked me if I had been in the restaurant and if I could walk. I probably said yes, and they told me how to get first aid. I don't remember walking. I'm so confused... I've been lying in this bed ever since. I feel terrible and I'm shaking."

Römpötti wiped her sticky hair with her trembling hand.

"Kari's blood is stuck in my hair. This is a nightmare."

Römpötti began to cry.

"Where's your phone?" Kulta asked.

Römpötti pointed to the floor and grimaced.

Kulta picked up Sanna Römpötti's phone. It had four text messages. He unlocked the phone and the first message opened. It was from Jaska. *Where the hell are you? We need you at work NOW!!! RIGHT NOW!!!!!*

Kulta wanted to reply for Römpötti, but decided against it. He quickly checked three points: The call came from an unknown number at 4:53 P.M. The operator was Elisa. Kulta jotted down Römpötti's phone number for the search.

He was about to slip the phone back in Römpötti's purse, when she managed to say between sobs, "I recorded the phone call; it's in the phone memory."

Kulta decided to take the reporter's phone with him.

"You've got quite a few messages from work," he said. "Would you like me to let them know you're alive, or something? Or I can call a relative."

"From work?" Römpötti said, swallowing her tears. "From Jaska?"

Kulta nodded.

Römpötti let out a heavy sigh and said, "Could you get his number from the text message and hand me the phone. My hands are too shaky."

Kulta looked up the number and handed her the phone.

The phone call was short. "It's Sanna, hi. Why am I not at the scene? Well, I am...at the Töölö hospital, and an hour ago I was in Mamma Rosa... I'll tell you later... I'm yelling because I can't hear anything due to the explosion. Talk louder. Send a camera crew over here. Yeah, of course I can... No, I'm not alright."

Römpötti looked at Kohonen and asked, "What's the room number?"

"Eight. It's in the ER."

"Did you hear that?" Römpötti said into the phone, and got a 'yes.'

"I'll make sure they get into my room, or I'll haul myself outside."

Römpötti ended the call and looked from Kohonen to Kulta.

"No information on Takamäki, Joutsamo, or Lind?"

"No," Kohonen said. "You've got blood on your face, too. Would you like me to wipe it off?"

"That's okay. It'll look better on television."

Kohonen didn't listen, but wet a piece of tissue and wiped Römpötti's dirty face. The reporter let her do it, and gave in to tears.

* * *

Suhonen had reached the end of Tarvo Street in Munkkivuori, when Kulta called.

"You've got the NBI guy in your car, right?"

"Yeah," Suhonen said.

"He needs to get caller data on this number ASAP."

Suhonen ran the red light, not wanting to wait at the intersection. Fortunately, traffic was light. The explosion and live TV news coverage kept people in their homes.

Suhonen complied and repeated the time, the provider, and the number to Nykänen, who wrote them down.

"This is extremely important. It was the number of the caller who lured Takamäki, Joutsamo, Lind, and Römpötti to the restaurant. A man with a hoarse voice said he knew something about Sandström's murder."

"Lind and Römpötti, too? Damn," Suhonen said.

"Yep. Tell Nykänen to forward the info. It's a direct link to the killer. Oh, and I forgot to tell you before, we found four sticks of dynamite in Sandström's apartment."

Nykänen was already talking into his cell phone, which was plugged into the car charger. The constant phone calls in the car had run down the battery.

"What? And you didn't mention this before?"

"I didn't remember."

"I mean before the explosion."

"It didn't seem relevant at the time," Kulta said. "Of course, from now on we'll fucking shut down the country's air space if we ever find sticks of dynamite in the apartment of a common thief who was murdered."

Suhonen didn't want to make Kulta feel guilty.

"I'll be there in a minute. Who's in charge of the investigation?"

"Guess we'll find out at eight thirty. The Ministry of the Interior, the NBI, and the Helsinki Police are doing a press conference. It'll be live on television."

Nykänen forwarded the information as Suhonen turned from Lapinmäki Street in Haaga toward the Hakamäki Street tunnel and Pasila.

Nykänen ended the call when they got to the tunnel.

"Sorry, I didn't have a chance to tell you, Keijo Partanen has been designated lead investigator."

CHAPTER 34
SATURDAY, 8:30 P.M.
HELSINKI POLICE HEADQUARTERS

The press conference started exactly on time. By the media's request, it was held at the Ministry of the Interior, because the room was already set up for press conferences. The media would have had trouble setting up connections at Pasila Police Headquarters, and especially at the NBI building in Jokiniemi, when most of the portable equipment was in Töölö at the scene.

The broadcast was live on the main television channels. Suhonen was watching it at Pasila headquarters, and Nykänen had joined him. They'd been trying to come up with their next move, but the broadcast on the conference room flat-screen TV had interrupted the meeting.

Suhonen refilled his cup from the coffeemaker. The atmosphere was anemic throughout the building, as if the Helsinki police force was in shock. News about Takamäki and Joutsamo had spread fast.

A blonde press officer from the Ministry of the Interior opened the conference and introduced the participants. In the second row were seated the minister, the Helsinki police chief, the police commissioner, Keijo Partanen—the lead investigator—and the chief resident at Töölö Hospital.

The Helsinki police chief in his immaculate uniform was first to speak. He leaned into the microphone.

"Today, about an hour and a half ago, at 7:03 P.M., an explosion at Töölö Square rocked Helsinki. The investigation is in its preliminary stages, but the explosion was quite obviously caused by a car bomb. The NBI is now in charge of the investigation."

The police chief glanced at Keijo Partanen from the NBI, and the tall, narrow-faced man took the floor.

"We're investigating this explosion as multiple attempted homicides. At this point we have nothing further to report."

Next, the chief resident spoke. "Based on the information I received ten minutes ago, seven people died and several dozen were injured in the explosion. Most of the injuries were caused by shards of glass from broken windows."

The police commissioner stood up and said, "This is an extraordinary act of violence, and the police will use any and all measures to bring the perpetrators to justice. Cost will play no part in the investigation."

Suhonen huffed at the mention of money at a moment like this.

Looking particularly stern, the minister of the interior added, "This is a serious attack against our society. We'll leave no stone unturned."

Suhonen knew that the police commissioner and the minister of internal affairs spoke in earnest. All roads leading out of Helsinki were blocked, and everyone passing through would have to show identification. The harbors and airports had additional security checks, and the border patrol was stopping ships and boats in the Gulf of Finland.

The police were visible in every possible way. They performed raids in apartments in Southern Finland; even though it was unlikely the places had anything to do with Aarnio, Saarnikangas, or Tanner. The police wanted to show criminals that none of them was out of reach. At the same time, law-abiding citizens could see that the police would act to keep them safe. A police car driving by with sirens on and lights flashing would bring a feeling of safety, they reasoned.

Saarnikangas and Tanner were still on the loose.

"Any questions?" asked the press officer, who chaired the conference.

Suhonen stopped watching the broadcast when Keijo Partanen uttered his fourth "No comment." He was surprised none of the reporters had asked why the investigation had been handed over to the NBI. They had a good reason: the violence had been aimed at members of the Helsinki Police Department.

He poured himself more coffee.

Suhonen was irritated at the lack of condolences expressed to the victims' families. On the other hand, he wasn't sure if the families even knew about the victims yet. In a case like this, it might take hours to get the word to families; identifying a severely disfigured body was difficult.

The fate of Takamäki and Joutsamo was still unclear. Suhonen had considered visiting them in the hospital, but the chase for Saarnikangas and Tanner took precedence.

Nykänen, seated by the wall, put down his phone and said, "That was Turku."

"And?"

"They set up a surveillance van by the prison."

Suhonen knew the van would serve as an undercover station and trace the calls made in the area without the caller's knowledge.

"And they traced a call from one prepaid phone to another," Nykänen continued. "Interestingly enough, it was the number Kulta had acquired."

"What was said?"

The surveillance van was equipped to record all phone conversations.

Nykänen looked apologetic when he said, "We don't have permission to listen to it."

"Shit. This isn't happening."

"It'll still be there on the hard drive when we get the permission."

"We'll get the permission," Suhonen said, looking at Nykänen. "The lead investigator is just busy with the TV broadcast right now. Hell, you tell the Turku guys to listen to the phone call and tell us what was said."

The men looked at each other.

"You're right. We can't sit around waiting for a judge. This is a big case."

"And another thing: where did the call come from?"

"That much we know."

"Where?"

"You can't go there," Nykänen said. "You're involved in the case, on account of the set-up of your teammates."

"You gonna shoot me?"

* * *

The clock on the wall said 10:02 P.M. when the nurse took Kulta and Kohonen to the hospital room. The detective lieutenant lay on his stomach on a bed with a monitor, with tubes attached to his body.

"Hello," Kulta said loudly. Maybe Takamäki's hearing was damaged, too.

Takamäki winced.

"Everything alright?"

"As you can see," Takamäki said with effort.

Takamäki's head was wrapped in a thick bandage. Blood-stained gauze covered wounds on his bare back.

The nurse had told Kulta that Takamäki had sustained wounds from shards of glass in his back and on the back of his head. A large piece of metal had slit his scalp. Had it hit only a couple of inches to the left, it would have killed him.

"Looks tough," Kulta said. It was hard for him to see his boss like this.

"Quit your complaining and do your job," Takamäki said with an attempted growl that sounded more like a whimper. "It was a trap."

"We know—Römpötti told us."

"I saw the guy. He was watching the restaurant through a pair of binoculars from across the square. He saw we were all there. He looked thirty or forty years old, athletic, and had short hair."

Kohonen wrote down the description.

"The NBI is investigating the case now."

"What the hell. Then nothing will get solved…"

"Suhonen is helping them," Kulta said, glad to hear Takamäki talk like himself.

"Well that's a relief. Least they've got someone with sense. Did you write down my observations?"

Kulta looked at Kohonen, who was holding a notepad.

"So, he was thirty or forty…" Takamäki repeated.

"Kohonen wrote it down, no worries."

"Good," Takamäki said with a sigh.

Kulta wondered if the shards of glass were still in Takamäki's back. It was likely Takamäki was still on the waiting list for surgery; those with life-threatening injuries would go in first, of course. Fortunately, medication kept his pain under control. His back looked awful.

"Mikko, I've been out of it… How are Anna and Nea doing?"

Kulta thought for a minute. He wouldn't keep information from his boss—and he wouldn't lie.

"Anna is in ICU. She sustained severe injuries, but she's expected to survive. Nea was hurt worse," Kulta said, regretting that he couldn't be direct.

"What are you saying? Give it to me straight. Nea was standing when the explosion happened."

"Nea died an hour ago. The doctor said there was nothing they could do. Her injuries were too extensive—loss of blood and such. One of the shards of glass had hit her in the throat. I'm sorry. My condolences."

Takamäki made a fist and said nothing.

CHAPTER 35
SUNDAY, 12:22 A.M.
HIGHWAY 24, PADASJOKI

A line of four cars sped along the dark highway. The clock on the Skoda's dashboard said 00:22. According to the road sign, Padasjoki was thirteen miles away. The destination address was in the GPS.

Suhonen was driving the first car and kept his speed at 87 miles per hour. The Volkswagen van, last in the line, couldn't have kept up at a higher speed.

Juha Saarnikangas, identified by a photo, had been caught at the West Harbor an hour and a half ago. He had used a passport under the name of Juha Rautio.

A border patrol officer had recognized the man trying to get on the last Tallinn ferry, despite the fake beard and glasses he wore. His duffel bag had over a hundred and fifty thousand euro in it, along with a plane ticket from Riga to Bangkok.

NBI had also arrested Vesterinen, the prison guard. In his pocket they had found the cell phone which had been used for the call the surveillance van had picked up.

On the phone, Aarnio had once again rattled off his religious quotes, after someone had reported a job done. He had talked about good and evil, light and darkness, day and night, and life and death.

"I got a text message on the victims. You wanna hear it?" Nykänen said.

"Yes," Suhonen said.

Nykänen read the message on his cell phone: *The explosion claimed the lives of server Francesco Togliatti, 33; teacher Laura Nurmi, 43; superintendent Mikko Nurmi, 48;*

student Joona Rantala, 21; American citizen Alex Sandstone, 66; master of economic sciences Viivi Ristola, 33; and attorney Nea Lind, 38.

Suhonen was quiet for a moment. He let his gaze sweep the autumn scene. A thin layer of snow covered the ground.

Suhonen thought about Takamäki. Kulta had given him a report on the detective's condition and he tried to understand how his friend must feel. First his wife had died in a car accident, and now Nea in a car bombing. Hell, Suhonen thought; he realized he had sped up to 99 miles per hour, and quickly lifted his foot off the gas pedal.

"I hope they release the list to the public."

"Why?" Nykänen asked.

"So everyone can see it's not just about numbers, age, and sex in cases like this. The victims were real people. It was a bad mistake to keep the names confidential in the two recent school shootings. Even though the media didn't release the names of the victims either, the cops were still nervous about making similar mistakes to the ones with the Jokela incident."

"Exactly," Nykänen said.

"Society today wants everything neat and tidy, as if nothing ever goes wrong; only anonymous people, not real persons, die as crime victims. As though nothing bad ever happens."

"Right," Nykänen said. "I'll talk to Partanen and our bosses—maybe they'll get it."

The GPS said to turn in a third of a mile. Suhonen slowed down to 50. They were going after Jari Tanner. He had switched cell phones, but he couldn't get rid of them altogether.

A cell phone display on the dashboard beeped and a woman's voice sounded in the speaker, "The cell phone is still in the same location."

The NBI had traced the number Aarnio had called using the phone Vesterinen had given him. The call to lure

Takamäki and the others to the restaurant had come from the same number.

Suhonen wondered about the slip-up, but he knew criminals always made mistakes. He thought of Tanner with disdain and wished he had put him behind bars back in Malmi. All this could have been avoided if he had realized the severity of the situation. But hindsight was 20-20, and that was the only way to view it.

The highway became a two-lane road, as Suhonen turned right. Tall fir trees lined both sides of the road and the only street lights were at the intersection.

The destination was 1.2 miles out. The police had checked Google Maps and found out it was an old school building. To keep the chase covert, they hadn't called the owner or asked about possible renters.

"Our guys will go in first, okay? You're kind of an observer here," Nykänen reminded Suhonen.

"Yeah, of course. Naturally," Suhonen agreed.

They were half a mile away and soon only a quarter mile. The street lights returned.

The operation was simple: they would drive as close to the location as they could, go in, apprehend the man, and get out. The K-9 unit had given the dog in the back of the van a piece of clothing from Tanner's apartment. If Tanner tried to escape into the woods behind the old school, the German shepherd would catch him.

Suhonen stopped the car three hundred feet from the school and jumped out. Nykänen said something, but Suhonen didn't catch it all.

The lights were on inside, so someone was probably there.

* * *

Suhonen jogged up the road and was the first to reach the door. He pulled out a pistol from a holster in his leather jacket. He seldom drew his weapon, but there was no telling what Tanner would do. Aarnio's assistant had a big ego.

Suhonen opened the front door before the two NBI officers reached the steps.

The foyer had a place for coats and shoes. The old school building had had twenty students at most. Suhonen wondered if the suspect had heard the cars, or if he was even there. The detective proceeded quickly.

The NBI officers in vests walked up behind Suhonen. They understood the situation; it was about work safety, not rules. The man had to be handcuffed first, and then they could decide who had the authority for what.

Suhonen opened the inside door, holding his Glock at the ready. The large space had probably been a classroom. It looked like it could hold twenty students. The same space might have been used for a lunchroom, too. No one was in sight. The back wall had one more door, and next to it was a table with a telephone.

Suhonen was walking toward the back door, when it suddenly swung open.

The man with a crew cut was startled as he stepped in the door.

"It's the devils themselves," Tanner hissed.

Suhonen pointed his gun at the man in the door. He could see from the corner of his eye that the NBI men had also drawn their pistols.

"Tanner, get on the floor like you're tanning your back on the beach."

"No can do," said the man with a chuckle.

Suhonen peered into the backroom between Tanner and the doorframe and saw electric wires on the floor.

"Do it!" one of the NBI men said. "On the floor, now. It's an order."

Tanner shook his head and refused to obey.

"Hit the floor! I'm telling you to get down!"

The NBI officer's orders had no effect.

"You don't understand. You don't fathom the fate of this sinful land. Sin... Celebration."

Tanner mumbled something and bent over as if with stomach cramps.

Three officers aimed their weapons at him, but none of them fired when Tanner picked up the phone on the table and laughed.

"I knew you'd hesitate... Damn losers... What would the American Special Forces guys have done when I grabbed the phone? They would have fuckin' shot me... No," Tanner said, "No, Lord help me."

Tanner kept his finger on the green call button.

His eyes grew wide and he said, "Rejoice daughter of Zion! Rejoice, daughter of Jerusalem! Behold, your king will come. He is righteous and victorious. He is humble; he rides an ass, his royal steed."

Tanner was shaking the phone in his hand.

Suhonen looked at Tanner through the Glock's sight. A slight pull of the trigger and the man would be dead.

"When I burn the offering on the altar, I know it'll be a scented burnt offering pleasing to the Lord."

Suhonen looked at Tanner. He clearly wasn't all there.

Tanner shook his head, as if to chase his thoughts away.

"Burnt offering...hah, guess we put a bit too much in the car...burnt offering... Oh well."

"Take it easy," said one of the NBI officers. "Set the phone on the table," he tried again, knowing it was pointless. "I order you to get down."

Tanner let out a laugh and said, "You assholes came a half hour too early. And this was all meant for you, Suhonen."

"You seem compelled to explain," Suhonen said. "Why? Explain that, too."

Tanner looked at the officers with a serious expression, and the phone moved in his hand.

Suhonen pulled the trigger and the bullet hit Tanner in the forehead, causing him to fall backward.

The phone fell on the floor, jumped a couple of inches, and landed upside-down.

No explosion.

It was only now Suhonen noticed Nykänen standing behind him.

"You made the right call," Nykänen said. "I'll support you in anything that might come from this."

One of the NBI men carefully approached the body. It was obvious Tanner was dead, but the officer wanted to see what was in the backroom.

He took a look inside and quickly said, "Full of explosives. Everybody out, now! Back off to a distance, at least a third of a mile."

Suhonen holstered his weapon and turned to follow Nykänen. He remembered Aarnio saying they'd get back to business. The easy cell phone trace was a trap and they'd fallen for it—fortunately, a little too quickly.

Suhonen was sure Tanner had picked a spot nearby where he would see the police coming and would then set off the bomb.

CHAPTER 36
SUNDAY, 11:00 A.M.
KALLIO, HELSINKI

The broadcast on the explosion was playing on television. The minister of the interior was now starting another segment with condolences to the victims' families. One of the state media consultants must have reminded her to do so.

Suhonen was watching the broadcast in his apartment. Takamäki's clothes were in a hockey bag in the corner of the living room and his sheets were folded on the arm of the couch.

The minister continued, naming the victims. She read them slowly and carefully, stressing that society needed to remember the victims of the horrendous incident and support their families.

They'd be forgotten, despite the speech, Suhonen thought. That had been the case in the Myyrmanni mall bombing and the school shootings in Jokela and Kauhajoki. The problem was that none of the promises or support from society could ever make up for the families' losses or heal their grief.

Lead investigator Partanen took the stand, and in a serious tone, reported that the police were making progress. He didn't comment on the motive, but said that the main suspect was in custody. While Partanen didn't disclose the name, it wouldn't take too long for the media to dig it up.

His expression solemn, Partanen said that a second man had been apprehended at the harbor, and a third had died in a conflict with the police in Central Finland. A special prosecutor was now investigating the officers' actions, as if anyone would be interested in that detail. But it was always easier to talk about organizations than actual events.

Suhonen suspected that the police commissioner had ordered Partanen to make a statement about the situation being under control in order to set the public and the media at ease. Releasing the information had no effect on furthering the investigation.

Partanen emphasized that the bombing had nothing to do with international terrorism, but the motive behind it would be found elsewhere.

The explanations seemed to satisfy the reporters; the media trusted the police.

Suhonen wasn't surprised Partanen didn't mention the bomb set up in the school building. That detail would only have caused panic about other possible explosives. The police and army bomb squads would have had a busy night searching for bombs in every location imaginable.

Suhonen wasn't sorry about Tanner's fate, and he didn't regret shooting him. He was annoyed that in the heat of the chase none of them had even considered the possibility of a second bomb.

After a short introduction, the media had a chance to ask questions. Keijo Partanen kept his answers brief. He wouldn't comment on information the media had attained, including whether the police had shot a suspect in Padasjoki. He said he could only comment on details concerning his jurisdiction as the lead investigator.

Suhonen yawned. They had spent hours at the Padasjoki school after he'd shot Tanner. A special prosecutor had driven nearly two hours from Jyväskylä to interrogate everyone in the room. Suhonen had ridden in the NBI van back to Helsinki around six that morning.

He had fallen asleep as soon as he hit the bed, but had woken up at ten thirty.

A reporter on television asked Partanen about justification for the shooting.

"I can't comment on that. I won't confirm any such action at this point of the investigation."

Suhonen let out a small chuckle and took a sip of his coffee.

He got a bitter taste in his mouth when the chief physician said on the broadcast that the number of deceased had risen to eight that morning. Neither the doctor nor the minister of internal affairs knew the name of the latest victim.

Based on the last information he had, Anna was still in critical condition, fighting for her life.

THREE WEEKS LATER

SATURDAY,

DECEMBER 22

CHAPTER 37
SATURDAY, 1:20 P.M.
HIETANIEMI, HELSINKI

"In the name of the Father, and the Son, and the Holy Spirit," the priest said.

Suhonen couldn't help it; the tone of voice and the choice of words of the round-faced man made him think of Kimmo Aarnio.

Suhonen, Takamäki, and Römpötti sat side by side in the pew, all dressed in black.

The priest spoke warmly, but Suhonen missed the message. The man of faith spoke of loss and how to cope with it.

Suhonen hadn't known Nea Lind, but he knew she had been dear to Takamäki.

Takamäki had been released from the hospital ten days ago. He had stayed at Suhonen's place, but was going to move to a rental apartment in Kamppi next week. He had three weeks of sick leave left, but the doctor had agreed to give him more, as needed.

Joutsamo was still in the hospital. She had sustained a nearly fatal injury when a metal fragment pierced her skull. She had undergone six surgeries. The doctors were hopeful—as hopeful as they could be in their profession. In any case, Joutsamo would be off for months.

Suhonen looked at the small cross at the end of the casket. The priest talked about how grief cast a shadow on daily life.

The NBI was continuing the bomb investigation. It would take months, but they had the basic information. The explosive used in the car bomb was stolen from a job site in

Mäntsä and the same kind had been found in Sandström's apartment and the school.

It was unclear who had stolen the explosives, but it could have been Sandström. That part might never be resolved.

Based on Takamäki's description, Tanner was the main suspect for setting off the bomb by Mamma Rosa. Saarnikangas had been quick to confirm it in the interrogation. Residue of the explosives had been found on Tanner's clothing.

Juha had tried to whitewash himself further by claiming Tanner had killed Sandström because he suspected Sandström of squealing to the police. Juha and Tanner couldn't think of any other explanation for Suhonen snooping around the bible group's apartment.

Juha said Tanner took care of all communication with Aarnio, whose name Juha had heard only in passing. He claimed the idea for the trap was Tanner's, who had forced him at gunpoint to make the calls to Takamäki, Lind, and Römpötti. Juha's statement was weakened by the fact that he had denied the charge in an earlier interrogation, but based on the recording of Römpötti's phone call the NBI's sound lab had been able to identify him as the caller. Juha said he had no idea there would be a bomb.

Takamäki's house must also have been burned down by Tanner or one of his accomplices. Juha said he didn't know anything about that, either.

Suhonen thought it was odd because, according to Salmela and Sandström, Tanner had been looking for an assistant.

Juha said that he viewed Tanner and Aarnio as nothing but nitwitted nutcases for him to rip off. They seemed to be loaded and that's why he had been involved. He talked about the religious meetings and prayer circles in the Malmi apartment, and said that if it hadn't been for the money, he would have left immediately. Tanner had told him that Aarnio had been irate about Takamäki dating Lind; apparently Aarnio felt Lind was his woman.

Juha considered the fanatic religious behavior a motive. He hadn't understood the concept at any point, and he had no chance to back out.

The priest went on with his sermon. Suhonen looked at the candelabras in the simple chapel. Each had seven candles; adding together God's symbolic number three and the number four for the Creation of Man and Earth.

Aarnio hadn't agreed to talk to the police. Based on a psychiatric evaluation, Aarnio, in his twisted mind, might have felt he had lost something very important a year ago when Takamäki tore Lind away while he was in the act of raping her. It got worse when he heard about Takamäki dating Lind. Aarnio's motive was purely revenge. He added Römpötti, Joutsamo, and Suhonen to the list, because they had each had something to do with the events. The sick distortion of religious behavior had blown his actions out of proportion.

Aarnio had been in isolation in prison since the explosion. Ronkainen, the assistant warden at the prison, said Aarnio preached daily to the plant in his cell.

Juha had told the police about the money. The Saramäki Bible Group had ended up in Aarnio's and Tanner's hands by chance. A prisoner sentenced for life had become seriously ill and sought Aarnio for salvation and grace. The man said he had been running a religious association on the outside. It had made some money, but was now slowly withering. Tanner had looked into it and found out the association's actual assets came from apartments given in a widow's will and amounted to a few hundred thousand euros. The gravely ill man knew nothing about the business. The association's annual meeting had been held in Aarnio's cell shortly before the prisoner was moved to a hospital. Tanner was made chairman, but it was Aarnio who was in charge. In preparation for the crimes, the men used the bible group's money, which Tanner had been gradually turning into cash over the summer.

A hundred and fifty thousand in cash was found in the Padasjoki school building. That was the same amount of cash Juha had on him when he was caught at the airport.

The police had wanted to know why Juha and Tanner shared the money equally, if Tanner had done all the work. Juha said it was strictly about a Christian distribution; Tanner had forced him to take the cash.

Suhonen had taken the story for nonsense.

Saarnikangas's explanations were in vain; his fingerprints were on a plastic bag full of teddy bears, found in the school building. That would connect him to the Töölö Square bombing, and his collaboration with Tanner meant he would be charged for several murders. Juha was looking at a life sentence.

"Time doesn't change things—people do," the priest said.

Suhonen glanced at Takamäki seated next to him. Takamäki's back was still sore and he was leaning forward.

"Nea Lind worked with no thought of reward, especially for victims of crime. Now she is gone. Life is fragile, but grace will carry us through sorrow."

Suhonen noticed tears flowing down Takamäki's gaunt cheek.

The priest ended his sermon, and the organ started playing a hymn.

Our path is toward heaven... Heaven is our homeland... I long for heaven with hope...

Suhonen felt the vibration of his cell phone in his pocket. Luckily, he had thought to turn the sound off. He pulled out his phone and saw a text message from Joutsamo.

The message was short: *"I'm out of ICU. Would be nice to see you guys. Come over. Anna."*

Suhonen thought for a moment, then tugged on the sleeve of Takamäki's dark suit and showed him the text message. The detective lieutenant smiled and nodded.

CPSIA information can be obtained
at www.ICGtesting.com
Printed in the USA
BVHW030158270720
584717BV00001B/46